What had they

His Margaret. His M̶̶̶̶̶̶̶̶̶ names they had called her by, years ago, sprang unbidden to Simon's mind. Worse still, what had she done to turn herself into a fashion plate, a sophisticated houri? By all appearances she was no better than she should be! Oh, he knew them well, these cool and haughty sirens; knew all the tricks they used to ensare men. And his Margaret—for she should have been his—had turned into one of them.

When was it that he had realised that he had loved the wild little girl who had refused him because he had made such a ham-fisted mess of his proposal?

Paula Marshall, married with three children, has had a varied life. She began her career in a large library and ended it as a senior academic in charge of history in a polytechnic. She has travelled widely, has been a swimming coach, and has appeared on *University Challenge* and *Mastermind*. She has always wanted to write, and likes her novels to be full of adventure and humour.

Recent titles by the same author:

LADY CLAIRVAL'S MARRIAGE
AN AFFAIR OF HONOUR
EMMA AND THE EARL
A BIDDABLE GIRL?
THE LOST PRINCESS

The author would like to thank the staff of the Wolfson Library of the Royal Zoologial Society, London, for their kind assistance in helping to make the visit of my characters to the London Zoo in 1828 as authentic as possible.

THE YOUNGEST MISS ASHE

Paula Marshall

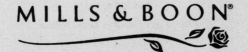

MILLS & BOON®

First published in Great Britain 1997
Harlequin Mills & Boon Limited,
Eton House, 18-24 Paradise Road, Richmond, Surrey TW9 1SR

© Paula Marshall 1997

ISBN 0 263 80199 3

Set in Times 11 on 12 pt. by
Rowland Phototypesetting Limited
Bury St Edmunds, Suffolk

04-9708-67543

Printed and bound in Great Britain

Chapter One

'**O**h, do hold still, Margaret,' complained Mrs Ashe to her daughter, the youngest Miss Ashe, 'you know how important it is that you look perfectly proper when Sir Simon comes to propose to you. And here you are, your hair awry and your gown creased, and he almost about to arrive. How is it, I ask myself, that however carefully Simpson dresses you, in half an hour you look as though you have been bird's-nesting with that wretched Julian Wentworth?'

Julian was the Rector's son with whom, not so long ago, eighteen-year-old Margaret *had* enjoyed bird's-nesting.

'I wish I were going out with Julian, or helping Wilkinson to pot plants in the hothouse. Anything would be better than sitting here like a prize heifer, waiting for its owner to claim it!'

'Dear me, Margaret, you do say the most indelicate things,' moaned her mother, trying to tidy her daughter's errant and undistinguished brown hair.

'No wonder your London Season was such a disaster.'

For the hundredth time she wished that Margaret was more like her sisters, who possessed bright golden curls, blue eyes, beautiful regular features and elegant figures, together with biddable dispositions. All of them, though virtually dowerless, had made grand marriages in consequence.

'Really, Mama, you mustn't expect me to chaperon Margaret again,' her eldest and most beautiful sister, Jane, Lady Vancourt, had told her mother. 'She makes no effort to please, finds polite society a dead bore and frightens off any pretty young fellow who might wish to marry her. Instead, she spends all her time either in the library with Vancourt's librarian, or in the stables with the grooms. . .

'No, she must stay in Leicestershire and marry some rustic squire who won't object to her lack of manners. Hetty and Phoebe are both of the same mind, so it's no use asking *them* to drag her about, either.'

Margaret, who much preferred to be called Meg, or Meggie, shrugged her shoulders and took her canvaswork from her mother with the instruction that Sir Simon Darrow must find her usefully employed when he arrived. It was, her mother thought despairingly, perhaps Margaret's most annoying attribute that she was so much more capable in everything she did than her elder sisters had been.

Her stitchery, her embroidery, her tending of the flowerbeds, her piano playing, her singing, her riding, as well as her ability to speak both French and Italian so fluently, were all to no avail if she despised marriage and the social round which were, after all, what women of their class were trained and destined for.

Such useful attributes would be sure to please a husband who was looking for sense rather than mere beauty in a wife, so it was more than ever distressing that the youngest and only plain Miss Ashe was so set against marriage.

'No one,' said Meg crossly to her mother, 'seems to understand that I don't want to be married, at least not yet. I'm not at all like Jane and the rest, you know. They never talk about anything serious and would faint if they saw a calf born. . .'

'Margaret!' shrieked her mother. 'What a thing to say! I knew no good would come of your father allowing you to run wild among the grooms and the gardeners. You really do need a husband to keep you in order. And, for goodness sake, don't say anything like that to Sir Simon—or to any other man, for that matter. Your reputation would be gone in an instant, and you would end up like your great-aunt Griselda, an eccentric old maid.'

But happy, thought Meg mutinously, giving a resigned sigh and beginning to stitch doggedly away at the tail of the peacock she had drawn upon a square of fine linen, which was destined to be a firescreen. I daren't upset Mama by telling her that, even though Lord Vancourt was the catch of the Season and Jenny caught him, she is most unhappy.

For what did he do, once the honeymoon was over, but start chasing bits of muslin again, even though he had vowed to her that his wild days were behind him. When I lived in London with them they only met at meal times—and not always then.

But that, she thought, doesn't explain why I don't wish to marry Simon. After all, so far as I know, he's never been interested in the muslin trade, and I'm sure that he would be faithful. Except that, like the heroine of that old play Papa gave me to read, *The Way of the World*, I think it was, I don't want to dwindle into a wife.

I suppose that it's all Papa's fault for encouraging me to read and to think, as well as learning what he calls the womanly arts. Jenny and the others certainly never wanted to talk about anything but lovers, dress, trimming bonnets and the season, and poor Papa needed *someone* to talk to!

Mrs Ashe had not ceased to harangue her about how she should behave before, during and after she had accepted Simon's proposal and was about to become young Lady Darrow instead of the youngest Miss Ashe.

'It will be such a relief to have all four of you married,' she proclaimed. 'And all of you so well, particularly since you—'

She stopped and coloured, realising it was scarcely tactful to tell Margaret quite so bluntly that her value in the marriage market had been so low, not only because of Margaret's lack of obvious charms, but because the Ashe family had been as poor as church mice ever since grandfather Ashe had gambled away all their land and property. He had left them just enough to live on, but not to keep Highmount Hall in the state in which their great-grandfather had left it.

'Are nowhere near as beautiful and biddable as any of your more fortunate sisters,' finished Meg for her. 'Say it, Mama. Tell me how lucky I am that Simon is willing to overlook my brown hair, green eyes and lack of figure, and marry me.'

'I am sure, Margaret Ashe, that you are the most contrary child a mother could have the misfortune to give birth to. I will leave you now to do your duty to your name and family,' was all that her unhappy mother could manage in answer. Margaret had always been able to run verbal rings around her.

'If I didn't marry, I should at least do my duty by keeping my name,' retorted Meg perversely. 'But I promise that I will give Sir Simon a fair hearing and then make up my own mind as to whether I accept him or not. Will that do?'

It would obviously have to serve. Before she left her to await Sir Simon's arrival, her mother could not resist offering her yet another piece of advice. 'Do not disarrange yourself once I am gone. A man does so like a tidy woman for his wife.'

But not for his mistress, thought Miss Ashe irrepressibly and irreverently, having had some of London's most notorious ladybirds pointed out to her, including Miss Laura Knight, who had been the *belle amie* of more than one great man. There had been nothing conspicuously tidy about *her*. Quite the contrary. She was more like the lady in the poem by Herrick, which Papa had once begun to quote when Mama had reproached her in front of him for untidiness.

' "A sweet disorder in the dress",' he had murmured slyly.

Only Mama had said sharply to him, 'Fie on you, sir! Not in front of the child.'

Seventeen-year old Meg had looked up the rest of the verse which went on 'kindles in clothes a wantonness'. So perhaps it wasn't surprising that Miss Knight, although richly dressed, had a certain air of invitation about her, which was best expressed by a curl which had sprung free from her otherwise carefully ordered *coiffure*, and a scarf which kept falling away to reveal more of a beautiful bosom than might be considered seemly. Another example, she thought wryly, of her Papa's fatal influence on her speech and conduct.

So she said nothing, and allowed her mother to leave her, unaware that a large part of her daughter's perversity had arisen as a consequence of another conversation between her parents: this time on the previous evening.

Her mother had been expressing surprise at the news that Simon had asked her father for the youngest Miss Ashe's hand in marriage.

Her father had replied in the pleasantly harried voice which he always used to her mother, 'But, my dear, consider. Simon is getting no younger. He is twenty-seven and unmarried. He has only that wastrel cousin, Peverel Darrow, for an heir, and needs a child of his own. Marrying Margaret would be most convenient for him, seeing that he does not wish to waste time running round the London Season, looking for a wife in the marriage mart.

'He knows that our Meg is a sensible girl of good

breeding stock, since all her sisters have provided their husbands with heirs with commendable promptitude. Besides, given everything, she is the homely sort who will always be faithful to him. She will be content to live quietly in the country, since she loves country pursuits and will never be the belle of the Season.'

'I had thought,' her mother had said, a trifle plaintively, 'that he might offer for Jenny, but he never did. She married Vancourt instead—which was, of course, a much better match than any Margaret is likely to achieve.'

'Marry Jenny? Never. That's not Simon's way. She was far too flighty for him. No, you may depend upon it, my dear, my practical and clever Meg is the one he wishes to marry. And I, for one, do not blame him. She will make him an excellent wife. We have trained her well between us.'

No, I shan't, Meg had thought savagely, I shan't make Sir Simon Darrow a wife at all. He's obviously only marrying me to have his children because I am of good breeding stock—like he chooses his cows and horses, I suppose.

And because I'm convenient. Convenient! As well as being plain and unlikely to attract any other man once we are married. Not that I should want to, of course, but it's horrid to be so taken for granted. I don't consider any of *that* makes marriage to him an honour at all.

Not that he was so bad a catch, all things considered, even if he were nowhere near as grand as Lords Vancourt, Wallasey and Zealand, her sisters' husbands.

Darrow Hall, its parkland, its tenant farms and adjacent coalfield in the heart of the Leicestershire countryside, not far from where the Quorn hunted, brought in a largish income. He could probably do far better than marry the only ugly sister in a beautiful family. He was a kind man, Meg was sure, but he wasn't the kind man the youngest Miss Ashe wanted, not now.

Now she would rather die an old maid like Great Aunt Griselda than marry him. Let him marry some other plain girl. The good Lord knew that there were plenty of them about for him to choose from. Which all went to prove that the old adage was true: listeners never hear any good of themselves.

Tears had filled her eyes as she had walked desolately away. Oh, if only she had not overheard them! If she had not done so, the prospect of marrying Simon would not have seemed so dreadful—he had always been a kind of jolly brother to her.

What is it that I do want, then? she had asked herself. I don't know. The only thing that I do know is that I don't want to get married—yet. I haven't seen the world. More importantly, I haven't seen anyone in it I wish to marry—marriage being such a lottery.

Now, stricken all over again, she pricked her finger and gave a slight moan just as there was a knock on the door. It was the butler, who announced that Sir Simon Darrow was here to see her if she were in.

'Of course, I'm in,' she replied. 'I couldn't be more in if I tried. Tell *him* to come in, too.'

She tried to smile as the butler bowed Simon

into the room. He was perfectly dressed for such an important occasion, which was also what she had expected. He was always so exceedingly proper in every way. And old. Racing towards his thirties.

With his deep-blue coat, cream breeches that were not skintight, perfectly blacked boots—without gold tassels—and a not-too-elaborate cravat, he was the very model of a country squire, neither carelessly dressed nor a dandy.

He might, Meg conceded, even be thought handsome if you liked big, strong men with harsh faces, grey eyes, slightly hooked noses and dark, waving hair prematurely shot with silver. Her own taste ran to blond Apollos who resembled the milder-looking Greek gods, of whom there were a number of statues in the entrance hall of her run-down home. Her father was considering selling them.

To her astonishment, Simon took her hand and bowed over it as solemnly and reverently as though she were the Season's toast, a beauty of the first water. Which was all a nonsense, of course.

He rose, and when she waved him to a chair, said, in that kind, fatherly voice of his which made him sound so much older than his years, 'Allow me to stand, my dear. I have something to say to you which I think would be better said standing.'

Well, what was she to say to that? Not the truth, which would have been something in the order of, Save your breath, Simon, I have not the slightest desire to marry you! So she said nothing, which was the cue for him to continue. 'My dear Margaret. You will allow me to call you Margaret, will you not?'

He stood there, head slightly bent, waiting for an answer.

What an odd way for him to begin! He had been calling her Meg, or Meggie, ever since she had run behind him in short skirts at the age of five. Then he had been a tall boy of fourteen, come to fly his kite with her big brother Jasper, who was now a cavalry officer in the Army, and she had been a little pest, wailing after them, 'Let me come with you, please. . .'

Or had he? Wasn't it true that lately he had taken to calling her Miss Margaret, as though she were already ninety? She really ought to give him an answer, for his air of pleasant command as he stood before the empty hearth was growing a little strained as a result of her delay.

'I'm sorry,' she stammered, 'I was woolgathering.' Which was hardly a gracious thing to say to a man who had come to propose to her, but never mind that. 'Of course, you may call me Margaret, Sir Simon.'

Belatedly, Meg realised how badly she was behaving. If Margaret, then Simon, of course; and so, politely and inevitably, he told her.

'Oh, I think that I may be Simon again, don't you?' he said. 'Particularly as I have come to ask you something, which I hope will result in what has been a pleasant friendship for both of us becoming something closer, much closer.'

Now his smile had taken on a genuine warmth, softening his harsh face, making him seem younger, more like his true age. If only. . .

If only, what? Meg couldn't think. What she

wanted to do was to prevent him from proposing,
but none of the books of etiquette which she had
read had ever given her any advice on that. There
was a general assumption in them that all sensible
young ladies could only have one thing to say in
such a situation and that was 'yes'. Would he be
very cross when she said 'no'? Might it not be better
to say 'yes' and please everyone?

Except herself, of course.

Better to bite the bullet. Let him have his say and
then decline him politely. She remembered Jenny
making them all laugh in the schoolroom when she
had told them how she had turned down some
impossible younger son of no fortune. Which was
not the same thing at all, for Simon was not a
younger son, and he certainly had a fortune, and he
did not deserve to be laughed at.

'My dear Margaret,' he was saying. 'I have known
you since you were a child, and have watched you
grow into a most attractive young lady of great prac-
ticality—a virtue which many young ladies lack. . .'

Was she really hearing this? Of course, she knew
what he meant. He had seen her doing groom's work
with Brutus; potting plants with Wilkinson and helping him to prune shrubs and roses; working in the
still room and, once, he had caught her churning
butter in their small dairy at the back of the stables.

He surely didn't know that she had been working
in the library, listing books for Papa so that he might
know which would fetch money if sold and which
would not. Or perhaps Papa had told him.

But most attractive? Now that *must* be a joke.

He was ploughing on, listing her virtues which

apparently and mainly included common sense and not much else. How little he knew of her! He was quite unaware of the Meg Ashe who read Minerva Press novels and imagined herself amazingly beautiful—like Jane—and running off with the errant and bedazzled heir to a dukedom, and saving him from the plots of his wicked uncle. . .

'And so,' he finally achieved, 'seeing that we have always been great friends, I thought that we might seal that friendship by becoming man and wife. Make me a happy man, Margaret, by accepting the hand which I offer you.'

At least he didn't go down on one knee as Jane had said Vancourt had done. Instead, he put his large and shapely hand out to her, doubtless certain that she would take it—and him.

Now that the moment for refusing him had come, Meg found that she had no heart for it. Yes, he had been a good and kind friend and his grim face no longer looked so grim. It was the face of the patient young man who had always had time to talk to her, lift her on to her horse, and make up for the fact that she had lost her brother Jasper to the Army.

He had always been kind to her—unlike her sisters. Simon, who had shown her how to hold his pet macaw and stroke his naughty monkey, trophies his sailor uncle had brought him from strange lands overseas. Simon loved all animals.

Alas, while she hesitated, he settled the matter for her and, in Jasper's slang, dished himself.

He smiled encouragingly and said, 'Come, my dear girl, do not be coy. This is not like you. I know how forthright you are, how free from the fashionable folly of most young women—how little you value sentimental flim-flam. Give me your answer.'

He meant it kindly, no doubt, Meg thought afterwards.

He believed that he was offering her a compliment by differentiating her from the pretty girls who were allowed to dither charmingly, prevaricate and titter before they made an answer. Had he not spoken so, she would have accepted him, and her whole life— and his—would have been different.

After all, she knew him to be a good man, kind even to his tenants when many landowners were not. He had never taken part in the careless round of pleasure like many young men of his station. He would make a splendid husband and father.

Alas, all her life she had been 'only Meg', and, in a sense, the manner of his proposal had betrayed that, to him, too, she was different from her sisters. So he had spared her—spared her!—'sentimental flim-flam'. Oh, if only. . . And that 'if only' had her disregarding his offered hand so that he dropped it, his face beginning to change a little, becoming sterner, the kind smile disappearing.

'I'm sorry, Simon,' she faltered, her voice breaking a little, 'but I have always thought of you as a brother, never as a husband.' Well, that at least, was true. 'So I am sure that, on reflection, you will agree that it would be wrong for me to consent to be your wife. I am sure, also, that there are many young ladies who would be pleased to accept you, but I cannot.'

'And this is your considered answer? You have

made it very quickly—you do not wish to ask for time to reflect on my offer?' His face had darkened, but to Meg's relief his voice was as cool and calm as ever.

'Yes, it is my considered answer. I do not think that I shall wish to change my mind.'

'Then I am sorry, Margaret. I had thought that we might deal well together as man and wife.'

Deal well together! Where was love? Where was passion in that? Vancourt might have been a deceiver, but Wallasey, Hetty's husband, had looked at her, and she at him, with such fire in their eyes. Where was Simon's fire when he looked at her? And, more to the point, where was hers when she looked at him?

'Your father thought. . .' Simon began. For once Meg saw him at a loss, which surprised her.

He stopped, started again. 'Your father thought that you would be very happy to accept me. He knows that we share the same interests—which is a good foundation for marriage.'

Meg thought fleetingly of kneeling beside Simon and his herdsman as they examined a newborn calf. Of his tenderness for the calf, and the pride with which he had shown it to her. He had told her that it was the first of a new breed. It occurred to her that he had never talked of such things to Jenny, to whom her mother had thought that he might propose.

Even so, she had made up her mind. She was tired of being the youngest Miss Ashe, taken for granted. She quailed a little at the thought of what her parents would say when they heard that she had refused such a desirable marriage, but it was her life, not theirs, and she was not afraid to live with the consequences.

In many ways Simon Darrow knew the youngest Miss Ashe very well, even if he did not know enough of her to frame his proposal correctly. He could tell by the set of her face, the tilt of her head, her whole posture, that her mind was made up. She would not have him. Or at least, not now. He was a patient man, he told himself and there would be another day—when she was a little older, perhaps, and marriage did not seem so daunting.

He would wait.

'Refused him!' her mother almost shrieked at her when Simon had left, his carriage disappearing down the drive. 'You wicked, thoughtless child! You are unlikely ever to get a better offer—or, indeed, any offer at all, considering how little *you* have to offer!'

Her father was more measured, and kinder in his speech, but Meg could tell at once how disappointed he was.

'Oh, Meggie,' he said sorrowfully, 'I thought you liked Simon. You have been friends for so long, and he would make you the best of husbands. On the other hand, it is your life, and I don't believe in arranged marriages, or I would have arranged your marriage to Simon.'

There was nothing she could usefully say to that, but, 'I don't think that I love him, and I'm not yet ready to be married.'

Her mother made a great scoffing noise, but her father looked thoughtful, and nodded.

'You may be right, my child. You are not like

your sisters.' He paused, then said rapidly before her mother could speak again, her colour high, her face set in lines of temper, 'My dear,' and now he was addressing his wife.

'My sister, Léonie, is coming to stay with us shortly. I think that it would be helpful if we asked her to take Meg back to Paris with her when she leaves. It would be good for her to learn to live away from us and her sisters. She has grown too used to being the youngest—and the least considered. A change of air might work wonders.'

Mrs Ashe's expected snort of disagreement would have amused Meg at any other time.

'*Margaret* does not need pampering. She needs informing what her duty is, and doing it. You must order her to write at once to Sir Simon and tell him that she has changed her mind. Going to Paris with Léonie, indeed! What will that achieve other than to convince her that she may do as she pleases— and be rewarded for it.'

Mr Ashe passed his hand wearily over his face. He knew that his wife detested her sister-in-law Léonie. Not only had she married a French *émigré* Vicomte and changed her name from an unpronounceable English Leonora to a pronounceable French Léonie, but she had the effrontery to be charming, civilised and witty—a great lady, in every sense. Everything, in fact, Mrs Ashe considered, which was not sturdily English.

'I have made up my mind,' he announced, his tone as mild as he could make it. 'If Léonie will agree to take her, Meg shall go to Paris.'

'Oh, I know that you only call her Meg to annoy

me,' her mother proclaimed. 'But you will have your way, I suppose, as she does.'

'No one,' said Meg, 'has asked me whether I wish to go to Paris.'

'Now, Meg,' said her father. 'Is that a declaration that you do not wish to go—or simply one of independence? If the latter, then I will ask you.'

She smiled. All was well again. Papa was not really cross with her; perhaps he even understood something of what had made her refuse Simon. He was already making the kind of mild joke that her mother would never understand.

'Really, Mr Ashe! Tell her what you wish her to do. Do not raise her spirits by asking her anything. *That* is what has brought us to this day!'

'Yes, Papa, I will go with aunt Léonie, if she will have me,' Meg said swiftly, in an attempt to prevent her mother from continuing to berate her father. To see Paris! Recently defeated at Waterloo though the French had been, Paris was still the *Ville Lumière*, the city of light and culture.

'Then that is settled,' replied her papa, equally swiftly, ignoring her mother's scoffing.

'Light in the attic, both of you. Nothing good will come of it, I can tell you, Margaret being what she is and Léonie what she is.'

And so it was decided.

Aunt Léonie, when she arrived at Highmount Hall in her usual continental state, took one look at a dejected and rumpled Meg and agreed that Paris was the only cure for such determined megrims.

'What is it, child?' she asked Meg when they

were alone. 'Are they determined to wed you to
some elderly ogre?'

Meg shook her head. 'No, not at all. It was Sir
Simon Darrow—Jasper's friend, who lives
nearby—whom they wanted me to marry.'

Inwardly, she was marvelling at her aunt. Would
she ever be like her? She made her beautiful sisters
look like dowdy milkmaids, and even if she went
to Paris to be groomed by Aunt Léonie—for that,
of course, was what Papa intended—would she ever
achieve such effortless elegance?

Her aunt had dark hair and green eyes, exactly
like her own, but her resemblance to Meg ended
there. She was so absolutely, exquisitely polished:
a perfect example of Parisian chic and sophistication. Her spoken English now had a pretty accent
to it—which added to her attractiveness.

Meg could see at once why her mother resented
her husband's sister so much. She was almost fright-
ening in her total command of life. The fact that she
was a rich widow was yet another offence to be
added to the long list that Mrs Ashe kept.

'Ah, yes. I remember. Somewhat older than you
are. Exactly the right age for a husband for you. A
good man—and kind. So why the refusal?

'I don't know.' Meg's eyes filled with tears. 'I
wake up in the night sometimes, and wish that I had
said yes. And then by morning I think no again. I
believe that the real truth is—and Papa agrees with
me—that I am not yet ready for marriage.'

'But not your mother? She would have you married and off her hands. Hmm.' She pulled Meg to
her feet—they were alone in the big drawing-

room—and held her away so that she was looking at her from a distance.

'I agree with you. You are so raw, so young, so *farouche*. Your Papa tells me that not only are you clever, but that you are practical as well, and that is why Sir Simon wishes to marry you. Tell me, are you tired of being clever and practical? Is that why you refused him? Do you wish to be, oh, so pretty and flirt, and have the young men at your feet, la, la?'

'Sometimes.' Meg was honest. 'The truth is, I don't know what I want.'

'Then you shall come to France with me and you shall find out. I shall make such a fine lady of you that no one will know you—and then, perhaps, you may come to know yourself.'

And when I do, what then? thought Meg, who was not sure that she wanted to go to Paris to learn to be a fine lady, until her aunt said,

'I will make you someone who will eclipse your sisters, for you have character and they do not.'

Oh, that did it, did it not! For then she would no longer be 'only Meg', the youngest Miss Ashe. Who knew what the future might bring?

'Yes, I will come to Paris with you,' Meg said, hanging her head.

Her aunt put her finger beneath her chin, saying briskly, 'No slouching, mind, no round shoulders, for deportment will be your first lesson.'

Meg had set her foot on a new path in life and she had no idea where it would take her, nor what pains, as well as pleasures, she would find as she walked along it.

Chapter Two

'If you must know, I am at *point non plus*, my dear, and I have no one to turn to—except you. I would never have thought, years ago,' she went on slowly, 'that. . .' Jane, Lady Vancourt paused, and looked across the room at Marguerite de Vaux, Madame la Comtesse de Mortaine, widowed these two years, who stood in the bow window of the drawing-room at the Vancourts' Piccadilly home, a book in her hand.

How to finish her sentence without saying the unsayable, '. . .I would need to ask you, of all people, for help and advice,' but something in the calmly serene expression on her sister's face stopped her.

Instead, she began again.

'I know that I was foolish to do what I did. But, as I suppose you know, Vancourt has never done me the honour of being faithful to me, not since the day we were married. I was so bored with being dull and faithful and good, and all the things that perfect wives are supposed to be.

'When Peverel Darrow made such a dead set at me, I was foolish enough to give way for once and have an *affaire* with him. Such a mistake. And I made it worse by writing him letters—and now he is blackmailing me with them. Well, aren't you going to say something?'

'Only, why Peverel Darrow, of all people? You have known for years what a charming rogue he is, never to be trusted. Did his pretty face seduce you? It can't have been his character—*that* is not pretty at all.'

'Easy for you to talk,' retorted Jane. 'I suppose that you were never tempted before André died—and not since, either.'

Her sister did not answer her, simply shook her head, put down her book and arranged herself carefully on the sofa opposite Jane, who stared at her in frank disbelief. Such coolly charming perfection of appearance and manner was an art in itself.

Marguerite's chestnut-coloured hair, smoothly polished and sleek with golden lights in it like a ripe conker, enhanced her green eyes. It was dressed in the latest, severer style, without clustering ringlets and the usual deep fringe. The lack of curls emphasised the austere planes of her face, giving it a grave and individual attractiveness.

'You are so like Aunt Léonie,' burst from Jane, 'so much so that it's almost unnatural.'

'*Vraiment*? Truly? And you are so like Mama—as are Hetty and Phoebe. One of us had to resemble Papa's family.'

'And that is not what I meant—it is your manner which is most like hers, as you must know.'

Marguerite inclined her head. 'What I do know—' and her tone was gentle '—is that you need my help. What can I do for you?'

Recalled to the point, Jane resumed her sad story. 'He has threatened to send my letters to Vancourt unless I pay him five hundred pounds—when he promises to return them. Despite the fact that Vancourt trades with every member of the muslin set and has a *maîtresse en titre* as well, he would never forgive me for having an affair. He would send me into the country forever.

'But. . .' and her voice degenerated into a wail '. . .I can't raise five hundred pounds, and he has told me that unless I pay it over to him at Lady Leominster's reception tomorrow evening, he will offer them to Vancourt for the same amount, and if he refuses he will sell them to Bayes who will publish them in his Radical paper as evidence of aristocratic corruption, and the need for reform. It might even bring the government down.'

Despite herself, Marguerite began to laugh. 'Oh, I doubt whether your letters will bring the Ministry down—' Vancourt was a minor member of the cabinet '—but I agree, the scandal would be *formidable*. Yes, I will help you. Do not trouble yourself about the money, I will lend you that.'

'Oh, thank you, thank you. I know it's a great deal to ask, but I wonder if you would take my place, hand him the money and collect the letters? I haven't the courage to face him. I'm sure I would do something stupid. . .but you. . . Oh, please, say yes.'

Marguerite had no wish to do any such thing, but

Jane had dropped her face into her hands and had begun a low dry sobbing which was more distressing than loud watery keening would have been.

'Yes,' she said, at last. 'Tell me exactly where your rendezvous is tomorrow.'

Jane sprang to her feet and flung her arms around her sister. 'Oh, thank you, thank you. I am to meet him in Lady Leominster's Chinese room tomorrow evening at ten of the clock. Oh, I knew that you wouldn't let me down! After all, we meant a great deal to one another when we were children, did we not? I am on my high ropes that you have returned to England in time to help me.'

Marguerite de Vaux, Comtesse de Mortaine, who, after eight years in France, was no longer 'only Meg', the youngest Miss Ashe, but a great lady of consequence in her own right, smiled a wry smile as she stared across the room at a group portrait of Lord and Lady Vancourt and their two children, prettily disposed in an Arcadian garden. Whatever she had expected when she returned to England, it was not this. Neither the knowledge of how much she had changed, or how little Vancourt and Jane had!

'There, there,' she said, as though she were comforting a child. 'No need to worry.'

'Oh, what a tower of strength you have become, Margaret. Whoever would have thought it when we were children together? You were such a gauche little thing. And you have become quite a beauty, too. Vancourt was making sheep's eyes at you, as I'm sure you noticed.'

'And that's a Banbury tale,' retorted Marguerite

de Vaux, who still thought of herself as Meg, the youngest Miss Ashe, 'that I am a beauty. I make no such claim for myself. And you may rest assured that I have no designs on Vancourt, or anyone else for that matter. I am content to remain a widow.'

'You've no need to. Others will make the claim of beauty for you. As for being a widow, that is the one thing about you which I do criticise. After all, André died over two years ago, and here you are, still in lilac, still in half-mourning.'

'It suits me,' said her sister, as simply as Meg Ashe would once have done.

'True, it goes with your eyes. How was it that, when you were a girl, we never noticed how beautiful they were?' sighed Jane who, at least, Meg thought, had the decency not to be jealous of her now that the tables were turned. For between two children, three miscarriages and Vancourt's overt unfaithfulness, she had not worn well.

The pretty plump girl with blonde ringlets and blue eyes had become faded and harried-looking before she had reached thirty-five. Meg, on the other hand, knew how much she had changed and bloomed after two years grooming in Paris by her aunt Léonie, her four years of marriage to André de Vaux, and her two years of widowhood.

Apparently inconsequentially, Jane asked, 'Have you spoken to Simon Darrow since you returned to England?'

Simon Darrow! How long was it since she had thought of him? In those early, dreadful days in Paris spent trying to live up to Aunt Léonie's apparently impossible demands and commands, Meg had thought of him often. Mostly in terms of bitter regret that, had she accepted his offer, she would have been back in the country with him and his dogs, cows and horses, instead of being pulled in and out of fine clothes, and being rebuked for her gauche behaviour.

At what point had the change come when she had turned from Meg to Margaret to Marguerite, Aunt Léonie's charming and amusing niece, who had half the eligible young men in Paris at her feet? Not until after a long and arduous tutelage, that was for sure! And when exactly had she forgotten Simon, so that to hear his name was something of a shock?

'He's never married, you know,' said Jane, watching her sister for some kind of telltale response. But, as usual, she was wasting her time. Behind that calmly perfect mask acquired in France, nothing showed.

'No, I didn't know.'

'And he's an MP, now. Doing well, Vancourt says. Won't be long before they offer him a post in the Government.'

Simon an MP! Simon, who always claimed that he loathed London and politics whenever the suggestion had come up in the days when she had known him. What a turn-up! Had he changed, too?

'He's greatly changed,' Jane offered, mind-reading a little, perhaps. 'Vancourt always thought him a bit of a prig—particularly where women were concerned. But he's certainly not a prig these days. Quite the rake, or so the rumours say.'

Simon a rake! Staid, somewhat solid, if not to say stolid, Simon Darrow. Decidedly, whilst she was out of England, forgetting all that she had left behind, things had changed more than somewhat.

What surprised Meg most of all was that learning that Simon was a rake hurt her—it was as though, at the back of her mind, she had always thought of him as her husband, so that to hear Jane say that he was a womaniser gave her a strong feeling of betrayal!

Which was ridiculous, to say the least. For if she had the right to turn herself into a Frenchified belle, and to marry a rich and powerful French aristocrat, then Simon certainly had the right to turn himself into a ladies' man.

For once, Meg was nonplussed. Fearful that she might betray her odd turn of thought to Jane, she was carefully considering her answer when Vancourt entered with a young man at his heels.

Watching him carefully, Meg saw that Jane's statement that he was attracted by her was no less than the truth. His manner to her was gallant in the extreme, and when he introduced the blond young man as 'my cousin, Mr Will Osborne', Will's answer betrayed that Vancourt had spoken of her in admiring terms.

'Delighted to make your acquaintance, Madame la Comtesse,' he said, bowing over her hand, his accent atrocious. 'I have heard so much of you, and all to your advantage.'

Meg smiled and inclined her head to him graciously in a gesture which Meg Ashe would have mocked, but which slew young Mr Osborne, who turned scarlet at her graciousness. He decided that all he had heard of the Comtesse de Mortaine's charm, sophistication and *savoir faire* was true.

'Vancourt tells me that you are accompanying him and Lady Vancourt to Lady Leominster's ball tomorrow evening. You would do me a great honour if you agreed to allow me to act as your escort.'

Jane watched, fascinated, as yet another pretty young fellow threw himself metaphorically at her sister's feet. She was no more surprised than Meg herself.

In France it had, even before she had married André, seemed perfectly natural for her to enter a room and capture the attention of nearly every man in it, but here in England—that was a different matter. She had feared that the shadow of being the youngest Miss Ashe might still hang over her and affect her confidence. But no such thing!

She took Will's homage as her due, and accepted his offer. She would arrive at her first public appearance in London on the arm of one of the Season's greatest catches. Jane had already told her that Will was the cousin and heir of the Earl of Stanyon and every mother in the marriage market was desperate to secure him for her daughter!

And if she saw Simon Darrow—but why was she thinking about Simon? He was part of her past, which was dead and gone.

Another dead bore of an evening, thought Sir Simon Darrow glumly. Ever since he had broken with Caroline, Lady Kenilworth, that lovely widow, who had been determined not only to add him to her list of conquests, but to marry him as well, he had found such occasions as the Leominsters' ball wearying.

Every Mama in society was in headlong pursuit of him.

It was not that he hadn't enjoyed his six years as an MP, although he hadn't expected to. Before his first Season had begun, he had decided that the end of it would see him married, and now, here he was, still a bachelor—and in the eyes of the polite world, a confirmed one.

He had taken up a position near the top of the stairs, watching Lord and Lady Leominster greet their guests: the strains of a waltz came from the ballroom behind him. George Vancourt was escorting a small party on to the landing at exactly the same moment that his cousin Peverel accosted him.

'How do, Sim? Thought you might not be here. Hard day in the Commons, wasn't it?'

Peverel had Jasper Ashe with him, a blond giant resplendent in full regimentals. It was some years since he had seen Jasper, although as boys they had been chums, always in and out of scrapes. Then Jasper had joined Wellington's army, in time to see action at Waterloo, and they had drifted apart.

'Happy to see you again, Darrow. How many years has it been?'

'Too many,' said Simon cheerfully—he preferred Jasper's Darrow to Peverel's over-familiar Sim— and then stopped.

His attention had been caught by an unknown woman in Vancourt's party. Her escort was that eager young puppy, Will Osborne, who was visibly dangling after her, adoration written in his eyes. She was just under middle height, with a perfect figure, a slightly haughty carriage and was dressed with extreme elegance and perfect style in amethyst silk; a colour which enhanced both an ivory face of great character and her lustrous chestnut hair.

The jewels she wore were discreet, not vulgar, but were worth a small fortune none the less. A tiny tiara of amethysts and diamonds adorned her shapely head, amethyst and diamond tear drops her ears. A single amethyst on a thin silver chain beautified a neck like that of a swan in its elegance, and a slender bracelet of the same stones showed to advantage an exquisite tiny hand. She was carrying a large fan— amethyst coloured, inevitably—with pale mauve lilacs painted on it.

Altogether she was a sight to draw every eye, male or female—and was obviously used to doing so, for the murmur which followed her progress apparently moved her not at all.

Simon drew in his breath. He remarked abruptly to his cousin Peverel, who knew everything and everybody in society despite his dubious reputation, 'Who is the polished piece of perfection with Vancourt who is causing all the excitement?'

For some reason his question appeared to amuse both Jasper and Peverel inordinately. Jasper laughed openly, and Peverel's accompanying smile was more than usually knowing and cynical.

'Come on, Simon,' Jasper said, grinning. 'You needn't bam us. We're old friends, remember?'

'Bam you?' Simon was genuinely puzzled.

So puzzled that Jasper, choking a little, said, 'Doing it too brown, old fellow. It's m'sister—as you well know.'

This merely served to confound Simon the more rather than enlighten him.

'Now *you*'re bamming *me*. That's neither Hetty nor Phoebe and well you know it.'

It was Peverel's turn to try to bait him. It was too good a trick to miss. Simon was usually the one coldly in charge, not the gull which he was now pretending to be.

'Not Hetty nor Phoebe, nodcock, but Margaret—Jasper's youngest sister—the Comtesse de Mortaine. Don't pretend you can't recognise her.'

'Margaret! *That's* Margaret?'

Vancourt's party was passing them at some little distance. The woman whom they claimed was his long-lost Margaret was walking quietly along, her eyes lowered. Suddenly, as though she had become aware that she was being closely watched, she lifted her head to turn to look in his direction, so that Simon caught a glimpse of a pair of brilliant green eyes.

Something clicked in his brain. It was as though Madame de Mortaine had been wearing a mask that had suddenly dropped to reveal a face far different from that which it had hidden. He briefly saw Margaret Ashe again, the youthful hoyden who had followed him and Jasper about.

The look of pain which passed across his face astonished Jasper, who moved between Simon and Peverel so that Peverel should not see it. So, Simon's proposal to Meg must have been more than one of convenience—even if Simon had not consciously known that when he had made it.

He had spoken lightly of it to Jasper when he had

seen him in London a year later, and Jasper had believed him. After all, Meg had scarcely been a great prize, either in looks or wealth, and Simon could have been expected to marry both.

Now, of course, she was one of the greatest prizes in society!

What had they done to her? His Margaret. His Meg. . .his Meggie. The pet names they had called her by, years ago, sprang unbidden to Simon's mind. Worse still, what had she done to turn herself into a fashion plate, a sophisticated houri? By all appearances she was no better than she should be! Oh, he knew them well, these cool and haughty sirens; knew all the tricks they used to ensnare men. And his Margaret—for she should have been his—had turned into one of them.

When was it that he had realised that he had loved the wild little girl who had refused him because he had made such a ham-fisted mess of his proposal? He looked away from Jasper and Peverel. Jasper, quick-witted, thought that there was only one thing to do, and that at once. Simon must take his medicine.

He seized him by the arm, and said, 'Come on, old fellow, and meet her again. How long is it since she left England? Eight years, is it not? You could scarcely have expected her to remain the same, could you now? Especially after living for so many years in France and marrying into their nobility.'

Whilst he spoke, he was urging Simon into the ballroom and towards Vancourt's party. By now Simon had sufficiently recovered himself to remark coolly, 'I should never have known her. Not only is she not in the least like you and your sisters, but she doesn't resemble the little girl I used to know in any way.'

'True,' said Jasper, nodding vigorously, to be supported by Peverel who was walking with them, determined to see the fun when Simon met Meg again. He had been greatly relieved when she had turned his cousin down. For, no doubt about it, had she not done so she would have dished any hopes that he had of inheriting Darrow Hall and all that went with it.

The Ashes were a prolific lot, and by now Simon would have been the father of a number of squalling brats, and all of them—to spite his former heir—sons. No need to think that Simon might up and propose to the merry widow, his former choice of wife, if the expression on his face, when he had discovered who the fancy madam was, was any guide.

Which was exactly what Simon was thinking, agreeing for once with his wastrel heir. The nearer he got to the woman who had once been Margaret Ashe, the less he liked the look of her. Meretricious in every vein of her body, and proud of it, was his savage conclusion. For some reason that he didn't understand, he had a burning desire to punish her for having changed so much that she was unrecognisable.

Oh, but she had recognised him, without a doubt! For as he drew near and she saw him coming, her eyes widened, and there was the smallest, slightest shift in the hands which held the big fan.

Simon had found, during his years as an MP and

in London society, that he could read not only animals, but also men and women. Now, eight years later, he would not have made the mistakes in his proposal which had lost him Margaret—except that now he did not wish to propose to her. By no means.

He was immediately before her, bowing, as Jasper said, 'Marguerite, I have brought over an old friend to see you,' and as she did not respond other than by a cool nod of that haughty head, and the holding out of a small hand to be kissed, he added, 'You remember Simon, surely?'

Marguerite, Jasper had called her. What the devil kind of name was that for Meggie Ashe? It took him all his strength not to say so. Instead he remarked, politely, if coldly, 'I would not have known you, Margaret, without Jasper's help—and scarcely with it.'

'Oh, I knew *you*,' she responded, unsmiling, and withdrawing the hand which he had refused to kiss. 'You have become London fine, I admit, but that has added polish, not change.'

She even had the temerity to speak English with the slightest of accents—something which doubtless charmed fools like Will Osborne, who stood there, worshipping her. It didn't charm Simon Darrow, and he would have liked to tell her so. At the same time, something inside him was wondering why he was so angry with her.

Jasper had drawn Peverel away, and was talking to Vancourt, another old friend of both of them. Judging by the way he was looking at Madame la Comtesse he was yet another of her admirers. Well, good luck to him, unless she was as cool in bed as she was in public. . .in which case he wouldn't be lucky. Damn him either way!

Margaret knew only too well that Simon was seething with rage. Like him, she had learned to read people in the years since she had last seen him. She had not lied when she had said that she recognised him. The only changes in him were for the better.

She had forgotten, or perhaps had never really understood, how attractive his harsh craggy face and powerful body were. There was more silver in his glossy black hair, but that merely served to add to his attraction, not diminish it.

He was quite different from the men she had known in Paris, and quite unlike her late husband, that blond Apollo.

'I understand that you are now a member of Parliament. When we last met, you always said that you would never be tempted into public life, that you had no talent for it, but Vancourt tells me that you are in line for a government post. Quite a transformation.'

'You are not the only one allowed to change,' riposted Simon drily. 'It was pointed out to me that if I did not like the way that the country was run, then I had a duty to take up a position where I might try to change it.'

She inclined her head, ignoring the first part of his answer. 'Very proper of you, and much to be commended. I trust that leaving your rural interests for so much of the year was not too great a wrench.'

Such patronage! And from little Meg Ashe! Simon's thoughts were savage. His face registered only cold politeness, so that something wrenched inside Meg. Had they descended to this? Banal and boring chit-chat which she could practise in her sleep. She was not surprised when, oh so frostily, he replied in kind.

'It is my rural prowess, I believe, which has given me a Parliamentary reputation. But—unlike many— I have not said goodbye to my roots. I am still Darrow of Darrow, you understand, not a fine gentleman.'

Unspoken were the words, 'As you are a fine lady who *has* renounced her roots!'

'Ah, but you are a remarkably good imitation of a fine gentleman, are you not, *Sir Simon*?' Meg paused, then added meaningfully, 'In every way. . .or so rumour says.'

They were icy with each other, but Jasper, who had rid himself of Peverel and was watching them both, could almost feel the fire beneath the ice. Hostility was in every line of their bodies, although their faces gave nothing away. That last *double entendre* from Meg, twisting Simon's tail about his amorous career, was enough to have any right-minded man thirsting for her blood.

Why in the world were they behaving in this odd fashion? Were they both light in the attic? He had hoped that, once Simon and Meg met again, they would realise that they were made for each other.

But were they?

Meg had turned into a haughty belle with a cruel tongue and Simon into a rake. Who would have thought that possible eight years ago?

Only by hanging on to her self-control as hard as

she could was it possible for Meg not to flinch at
the silent fury on Simon's face after she had flung
her insult at him. But it was her own fault, was it
not? Whatever had provoked her to be so unpleasant
to him?

'My dear Madame la Comtesse,' he told her
softly, 'it would please me greatly to demonstrate
to you the truth of your innuendo in the most time-
honoured fashion! You understand me, I'm sure.'

So she did. But she had never thought to hear
Simon be so unpleasantly cool to her, and at the
same time offer to seduce her!

'Oh, I do hope not.' Her tone was as sweet as her
smile. 'Sometimes, I fear, my understanding proves
faulty. A feminine frailty, perhaps.'

Frail! She was as frail as a six-foot-tall Grenadier
Guardsman, and apparently about as sensitive!
What, though, was appalling was that the mere sight
of her, added to his covert suggestion, sent a spasm
of desire through him so strong that it was shocking.

For the one thing which he had never done was
lust after little Margaret Ashe! But this woman was a
different proposition altogether.

He had heard some of the unpleasant gossip about
Madame la Comtesse de Mortaine, never thinking—
for how could he—that she was *his* Margaret; that
she was accustomed to men who wanted nothing
more than to bed her, and was happy to oblige them.
Damn everything, he now had a burning desire to
be obliged, and a determination to achieve it.

Well, she was his Margaret no longer, just a
Frenchified barque of frailty, fair game for any man.
Fair game for Simon Darrow. He could only hope

that his good friend Jasper Ashe had no notion of
what he was thinking!

'I'm sure,' he returned, his smile both sweet and
false, 'that there is nothing wanting in your understanding which I could not easily supply. You have
only to say the word.'

'But if that word has been torn from my diction-
ary, Sir Simon, what then?'

'That I will lend you mine—to our mutual
advantage.'

Meg was torn between a desire to laugh at his
impudence, and an equally strong desire to slap his
face for his easy supposition that she and virtue
were no longer bedfellows—and endure the scandal
which would follow such a public act.

So this was what Simon Darrow was really like
beneath the mask of virtue which he had shown the
world—and her—eight long years ago. Would she
have accepted him then, had she known? Especially
since she had partly refused him because of his supposed iron rectitude. Now, where on earth had that
gone to? Or had he been a hypocrite then?

An overwhelming desire to end this surprising
conversation before she said something unforgivable
caused Meg to end their tête-á-tête. She raised her
large fan to look at him over the top of it, and said,
'I really must ask you to allow me to leave you. I
see that there are a number of friends present from
my days in France whose acquaintance I wish
to renew.'

Simon stared into the brilliant green eyes which
were, he was sure, mocking him, and murmured as
softly as he could, 'So long as it is understood,

Madame la Comtesse, that this is *au revoir* and not goodbye.'

She lowered her fan for a moment, to reply in kind, 'Oh, that is entirely up to you, sir,' which she was sure was the kind of flirtatious coda which the siren he obviously supposed her to be would make.

Simon almost laughed aloud as she moved away, but refrained out of respect for Jasper's hurt feelings.

'What in the world has happened to your old rapport with Meg, Simon?' Jasper asked mournfully. 'You used to be such friends.'

Simon parried Jasper's criticism of the pair of them by remarking easily, 'Oh, too many years have passed for us to take up where we left off—and I'm not quite sure what our true relationship was then. Meg was such an unformed child.'

Jasper opened his mouth to say something further, then shrugged his shoulders. Oh, to the devil with both of them—no one else would want such a cross-grained pair!

'You're sure that you are really happy to do this favour for me, Meg? It is a great imposition, I know—but I shall be truly grateful.'

'I wouldn't say that I am exactly happy to meet Peverel Darrow for such a reason—but I am willing. Will that do?'

Which was exactly the kind of barbed remark which her sister was fond of throwing into the conversation, was it not? Meg saw by the shadow on her face that she had hurt Jane's feelings. Remorse seized her. Jane's life was unhappy enough without her being needlessly teased.

Dropping her mask of cool control, Meg impulsively put an arm around her sister and hugged her. 'Oh, Jane, forgive me. I'm a little overset tonight. Forget what I said. Remember only that in about an hour, with any luck, you will have your letters back—ready to throw into the nearest fire after you have checked that he has returned them all.'

'Oh, dear, I never thought of that. Surely even Peverel wouldn't do such a thing!'

'Always as well to be sure. Just tell me where the Chinese room is, so that I arrive in time to beard the wolf in his den.'

'Oh, how serene you are! I suppose it is all those years in Paris with Aunt Léonie, and then being married to André. I wish that I possessed your composure.'

Meg forebore to tell her sister the hard price which she had paid to acquire that composure. Later, when she quietly left the Vancourts' party to make her way to the rendezvous with Peverel Darrow, she wondered ruefully whether jousting with him would be easier than jousting with his cousin Simon.

He was far more handsome than Simon, that was for sure, and far more easy in his manner. Where Simon was harsh he was soft—in every way.

Meg found him standing in a dimly lit room, by a fire place flanked by two large bronze urns with roaring Chinese dragons twined around them. The mantelpiece was adorned by a pair of blue and white Chinese vases. All that was wanting was a haughty mandarin to preside over them. Peverel's brows rose in surprise when she entered. Her arrival, instead of that of Jane, did not put him out of countenance.

'Ah, an emissary, I see,' he murmured, offering her a low bow, and motioning her to a seat on to a long divan, which she refused. 'But then, your late husband was a diplomat, was he not? I suppose that you learnt something of his trade. Have you come with a yea or a nay for me?'

Meg lifted the reticule which depended from her waist. She had not done him the honour of acknowledging his bow, or his attempt to take her hand. Instead she took a piece of paper from the reticule, but she did not give it to him as he expected.

'I have here that which you have demanded, sir,' she told him, her voice as frosty as she could make it. 'But I shall not hand this bank draft to you until you give me *all* the letters that you are misusing so wantonly. Blackmail, sir, is not a pretty word, and you are far from a pretty fellow to practise it.'

He bowed again. 'Oh, what a fine lady the little country cousin has become! And so worldly wise. I congratulate you, Madame. Your caution, however, is uneccessary. I am prepared to hand over all the letters, retaining none. I am not a complete villain, you see.'

If it were not for the pain which he had caused her sister, Meg might have been amused by his impudence. Caution had seen her refusing to speak Jane's name, someone might enter, and hear them, and she would rather risk her own reputation—which she knew to be shadowed—than that of poor Jane, who had too many crosses to bear already.

Peverel was also employing caution in naming names—presumably for similar reasons. His eyes on the bank draft which Meg was holding, he pulled from an inner pocket of his fine coat a small packet of letters tied with blue ribbon.

'Reputation restored again,' he had the effrontery to say. 'I need not tell you that burning them would be an excellent notion—never having written them at all, a better.'

Meg did not deign to answer him. It was bad enough to act as a go-between in such a sordid affair without having to endure the excesses of a villain's impudence. He laughed soundlessly at her silence when she handed him the draft, and took the little bundle of letters from him.

As she withdrew her hand, and before she could stop him by moving away, he seized it and kissed it saying, 'Allow me to assure you, Madame la Comtesse, of my utmost admiration for your courage and daring in coming here tonight, and for the manner in which you have behaved. You have surpassed all that I know of you.'

It was plain that, having seduced Jane, he was now prepared to seduce her sister.

To no avail. Meg withdrew her hand as haughtily as she could, gave him a cold stare and averted her head. He was not in the least distressed by her rebuff, merely smiled and murmured, 'One day, Madame la Comtesse, one day you shall give me a different answer. Even the strongest fortress falls at last.'

Still she made him no reply, simply watched him kiss the bank draft, signed by her, proving to him that Jane had not dared to ask her husband for the money, before he left her alone. Meg gave a great sigh, patted her reticule, which now held Jane's letters, and prepared to leave herself.

But as she put her hand on the door knob a sardonic voice said behind her, 'So, Madame la Comtesse, not so discreet after all since you had to hand over money to my rascally cousin Peverel to recover your incriminating love letters and save what is left of your reputation. I cannot say that I admire your taste. . .'

Simon Darrow had been afflicted by an excess of remorse as soon as Meg had left him. How could he have spoken to her so cruelly? What devil had possessed him, so that first he lusted after her and then insulted her because he had done so? Useless to say that she had been as rude to him as he to her. Jasper was right to reproach the pair of them.

The rumours must be wrong. His little Margaret could not have changed so much for the worse. Behind the mask of experience was surely still the frank child she had once been. It had been his duty to find her. Instead, he had most likely driven her away for ever. He was so disgusted with himself that he could no longer bear to be in the company of so many visibly enjoying themselves.

Shame had driven him out of the ballroom and along the corridor to seek solitude. He would have left Leominster House immediately, except that he had engaged to meet Jack, Earl Devereux, later. Jack was coming on from another engagement in order to discuss two matters with him. The first related to the agricultural policy of the present government, which was of great concern to all landowners, and the second to the business of the new Zoological Society of London, which he hoped to join.

He had opened a promising-looking door to discover a dimly lit room furnished in the Chinese style. He remembered that he had been told once that the present Earl's father had been a great Chinese fancier. There was a low divan before an empty hearth. Another, a high-backed one, faced away from the door towards long curtained windows.

Having no mind to be found by any passing busybody, he picked an interesting-looking book from a shelf in a niche by the fireplace, sat on the high-backed divan out of sight of anyone entering, and began to read. . .

And then, after a time, he dozed—he had passed a long and hard day—to be awoken soon afterwards by the noisy entry of someone whistling happily. He peered over the back of the divan to discover that it was his cousin Peverel—on some dubious assignation, no doubt.

For a moment, Simon debated whether to make his presence known, but decided against it. The devil which had possessed him earlier now prompted him to wait in silence in order to discover exactly which light-minded woman it was whom his disreputable cousin was expecting.

Alas, when she arrived, it was none other than Marguerite de Vaux, Countess de Mortaine, late the youngest Miss Ashe!

Oh, how stupid he had been to feel remorseful, to doubt that his fondly remembered Margaret had turned into the lightskirt which gossip said that she was. He was compelled to believe that all that he had heard of her was true: that her husband had died in a duel over a woman's honour, and that woman his wife. That her conduct was no better than it should have been, and had brought her husband to his death.

Every word in the conversation which he was overhearing struck his heart like a dart piercing it. What was worst of all was that she should not only engage in an *affaire* with his worthless cousin, but that she should be foolish enough to write him incriminating love letters as well.

He was not to know—as Meg did not—that her care never to mention Jane's name, in order to protect her, had only succeeded in proving to Simon that his suspicions about her were true. Worse than that was the knowledge that he had behaved in such an ungentlemanly fashion by continuing to listen to their conversation without revealing himself.

He should have announced his presence the moment that they had begun to speak, but at first their voices had been low, and he had not been sure immediately that it was Meg he was overhearing— and by the time he was, it was too late.

The anger which he felt over his own misbehaviour found relief in being turned on Meg—who, having had an unwanted encounter with one cousin, was now faced with a verbal duel with the other.

For a moment she was bewildered, then understanding flooded in. Her carefully worded tête-à-tête with Peverel had only served to convince Simon that *she* had been Peverel's mistress; that the letters she had recovered were hers.

She opened her mouth to confound him—only to realise that, in order to do so, she would have to betray Jane who had trusted her. No, indeed, she would deny nothing. If Simon was intent on believing her to be a Jezebel, then so be it. He did not deserve to know the truth—even if she could tell it.

Oh, she had weathered worse than this, although the sight of his hostile, condemning face was enough to make her feel physically ill. Holding her head high, keeping her voice level and her hands still—she knew that twisting and shaking hands betrayed an inward confusion—she confronted him. He thought that she was Jezebel: then she would behave like her.

'Why, Sir Simon, I do believe that you are jealous of your cousin. Is it because open rascality appears to conquer, whilst hypocritical virtue cannot?' This sword thrust to the heart was all the more cruel for being so calmly delivered. Its effect on Simon was immediate and shocking—it broke the fine control on which he had prided himself all his life.

He was around the divan in a trice, and was upon her, saying hoarsely, 'Why, Madame la Comtesse, seeing that you are any man's whore, why should you not be mine?' His arms were about her, his lips were on hers, and if Meg's first instinctive reaction was to welcome him and his insistent searching mouth, her second and more considered response was to tear her betraying mouth from his and push him away from her, while still retaining her composure.

'No, indeed. I always choose my lovers myself, they do not choose me, and I certainly have no intention of choosing you. You are more of a savage than Peverel was. He, at least, had the decency not to continue to pursue me when he saw that I was no longer willing.'

On hearing this further insult Simon, who had begun to feel ashamed all over again at yet another breach of his precious self-control, lost both his temper and his newly recovered remorse.

'That being so, Madame, if I am the savage you proclaim me to be, then I beg leave to enjoy the privileges of a savage.'

He was almost upon her again before Meg, seeing that she had unwittingly roused a tiger, had it by the tail, and could not control it, ran to the door.

But he was there before her, a strong arm holding it shut, demanding, 'What, may all the world have you, but not I?' A sentence which afterwards, when cold reason ruled him once more, set him shuddering. What in the world had possessed him to make him rant and behave like the villain in a Drury Lane melodrama? And how, in the name of everything precious to him, had they reached such a pass so quickly?

Even at the time, the enormity of his conduct suddenly struck him as he began to take Meg in his arms—to do what? He released her, and stood back, visibly fighting for self-control, so roused was he.

If he continued in this fashion, logic said that there would be only one end, and that something which he had always believed that as a man of honour he could never commit—the rape of an unwilling woman. Whatever had happened to the man of virtue he had once thought himself to be?

Meg refrained from asking him that question, which had also sprung into her mind. She leaned back against the door, paralysed, shocked by her own response to his wildness. One part of her wanted him to go on, wanted to lie in his arms, was hatefully pleased that she was able to rouse the devil in him.

The other, sane, part, said to her; 'If you surrender to him, then afterwards, he will hate both himself and you for such a betrayal of all that he lives by. And do you wish to lie with him in despite, with him thinking you a lightskirt, and you resenting that even as he pleasures you? What would the pleasure be worth that was founded on an untruth? How hatefully fleeting would it be?'

The same thing which had shocked Simon was shocking her: the speed with which they had found themselves in this situation. It was barely two hours since they had met again after eight long years, and here they were, at such surprising odds that they had almost consummated their unruly passion on the floor of the Leominsters' Chinese drawing room!

Still composed, although inwardly shaking, Meg began to try to placate him. 'If I were to assure you that I have nothing to reproach myself with so far as your cousin Peverel is concerned. . .'

Alas, Simon allowed her to say nothing further.

'Oh, no lies, please, Madame. I heard you both— remember? Accept my apologies that I assaulted you so rudely, that was scarcely the act of a gentleman— but I was most damnably provoked, not only by what I had earlier heard, but what you said to me afterwards.'

This only served to enrage Meg once more. She knew that she should leave, that she was in danger of rousing him again, but she could not prevent herself from saying, 'Provoke you, sir? You are as amusing as a comedian in a play by Sheridan.

'In the first place, were you the gentleman you pretend to be, you would have made your presence known when I came in, not skulked in the shadows listening to what was no concern of yours—and then claiming to be provoked by it. In the second place, whatever I said to you was in response to *your* unwarranted conduct, and should have driven you to reconsider your own behaviour and not animadvert on mine!'

Such a piece of cold-blooded legalistic pont-ification in the middle of a passionate amorous encounter, by the woman who had been subjected to attack, apparently struck neither party as at all untoward or odd. On the contrary, Simon replied in kind, saying stiffly, 'You cannot reproach me more than I reproach myself. But I must ask you to subject your own conduct to the same scrupulous examin-ation to which you have subjected mine.'

This was really the outside of enough! To blame her for his own misconstruing of her character! Meg would have stamped her foot had she not been so busy living up to her own legend as a woman of experience whom nothing could annoy or shock.

'It is plain, sir,' she told him, 'that we shall never agree on anything, so that further conversation is useless. Let us try to bring this unfortunate meeting to an end, and agree to avoid one another in future, since intercourse between us appears likely to bring out the worst in us both.'

Simon nodded a miserable assent, bowed, and held the door open for her. So this was how the friendship between the youngest Miss Ashe and Simon Darrow was to end—in hateful antagonism.

Walking along the corridor to the ballroom, looking around her for Jane, to reassure her that her letters were recovered, that her reputation was saved, Meg was astonished to find that her eyes were wet with tears.

Whether they were for herself or Simon, she did not know.

Chapter Three

'I cannot thank you enough, Meg, for what you have done for me. Peverel seems to have returned all my letters—which was more than I expected—and last night when I was alone, I burned them.'

Jane and Meg were seated in the Vancourts' pretty drawing-room, waiting for Jasper and Vancourt to arrive home after a session at a gymnasium run by an ex-member of Jasper's regiment.

'No thanks are required, Jane,' replied Meg, looking up from her work—she was painting Jane's portrait in watercolour. 'I was only too pleased to be able to help you.'

She had told no one, least of all Jane, of her unfortunate encounter with Simon. Since she appeared to be doomed to keep a large part of her life in France a secret from her friends and relatives, to keep quiet about this latest incident should not have seemed too great a burden—but it did. She felt like the old man of the sea himself, his back bowed beneath the weight of his past and his knowledge.

'Now that I can breathe freely again,' Jane con-

tinued happily, 'I can spend some time introducing
you to as many eligible *partis* as possible. I am sure
that you will wish to marry again—life can be hard
for a widow, I am given to understand.'

Meg shook her head. 'Oh, no. I have not the
slightest desire to remarry, so you may rest easy.
And I have found that there are many advantages
in being a widow.'

'So you say now, but you may not think so when
you are a little older. And there is one match that
one would expect you to make, one which we all
thought that you would agree to long ago.'

'Really, Jane?' replied Meg with false innocence.
'And, pray, what match is that?'

'Oh, come now. You must know that I am referring to Simon Darrow. Mama and Papa thought it
inevitable that you would accept him and were
shocked when you did not.'

'I would have been more shocked if I had
accepted him,' riposted Meg without looking up
from her work.

Jane ploughed on regardless. 'Oh, it wasn't just
Mama and Papa, you know. The rest of us, particularly Jasper, were equally surprised. After all, you
worshiped him when you were a little girl—you
never left him alone.'

'Well, I am not a little girl now, and I don't
worship anyone, least of all Simon Darrow. Is that
Vancourt arriving?' For there were voices in the
corridor outside and this was not a topic which Meg
wished to pursue.

It was not Vancourt, however, but Caroline, Lady
Kenilworth, come to call in a cloud of French

perfume and, Meg naughtily noted, a cloud of false French hair, neatly adjusted to hide her own thinning locks. She was dressed *à outrance*, and had a manner to match.

'I have heard so much about you, Madame,' she trilled at Meg, once the niceties were over, 'and I regret that I never found an occasion to be introduced to you at the Leominsters' ball. Simon Darrow told me that you were staying with your sister, so here I am.'

She strolled across the room to stare at Jane's portrait, which was nearing completion, then swung away again, without further ado, saying over her shoulder to Meg, 'Of course, as you may not know, Sir Simon and I are bosom bows these days.'

Meg offered Caroline her sweetest smile. It was plain that someone had informed Caro that Simon had proposed to Meg eight years ago, and now she was being warned off, as Jasper said of some punter at a cheap gaming hell who could not pay his dues. Well, she could have Simon Darrow, and welcome to him, nasty tongue and all.

'Oh, I know nothing of London society and its *on dits*,' Meg announced cheerfully, in a tone which hinted at an unspoken 'and have little interest in hearing them'. Instead, she added, 'And am I to offer you congratulations, m'lady?'

'Call me Caro, do. Now that Caro Lamb is no longer with us, the name has become respectable again. As for congratulations, you may defer them for a little. The gentleman and I are in full agreement that, being of mature years, we need not rush matters, but may settle them in our own good time.'

You may settle them in Hell, for all I care, remarked Meg's internal devil nastily. Aloud she said, 'Very wise of you, very proper. Second marriages for the bride are always dangerous—particularly when the groom has been such a determined bachelor as Sir Simon.'

'You speak from personal knowledge, Madame?' Caro Kenilworth was being as poisonously sweet as Meg whom she undoubtedly—and mistakenly—saw as a rival.

'Not at all. From observation, not experience. It was a first marriage for both my poor André and myself.'

Meg wondered if a handkerchief to her eyes might be a useful piece of business at this point. If nothing else, it might shame Lady Kenilworth into silence. She was not to know how little Meg mourned her lost husband. The real question was: how could Simon have become so lacking in taste as to have this aging houri for a *belle amie*? Opportunity, doubtless, was the great thing here!

Behind Caro's back Jane was mouthing something, her pleasant face a little alarmed. She had always been frightened by women of the world like Caro, but Meg had no intention of being warned off, put down, or battered into submission by such an elderly charmer.

The elderly charmer was roaring on. 'I believe that you are expecting Vancourt and Sir Simon here this afternoon. If so, it would be a great convenience for me to let him know that I am attending the Devereuxs' outdoor fête. They are so rarely in London and their grounds are so fine that it is an occasion not to be missed. You will be there, of course?'

'Of course,' murmured Meg.

Jane said, 'I am expecting Vancourt and my brother, but not Sir Simon. I fear that you will be disappointed.'

'Oh, I think not,' drawled the ineffable Caro. 'My understanding was quite otherwise.'

Fortunately for Jane, whose *savoir faire* had been greatly undermined by Vancourt's continued and open unfaithfulness, voices in the corridor announced that this time it *was* her husband and Jasper who were arriving and who would assist Meg in fending off Caro's practised nastiness.

Unfortunately when they came in, laughing and talking, and all aglow from what Vancourt cheerfully announced was a famous piece of exercise, Caro was proved to be right, much to the inward consternation of both sisters. Simon Darrow was with them, being congratulated by Jasper and Vancourt on the splendid state of his athletic prowess despite 'sitting about in the Commons, prosing', as Jasper inelegantly put it.

Meg had already realised that it was plainly going to be impossible for her and Simon to avoid meeting one another frequently. London society—the cousinry, as it was always known—was numerically small and inter-related, into the bargain, to such a degree that everyone knew everyone else and was constantly coming across them.

Meg privately thought of it as a public quadrille with partners, advancing and receding, sometimes in a group, at other times separately.

Simon's bow to her was impeccable, if indifferent; Caroline received a similar accolade, Meg was pleased to notice. Not that Caro took any notice of *that*. She had a hide like one of the rhinoceroses in the new Zoo which the London Zoological Society had recently founded at Regent's Park.

'And then we played tennis, or rather Ashe and Darrow did. And Darrow won.'

'As usual,' grumbled Jasper, who had walked over to where Meg was finishing her watercolour. But his grumble was a friendly one.

'Of course,' cooed Caro, in Simon's direction, 'one expects it of Sir Simon. To win, I mean. I can only say that I am sorry that ladies are not permitted to be spectators.'

'You would be bored,' announced Simon somewhat ungallantly. 'The fun is all for the players.'

'In that case,' remarked Meg, sparking at him before she had time to tell herself not to, 'it is a pity that ladies are not allowed to play and join in the fun.'

Exactly the sort of thing a forward, Frenchified hussy might come out with, thought Simon, but had enough self-control not to say so aloud. He had to admit, though, that annoyingly enough, Caro's faded charms looked the more so beside Meg's fresh elegance, French though it might be.

She was wearing lilac again, and the green eyes looked even more remarkable—and even more challenging when they were turned in his direction. He did not pause to think that his own stern grey ones, when turned on her, were equally challenging. Abandoning the importunate Caroline, he walked over to join Jasper and Meg, whereupon Jasper moved tactfully away to pacify Caroline, by employing all the charm with women that he had learned during his Army career.

Meg looked up at Simon. He said, without preamble, staring into the distance to avoid the distraction of those amazing green eyes, 'I have been thinking over what you said the other evening at the Leominsters'—that we should avoid one another. I agreed at the time, but I think that I was wrong. We are civilised human beings. It should not be beyond us to practise common politeness when we meet. It is my earnest wish that you will agree with me over this.'

Meg swished her brush around in her water pot in order to clean it, and avoided looking at him.

She said, using her most aloof Parisian manner, 'Indeed, Sir Simon. London society is so small that we should occasion remark if we were to be seen at odds. Particularly when there are many who will remember how close our families were in the past.'

He bowed. Punctiliousness was to be everything, it seemed. Meg, for once, had difficulty in keeping a straight face, so serious was he.

'Let us begin now,' he said as he straightened up. Then, in what Meg privately and naughtily thought of as his House of Commons voice, he remarked politely, 'I see that your painting skills are greatly improved. That is an excellent portrait of Jane.'

'Thank you, Sir Simon. I fear that you flatter me—but I did have lessons from an excellent French master in Paris.'

The moment she had spoken Meg was dismally

aware of the possible *double entendre*.

Matters were not helped by Simon producing one of his own. In an effort to mend matters between them, by complimenting her on something more, he offered unluckily, 'Ah, but one sees quite plainly that this is not your only talent which excellent French masters have enhanced. . .'

If Meg's first reaction was to be angry with him all over again for this revived memories of the way he had taunted her at the Leominsters', her second—when she saw his scarlet face—was to remain silent and do nothing.

'Forgive me. I did not intend to say anything which would provoke you.' This was so unwillingly wrenched from him—he was a man who had rarely needed to apologise—that Meg not only forgave him, but sought to reassure him.

'Why, sir—what should you mean? Pray do not spoil your compliment. It was doubtless expressed from the heart and will be received as such. And now I must show Jane her portrait. She has been most patient with me whilst I have been at work. I know from experience how wearying it is to sit still for an afternoon whilst a painter expresses him—or her—self.'

It was neatly done, Simon had to admit. He had been forgiven. And perhaps it would be possible for them to start again. He bowed and watched Meg walk over to Jane and the others. The only troubling thing was that merely to see her was to undo him. He had little time to reflect on this, however, for Caro was beside him in an instant as soon as she saw that Meg had left him.

'So *that* is the famous Madame la Comtesse de Mortaine. I cannot say that I am impressed.'

'No? Madame appears to me to be all that is claimed of her. But one lady can hardly be expected to see the charms of another—as you have frequently told me yourself.'

Even Caro's brass-faced composure was scarcely proof against this rebuff, so icily delivered. She was not to know how two-edged Simon's comment was!

She recovered herself, and replied smoothy, 'Ah, I had forgotten. Rumour says that you knew her when she was little more than a child, and have not seen her for many years. The change in her from being a country mouse must be remarkable. But I would have expected her to have more. . .' She paused significantly, largely because she could not think what to say that might not invite a further barbed remark from him.

'More what, Caro? And yes, the change is remarkable.'

'More. . .nothing. . . Oh, this is becoming tedious—like the lady. Let us *parlons d'autres choses*, talk of other matters. Say you will escort me to Devereux House tomorrow.'

Well, one thing was for sure. Caro's French was not a patch on little Meg Ashe's these days, was Simon's inward and ungallant comment. He had no wish to escort Caro anywhere. They had agreed to part, but the lady was not living up to her agreement. Nevertheless, his conscience told him to make up for his earlier rudeness to her by acceding to her wishes.

Simon wondered what in the world had come over

him during the last twenty-four hours or so, and reached the sad conclusion that he might not be behaving like a savage if Margaret Ashe had not taken his cousin Peverel for a lover and chosen to visit England!

All the world—or rather, most of the cousinry— was at the Devereuxs' afternoon party, as Jane and Caro Kenilworth had foretold. The gardens of Devereux House were as delightful as Jane had told her they would be; Countess Cassandra was as charmingly eccentric, and her husband as physically impressive, as rumour had said.

The Countess was wearing what looked like an Indian sari in vermilion and saffron, belted at the waist with a narrow cloth of gold sash. This should have appeared a very much overdone toilette, but she wore it with such careless panache that it looked entirely appropriate for an English summer afternoon.

Her husband, the Earl, was an Englishman out of the same mould as Simon. Large and craggily handsome, he looked like the cavalryman he had once been. They both greeted Meg as though they had longed to meet her. Will Osborne, who was her escort for the afternoon, was obviously an old friend. He recommended them to take a stroll down a pretty path that led to a small lake at the far end of the gardens.

Walking along it, being stared at by half of London society, it soon became plain to Meg that her presence was creating a great deal of excitement—her dubious reputation had obviously preceded her, she decided wryly.

Peverel Darrow came towards them when they reached the lake. An elegant wooden summerhouse or gazebo stood before it. Like all the company he was dressed *à outrance* by one of London's most fashionable tailors. His royal blue coat was by Stultz and his shiny black, gold-tasselled boots were by Weston. His cravat was a dream of a thing. More than one spectator wondered where the money was coming from to pay for such elegance.

No need to wonder, was Meg's irrepressible response to that thought. It was the banker's draft, which she had handed to him the other night, that was doubtless responsible for his impeccable turn-out. He greeted her and Will as though they were his dearest friends.

'Osborne, Madame, delighted to meet you both. The gardens are all and more than they are claimed to be, are they not? And the Countess even more so. A true original, if ever there was one. I believe that you thought so at one time, eh, Osborne?'

Will's honest face crimsoned. 'Oh, nothing to that, Darrow. It was long ago—and we were friends only.'

'Oh, I don't doubt you. Devereux a bit of a wild man, you see, Madame. Not a man of peace, like Osborne and me. By the by, Osborne, your Mama was asking after you. Told me to tell you that, if we met, she was seated on the terrace and wished to speak to you. I'll look after Madame whilst you do your duty like a good son.'

This brash and cold-blooded attempt to detach a rival from Meg's side could only succeed because

Peverel was older and brazen and Will was younger and naïve.

'If Madame does not object. . .' Will began a trifle desperately, only for Peverel to say in a cheery voice,

'Of course, she won't, old fellow. Must do your *devoir*, mustn't you? A single man's duty is to his mother first, after all.'

If anything had been needed—which it wasn't—to convince Meg that Will was too lightweight to be considered as a serious suitor or a possible husband, his surrender to Peverel's overt blackmail would have done the trick.

As he galloped away, Meg put up her parasol—she was wearing lilac again, and the parasol was a deep purple with a long white fringe—and drawled at Peverel in her most distant great-lady manner, 'It would have been better-mannered of you, sir, to ask me first whether I wished for your company before you sent Mr Osborne away.'

He offered her a deep bow, remarking in his most carelessly charming manner, 'Oh, I am sure that you would infinitely prefer to be escorted by someone less of a puling boy with his mother's milk still around his mouth than Mr Will Osborne. Besides, you made no objection to my proposal, none at all.' His smile was complacent and self-congratulatory.

'Only because I had not the slightest desire to be turned into a public bone to be fought over by two dogs. Moreover, you might be able to bam poor Will in such a high-handed manner, but you must remember, Mr Darrow, that I know you for what you are, and I will have no problem in bidding you *adieu*—which I do now,' and she made to go.

'One moment, Madame,' he said, and put out a hand to detain her. 'I do not choose to allow you to leave—yet.'

'Choose, sir, choose? I will tell you what I told your cousin. It is I who choose my companions, sir, not they me,' and Meg turned to go again. His impudence was unsufferable—and it was not yet over.

'I think not, Madame. I have no further interest in your sister. You have fire and spirit beneath that cold mask you wear, whilst she—like Will Osborne—is shallow. I have a mind to marry well, and you, unlike your sister, are free to marry and I am assured were left a vast fortune by your husband.

'We should, I believe, deal well together as husband and wife. When you handed me that bank draft drawn on your account, you created the assumption that *you*, and not your sister, were paying me for something—services rendered perhaps, or the return of *your* incriminating letters. It is your reputation which is now at stake, if I choose to be indiscreet.

'Furthermore, I know something of your life in France, which you would not care to become public knowledge—particularly since your reputation is already a trifle. . .spotty, shall we say? My courtship of you will be both short—and public. You would do well to take me seriously.'

Perhaps the worst part of Peverel's blandly threatening speech were not his threats but the words 'We should, I believe, deal well together.' They revived in Meg unfortunate memories of his cousin Simon's otherwise quite different proposal.

But he had Meg's attention, and knew it. Unknown to them both, however, their seemingly intimate *tête-à-tête* was being watched by his cousin Simon, who had come upon them as he strolled alone through the gardens, having abandoned his unwelcome companion, Caroline Kenilworth, to another gentleman whom she was hoping to fascinate.

So, Madame had no more sense than to be up to her tricks again with his worthless cousin, having managed to shake off that fribble Osborne! Would she never learn sense? He watched them, watched Peverel put an intimate hand on Meg's arm when he said, 'Oh, I have your attention now, Madame, have I not?'

'For a moment, only,' returned Meg coldly. 'I am not poor Jane. I will not be blackmailed, sir. And, in any case, I do not believe that even you would stoop to blackmail me into marriage.' Alas, she knew him only too well, and that he would stoop to anything—but she would fight him to the end. Peverel's smile told her that she had read him aright.

'I would advise you to stay—' he began, but before he could say any more, Simon was upon them, remarking,

'Ah, Peverel, I see that you are already acquainted with Madame. I was not aware that you knew her.'

They had been speaking in such low tones that Simon had heard nothing of what was being said— only that it was being said intimately. He was unaware that the intimacy was unfriendly. He only saw that they were close together and his suspicion of Meg was so strong that he always drew the worst conclusion about her behaviour, particularly when she was associating with such a known bad hat as his cousin.

Meg read Simon's body language correctly—and was furious with him. He was judging her to be a whore again, which was particularly galling when she was being bullied so determinedly by Peverel—who had, as usual, an answer for anything thrown at him.

'Oh, Madame and I knew one another in Paris,' he began to say in a way that suggested a much deeper relationship than the passing one they had enjoyed, if that were the right word. 'When Madame was married to André de Vaux.' This was also said as though André had been his dearest friend instead of someone with whom he had exchanged a few brief sentences—and none of them amicable.

Which successfully served to convince Simon of Meg's perfidy. She closed her eyes and her parasol, and said, 'I am sure that you have much to say to one another, since you meet so rarely. I will leave you. Lady Devereux is to give us a harp recital; as I understand that she is a most accomplished performer, I do not wish to miss it.'

She bowed to the cousins, who were glaring at one another, heads down, like a pair of angry buffalos, and moved away, amused at herself for taking a leaf out of Peverel's book and disposing of the unwanted third in a group without asking the others' permission. That unwanted third being herself.

Lady Devereux was an accomplished performer

and Meg enjoyed her playing, even though at the back of her mind she was worried by what it was that Peverel knew—or thought that he knew—about her.

Chapter Four

'**M**y dear Madame,' said Cass, Lady Devereux, to Meg, who had approached her after the recital was over, and had complimented her on her performance, 'I believe that we met briefly in Paris some years ago shortly after your marriage. Pray allow me to commiserate with you on the sad death of your husband.'

Meg inclined her head graciously and murmured her thanks. The acid voice of her inner demon commented that she was becoming so practised at this kind of polite nothingness that she would soon be able to do it sleepwalking.

Something of this perhaps showed, for Cass, one of the most shrewd members of London society, said briskly, 'Now that we have got rid of the niceties, may you also permit me to say that, if ever you become bored with conversations confined to *on dits* and the discussion of how best to trim a bonnet, there will always be a welcome for you at Devereux House. Something tells me that you suffer fools gladly no more than I do.'

Meg's laugh was, for once, a genuine one. This she had not expected. 'Oh, dear,' she exclaimed, 'was I so obvious? Were my good manners so excessive that they were enough to induce nausea?'

Cass's smile was as genuine as Meg's laugh. 'Indeed not. Jack, my husband, sometimes accuses me of mind-reading, usually after I have detected him in some monstrous piece of crinkum-crankum designed to deceive me as to what he and his one-time corporal got up to in one of their periodic reunions.

'You may or may not know that he served as a cavalryman in the ranks during the late wars and rose to the ineffable height of being a sergeant. Better that I tell you that than someone who might wish to cause trouble between us. You see, my dear, my mind-reading has told me that we are to be friends, nay, bosom bows.'

She was in no way pretty, Meg decided, but was something better. She had character and a sense of fun. As Cass was to say to her later on in their acquaintance, 'The trouble with me is that cheerfulness will keep breaking in, however determined I am to be solemn.'

In that sense, she was a happy counterbalance to Meg, who had, these days, a tendency towards sadness, and consequently solemnity. But this was to be in the future.

For the present, Cass, whilst drawing her attention to a portrait of a pretty boy carrying a hawk who turned out, improbably, to be her craggy-looking husband as a very young man, concentrated on saying as she turned away from it, 'Jack does not look

like that at all now—he rather resembles Simon
Darrow than his cousin Peverel, and not merely in
looks. Peverel, as I am sure you know, is not to be
trusted.'

Now this was mind-reading with a vengeance! Or
someone had been talking. But the look Cass turned
on her was so innocent that Meg decided that she
was reading meanings into what was being said that
were not there.

The rest of their conversation was innocent
enough, with Cass offering her a friendship which
Meg was coming to understand that she needed.
'You will,' she said, 'visit me soon, my dear
Comtesse, won't you? For if you do not, I shall
haunt Vancourt House until you do.'

To her astonishment, Meg found herself saying
something quite unexpected and of which she had
not previously thought. 'I shall not be staying
overlong at Vancourt House. I am determined to set
up my own establishment, and would value your
recommendation of a *dame de compagnie* to keep
me respectable.'

Now where had that come from? Perhaps the
knowledge that Vancourt's manner to her was
becoming over-warm, and Jane had enough to contend with without suspecting that her husband had
designs on her sister. Not only Jane, perhaps. It
was bad enough to have Simon suspecting that she
possessed no virtue and Peverel having designs on
her pocket, if not her virtue, without having to suffer
Vancourt having designs on her virtue, if not her
pocket.

Or was it the effect of Cass Devereux's downright

commonsense, which was reminding her that to remove the temptation which she apparently presented was, like discretion, the better part of valour?

No matter. At least, if she had her own establishment, Peverel's attempts to visit her would not arouse the suspicions of Jane and her husband, and she would be able to refuse to see him without causing comment. Meg was growing tired of living her life in public.

'Oh, I know just the person for you,' Cass said eagerly, 'A Mrs Hollis, a young widow who lost her husband, General Hollis, last year. He left her with very little to live on. She is a dear friend of my old governess, Mrs Dickson, and is so upright that she could almost confer respectability on the King himself! My husband's secretary will give you her address before you leave.

'In return, you will do something to rescue my guests from possible boredom. I understand from your brother that you and Sir Simon Darrow used to entertain your father's guests—he by singing, and you by playing for him. I would be greatly pleased if you would agree to do so again, this afternoon.'

Jasper! thought Meg wildly. It was Jasper who had put Cass Devereux up to this. . .this. . .trick, to try to get us together again.

Well, he would not succeed. She would refuse, politely, but still refuse. And then she looked at Cass Devereux. There was a transparent honesty about her, which she proved by saying gently, 'Oh, I know that you will feel that you are being coerced into this. But your brother—who knew my husband when he was in the ranks—believes that you and Sir Simon should be friends again, and asked me to do him this favour. You can, of course, refuse.'

After that, how could she? But first she had a question for Cass. 'Sir Simon? Has the request been made to him?'

'Oh, indeed, and he has agreed to it—but only on the condition that it would be pleasing to you.'

An olive branch from him, no less. She could scarcely, now, be so graceless as to refuse Cass.

Simon was waiting for her in the Devereuxs' splendid drawing-room, where the company were already seated for a resumption of the afternoon's entertainment. Caro Kenilworth was standing near him, her whole posture betraying the anger which she had felt on hearing that 'that woman' and Simon were to sing and play together.

He bowed over her hand as Cass's major-domo announced them. Caro flounced to a seat near the front, announcing loudly, 'Oh, I do so detest being compelled to listen to amateurs,' a statement that endeared her to no one.

Meg found that she was trembling. Simon said, below his breath. 'Come, we must not disappoint Jasper and the lady. I know that it is many years since we sang and played together but, knowing you, I am sure that you have not neglected your music. Here is the score for the "Last Rose of Summer". I remember that it used to be a favourite of your father's.'

So it had been. He had liked all the songs in Tom Moore's collection of Irish airs. Meg took a deep breath and sat down. She said nothing to him. Indeed, he did not seem to expect it. Her simple agreement had apparently been enough.

She sat down at the Broadwood pianoforte and played a few tentative chords. Simon placed the score before her, but it was not needed. Meg had played it so often in those long gone years that she knew it by heart. But again, she said nothing but a simple thank you—which appeared to serve.

Simon was ready, too. He was standing by the piano as he had done so many times before, waiting for her to begin. Meg was suddenly overcome. Panic struck her. She could not do this. And then Simon looked down at her, and smiled. For a moment it was almost as though she were little Meggie, the youngest Miss Ashe, again, and he was the tall young man whom she had adored.

Courage ran through her. She lifted her head and began to play the introduction, pausing at the end of it for a fraction of a second to allow him to begin.

Tom Moore's poignant and well remembered-words, sung by Simon's mellow baritone, filled the drawing-room. And if there had been a few who had, beforehand, silently echoed Caroline Kenilworth's unkind judgment on them, they were silenced by the simple purity of their performance.

The applause, which followed a short silence once the song had ended, was long and sincere. 'Another,' said Simon, and it was not really a question. 'You will consent to join me in another song.'

Meg nodded dumbly. Astonishingly, she was near to tears—she, who never cried.

'I thought,' he murmured, a trifle tentatively, 'that "*Partant pour la Syrie*" might go down well, you being a Frenchwoman these days.'

It was, Meg acknowledged, a suitable choice, being a French love song written during the late wars that had been adopted by France's enemy, England. It told of a young soldier leaving behind his own true love in order to go to war, and promising to win her hand by his bravery.

'And you will sing it with me?'

The tears were near to the surface again. Meg told herself that he was simply being kind because Jasper had put them in this impossible position, and he did not wish society to know that they were at odds.

Time turned back upon itself again. The lost years were gone. She was fifteen-year-old Meg Ashe, practising her singing, her piano playing and her ability to do both in public. Singing, she remembered how Simon had always encouraged her and, as contralto met baritone, their voices mixed and mingled as though they had never been parted.

When the song ended, he looked down at her, and she looked up at him. Their eyes met: tenderness in his, hope in hers. But for a moment only. In a trice Simon's eyes on hers were as hard as ever, and hopelessness took over again in Meg's. Their moment of rapport was over.

This time the silence after they had finished was long and profound. Cass led the applause. She rose and walked over to them. Something in the set of Meg's shoulders told her of the strain she was under.

'That was quite splendid,' she said. 'Particularly since this was sprung upon you both without warning. It is quite plain, though, that you have sung together before. I offer you my congratulations as well as my thanks.' If she thought that Simon, like

Meg, was also somewhat constrained in his manner, she said nothing to indicate that she was aware of it.

'I was right,' Simon told Meg coolly as they walked away from the piano to receive the thanks and congratulations of many of the company. 'You had not forgotten your past entirely. And your technique has improved immensely.'

'Nor had Jasper forgotten, apparently,' said Meg drily. 'I wonder that he does not consider joining the *corps diplomatique* since he seems to be so adept at arranging cunning plots. I take it that he also proposed that you, as well as I, should perform without a word of warning.'

Simon gave a short laugh. Like Meg, he thought that at least Jasper's ploy had set them talking in a reasonable fashion—which was doubtless what he had intended.

'Indeed, and I shall have words with him before we leave. I must, however, remark that eight years in France has done wonders for the purity of your accent. It quite shamed mine.'

Meg made no direct answer to this, other than to say, 'And here comes brother Jasper, who needs a little shaming of a different sort—from the pair of us.' She was not sure whether Simon's remark on her French accent was meant to be a compliment or not.

Jasper was as forthright as usual; as forthright as Meg had once been and was no longer.

'Well done,' he offered cheerfully. 'And at least my suggestion had the pair of you speaking to one another again in a civilised manner, not snarling like dogs over a bone!'

United for once, both Meg and Simon glared at

him. Meg, retaining her aloof self-control, merely murmured, 'You might at least have had the courtesy to speak to Simon and myself before approaching Lady Devereux. I had not expected such blackmail from a brother.'

Jasper's withers were quite unwrung, 'Oh, if I had done *that*, neither of you would have consented. As it is, no harm done, and the company was entertained. I must compliment you, sister, on your playing and singing. You have become quite the professional since you went to Paris.'

'And for my part, Ashe, I shall not forget this piece of arm-twisting, I assure you. I shall take my revenge in the gym, or the *salle des armes*, a true duel being a trifle overblown as a form of punishment.' Simon's tone was jovial enough, but there was more than a hint of savagery in it.

'Oh, come.' Jasper was all smiles, and ran an arm through Simon's. 'It's time for the tea board, I see, and Will Osborne is panting towards us to look after Meg. Why don't you put Caro K. out of her misery, and I will bring Lucy Seymour along.

'You may then inform us about the new Zoological Society of which *The Times* tells me you are a member, and after that you may invite us all, including our host and hostess, to stroll around the gardens in Regent's Park and feed buns to the bears.'

Unwillingly, Simon began to laugh. 'I had forgotten what a fellow you are, Ashe. I suppose, knowing you, that you have already made this suggestion to Lady Devereux.'

'Now, Darrow, there you are wrong. I spoke to Jack Devereux, not Cass, and he wishes to enrol as a member also, and would be delighted if you saw fit to propose him and to show him around the celebrated five acres of Regent's Park that Lord Lansdowne managed to gouge out of the Commissioners of Woods and Forests. Quite an achievement, that.'

'Nothing to yours, Jas,' said Simon, suddenly as cheerful as Jasper, and using his boyhood name to him to show that no real offence had been taken by his trickery, 'in manoeuvring me before a piano again. I suppose that you expect me to invite the whole Vancourt brood and young Osborne as well. In for a penny, in for a pound.'

Will, who had just arrived, heard this last statement with some surprise. He quite thought that Sir Simon Darrow had taken against him, as the slang saying had it.

'Eh, what's that?' he asked after claiming Meg as Jasper had prophesied. 'The new Zoological Gardens? I should be delighted to make up the party—if I am invited, of course. Have always wanted to see the bears.'

'So that's settled,' proclaimed Jasper cheerfully, before Simon, or anyone else, could demur. 'All that remains for us now is to set a date for this delightful expedition!'

And so it was arranged. Simon, who had every intention of having as little to do with Meg as possible, had been coerced by her brother into agreeing that she should be one of his party, in an expedition which he had not arranged!

All in all, Meg left Devereux House feeling happy for the first time since she had arrived in London.

Despite Jane's many quiet virtues, she could not share in most of Meg's interests: to find in Cass Devereux someone who did, and who could enjoy her witticisms almost before she had uttered them, was a boon indeed.

Not only that: Cass Devereux had become such a power in London society that if she accepted Meg, then so would all the other hostesses. It seemed that she was not destined to be a pariah after all.

And for a few happy moments she and Simon had shared—if only briefly—a little of the rapport which had once been theirs. Perhaps, when they were at the Gardens together, they might recover a little more ground.

Sir Simon Darrow was not quite so happy. The even tenor of his life had been disturbed by the reappearance of Meg Ashe to a degree that he would not have believed possible had he known of it beforehand. At least, he thought, unaware that Meg was spending her days dodging Vancourt's advances, she would have to behave herself whilst she was living with her sister, and she had been much more quietly reasonable with him during their songs together.

'Oh, Aunt Marguerite, are we really going to see the animals today? Oh, I do hope Papa wasn't teasing us when he said that we could go with you.'

Little Georgie Vancourt turned a pleading face to his aunt. He had already discovered that she was much more reliable than either his mama or his papa, and if she said something would be so, it was so. Now Papa would promise one thing one day, and quite another thing on another. As for Mama—well, she never seemed to know quite what she was doing.

His sister, Harriet, who was not sure that she wished to see wild animals—she remained unconvinced that they were safely penned away from visiting little girls—added a rather doubtful voice to Georgie's pleadings.

'Of course you shall go, my darlings. See, Nancy is coming to dress you. It is a cold day for June so you must both wear your pelisses.'

Meg was not quite so calm about this Sunday afternoon trip to the Zoological Gardens at Regent's Park as her comforting words to her niece and nephew suggested. One part of her was looking forward to seeing Simon—they had not directly encountered one another since the Devereuxs' afternoon party—the other part was asking herself why she should look forward to being hurt again.

Simon had made it quite plain that he considered her to be a loose woman, corrupted by her marriage and her years in France, and nothing she could say or do appeared to be able to change his mind.

Peverel's behavior was not calculated to improve matters, either. He haunted her, constantly reminding her that she was, to some extent, in his power, and that the day of reckoning might be soon. Until she had her own home, it would be difficult to avoid him. Vancourt had taken a fancy to Peverel— probably to annoy Jane who disliked him—and he was constantly at Vancourt House.

The rumours about her own past had died down a little since Cass had taken her up, and today's party would help to silence them even further.

The irony was that Vancourt's patronage was conferring respectability on her although he was the loosest fish around, whilst she, whose own conduct had been impeccable, was regarded with suspicion. It was enough to make the angels weep!

Nevertheless, she was calmness itself when she walked into the massive hall of Vancourt House, ready to be driven by him to Regent's Park, Jane by her side, and the children following in a dog cart driven by the chief coachman.

'How splendid you look, Meg. Exactly right for a fine day in the open with the animals. Neither too elegant, nor too *farouche*.'

Meg looked down at the pretty blue cotton dress she was wearing. It had a round linen collar embroidered with forget-me-nots. The sash which cinched her slender waist was of a deeper blue. Her shoes were made of a serviceable but light cream kid, ornamented with the tiniest silver rosettes. Silk forget-me-nots decorated her straw hat, and she was carrying a white parasol decorated with the same modest flowers. The shawl, draped so artistically around her shoulders, was a dream of a thing in the finest cashmere, and was also blue and white. She was slipping on exquisitely delicate white lace gloves as she turned to Jane.

'Parisian chic,' sighed her sister, whose own sage-green toilette did neither her figure nor her colouring any favours. She saw at once that her bonnet, her shoes, her everything appeared irretrievably clumsy beside Meg's elegance. 'Aunt Léonie's tutelage, I suppose.'

And so, unkindly, Vancourt told her when he

drove the carriage round to the front doors for them to be handed in by various subservient footmen. As usual, he was very late: he liked to keep his wife and children waiting.

'Really, Jane, if you can't manage a more suitable turnout than the one that you're wearing, then do have the goodness to ask your sister for advice.'

Jane flushed an unlovely crimson and his brutality set Meg shuddering. He had ruined Jane's day for her before it had begun.

She put an arm around her sister's shoulders. 'Certainly not, Vancourt,' she said, her voice icy. 'Jane is far more sensibly dressed than I am. Indeed, if there were time, I would beg leave to return to my room to put on something less suited to a drawing-room. I find the afternoon cooler than I thought. But I will not cause you further delay.'

'Thank you,' Jane whispered as she settled herself in her seat.

Meg being on Vancourt's other side afforded him the opportunity to whisper into her ear, once the grooms let go of his horses' heads and they set off, 'I like a woman of spirit, m'dear, and God knows my poor wife has little enough.'

'And small wonder at that,' retorted Meg in a fierce undertone, 'seeing that, by your behaviour, you have extinguished what little she had!'

If she thought this would deter him in any way from his pursuit of her, she was wrong. Rather, her spirited response to him and his behaviour served only to encourage him the more.

By God, it would be a pleasure to have such a proud filly beneath him. She was like an apparently extinct volcano with passionate fires beneath a cold exterior. Unlike her suet pudding of a sister, she was strawberries and champagne of the very best! His greatest pleasure would be to tame that proud spirit and have her his submissive slave. How to bring her to his bed was his present problem, particularly with that sly devil Peverel Darrow after her. Probably not such good tactics to have him constantly in his home in order to annoy his wife by his presence.

Meg knew quite well what her brother-in-law was thinking, and had there been room would have shuddered away from him. Fortunately for her and Jane's composure, the world and his wife were taking the air that morning, and it needed all of Vancourt's concentration to manoeuvre his way through assorted gigs, dog carts, curricles, broughams, landaulets and chaises, to say nothing of gay young bucks on horseback.

Many of them were on their way to Regent's Park. The Zoological Society was now so large that, even though only its members were allowed to visit the Gardens on Sunday, they were nearly as busy as on weekdays when the general public might pay to enter.

'God damn the traffic,' cursed Vancourt morosely. 'We shall be late.'

'And so I told you,' nagged Jane unwisely. 'And I do not, my lord, appreciate blasphemy indulged in before myself and my sister.'

'Damn that for a tale,' swore Vancourt. 'You never appreciate anything, so that is no matter to me. Your sister has heard worse in Paris, I dare swear.'

'Not often,' retorted Meg sweetly as they neared

the entrance to the Zoological Gardens, after they had negotiated the splendid Nash terraces which ran alongside them. 'And then only in the worst possible company.'

Her reward for that was a roar of happy laughter from her brother-in-law.

'Would hardly guess you were my poor wife's sister, Madame. Why in the world did you always tell me she was a plain, poor-spirited little thing, m'lady? Might have known that you were wrong, as usual. You should try imitating her.'

If Meg could have borrowed a pair of angel's wings and flown out of the carriage, she would have done so. As it was, she remained quiet with some difficulty. To say anything at all to Vancourt was merely to encourage him to torment poor Jane the more. Best to ignore him and hope that the drive would soon end.

To her great relief, it was not long before they reached the Grand Drive that ran round Regent's Park, which meant that their journey was nearly over and she and Jane and the children would be free to leave the carriage and roam around the Gardens. Her recent experience with Vancourt had served to confirm her in the belief that she must find another place to live.

I am becoming a nomad, she thought wryly, as Vancourt drove them to the entrance, a female wandering Jew who has no place which she can truly call her own: I must shuffle the cards and deal again...

Chapter Five

Simon was waiting for them by the gates. He was driving a stylish curricle picked out in blue and silver, a tiger behind, and Caro Kenilworth up front with him. She had a discontented expression on her face, most probably because the Vancourt party was late and she was being compelled to wait for it in public. Will Osborne had arrived on horseback, and his steed was being led away by his attendant groom.

Outside the entrance to the Gardens, which was flanked by two small rustic sentry boxes, Jack and Cass Devereux and their children were already dismounting from a staid family carriage.

'I told you that we would be late,' fretted Jane unwisely to Vancourt. 'They have been waiting for us.'

A further angry explosion from her husband was only averted by Simon's approach, Caro on his arm. Simon had his own reason for being annoyed: Peverel had just driven up, also in a spanking new curricle, and was now walking towards them, arm in arm with a stranger.

Now who the devil had invited him? Peverel read Simon's face correctly, and remarked gaily, 'No need to frown, cousin, I'm not a gatecrasher! My sponsor today is Acland, here like yourself as one of the Society's founder members. A splendid day to see the animals, is it not?'

Watching Simon bow stiffly to Peverel and his friend, Sir Thomas Acland, who was by way of being one of Vancourt's, too, Meg could not help being amused by Peverel's jaunty insolence, and by his flaunting of his new curricle, doubtless bought with the money that she had given him on Jane's behalf. Rogue he might be, but she could see exactly how he used his charm to achieve his criminal ends and stay afloat in an unforgiving society.

'Like my new turn-out, do you?' he asked Simon confidentially. 'Thought I might pamper m'self a little. Tired of driving round in other men's hand-me-downs.'

And where did he get the money from for *that*? was a question Simon would have liked to ask, but Peverel was moving on, a smile on his lips, and the friends whom Simon had invited were waiting for him.

'No need to pass me in,' announced Jack Devereux jovially. 'I was accepted as a member last week. Promised to help buy a giraffe when one becomes available. Cass says that she's always wanted to see a giraffe.'

He gave a great burst of laughter, and said affectionately, 'Mark you, I wouldn't put it past m'lady wife to ask to lead it round with her! Most disappointed that she couldn't bring her dogs in today, but rules are rules.'

This brought more laughter from all those who knew that Cass Devereux was famous for the size and splendour of the dogs which always accompanied her on walks and jaunts to Hyde Park. The lady herself enjoyed her husband's teasing most of all.

'And parasols are banned, also, I'm afraid,' said Simon, 'so I must ask the ladies to hand them to Stephen to take back to the carriages before we enter.'

Meg and Jane handed theirs to the waiting groom, but Caro complained angrily, 'Oh, this is really the outside of enough. I am sure that the sun is about to become over-warm at any moment and, of all things, I do detest a brown face! What can be the reason for such an absurd rule?'

'Not absurd.' For once Simon was short with Caro. 'The members have decided that the danger of visitors poking the animals with walking sticks, umbrellas and parasols and thus causing injury to them is too great a risk to take. I should have warned you all beforehand,' he admitted, 'but rarely carrying a stick or an umbrella myself, I quite forgot.'

He saw with pleasure that the guard at the sentry box was making Peverel surrender his elegant silver-topped cane.

To the delight of all the children, it was not long before they were through the gate and walking along the broad path on either side of which were animals exhibited in a variety of cages and houses.

George Vancourt and Ritchie Devereux, who had

already become great chums, were urging Ritchie's father to take them to the bearpit, 'at once'. Georgie had seen immediately that Jack was quite a different sort of papa from his own, who was sauntering along, looking supremely bored at the prospect of spending his afternoon with a pack of children gaping at animals, since he possessed not the slightest interest in either species.

Jack, on the other hand, had taken his small Sophie in his arms to show her the kangaroo, and was promising George and Ritchie that, as soon as they found the kiosk which sold food for the animals, he would buy them some buns to throw to the bears.

Harriet Vancourt was holding tightly on to Aunt Marguerite's hand. Her nursemaid had taken a light fever and was thus unable to join the party, but Meg had promised Jane that she would look after her, rather than allow her niece to lose her treat. Simon, who was walking parallel with them, Caro by his side, watched in some surprise as Meg gently helped her niece to kneel down in order to inspect more easily the cranes and bustards which were running around an enclosed lawn with a pond at one end.

For a moment he saw again the little Meg Ashe whom he had thought he had lost, so tender was the expression on her face as she cared for the child whom both her parents were ignoring, lost in their own grievances against one another. Impulsively, he moved forward to speak to her—but a possible moment of *rapprochement* was lost when Will Osborne, who had detached himself from Acland, moved forward to attach himself to Meg.

Will was big with information about the Gardens,

gleaned from Acland, who was strolling along in his wake, and which he was bursting to impart to Meg in order to impress her with his knowledge.

'Decimus Burton, the great architect, has designed the Gardens, and the Gothic building in which the llamas are to be found,' he announced portentously. 'They say he intends to build a turret with a clock tower on to it.'

'Oh, can the llamas tell the time, then?' asked Harriet eagerly: she was having difficulty in learning to tell the time herself, and was prepared to admire the llamas for being able to do so.

This naïve comment completely overset Will, whose understanding of small girls was as deficient as his understanding of their elder sisters. Meg rescued him by saying, 'Not at all, my dear, but the grown-ups walking around the Gardens will be pleased to be able to check their watches with it, I am sure.'

Will's attempt at an answer was drowned in the noise of George and Ritchie running up and exclaiming together, 'Oh, Aunt Marguerite,' from George, and 'Oh, Mama,' from Ritchie, 'we are all going to the bear pit to feed the bears. You must come with us. The bears are simply not to be missed, Uncle Peverel says, and they are nearby.'

Uncle Peverel! Both Simon and Meg reacted to this remarkable statement in the same way. So, it had not taken the wretched swindler more than five minutes to win the hearts of two small boys.

Well, if Meg and little Harriet were to decide to join 'Uncle Peverel', then he, Simon, was bound to go with them to keep Meg apart, if possible, from his worthless, blackmailing cousin. He was, however, checkmated even before he could announce his intentions, by Caro passing a fine lace handkerchief over her face and announcing that she needed a seat: she was far too tired to walk any further.

'But we've only just arrived.' Simon uttered this incontrovertible truth as gently as possible. 'So far you have only seen the kangaroos, and the bears are not far away.'

'And seeing the kangaroos is quite enough for me,' shuddered Caro. 'The wretched animal is an offence against nature. Carrying its young in a pouch, indeed! Quite improper to allow little children to see it—or the bears either, nasty dangerous things!'

Nothing to do but summon one of the young keepers and ask him to arrange for a chair to be brought for Lady Kenilworth, 'who is feeling the heat,' Simon explained as he watched Meg, Harriet, Cass Devereux and all the little Devereuxs, plus Will Osborne, join Jack Devereux, his Sophie and 'Uncle Peverel' in front of the bear pit. They were all busy buying buns to throw to the bears—particularly to the one who had climbed up his pole to watch *them*.

At least Peverel couldn't get up to any of his underhand tricks in the middle of that mob, was Simon's glum thought as he left the main party behind on his way to the beavers' enclosure.

And where were Jane and her husband, who had apparently abandoned their offspring to others? That question was partly answered a few minutes later when Jane suddenly appeared, scarlet in the face, at the exact moment when the young keeper was reverently setting out a light chair for Caro by the beavers' pond, which was situated in the shade of some trees, far away from the offending kangaroos and bears.

'Oh, splendid,' she exclaimed. 'I am already quite exhausted, and I had no notion that one might obtain seating. Vancourt is too busy staring at the camels to care for my comfort.' The young keeper was promptly despatched to fetch her a chair also.

'In that case,' said Simon, ever ready to seize opportunity by the forelock, 'you may keep Lady K. company whilst I rejoin the main party. I have a mind to throw buns to the bears, too!'

'Buns to bears!' shuddered Jane. It appeared that she was as impervious to Zoological delights as Caro. How in God's name, thought Simon, did I become entangled with such a silly. . .woman? And she wasn't even very good in bed, either, despite all the rumours.

Simon did not leave the two women until he had seen Jane settled beside a discontented Caro, who had expected him to remain with her. They had a good view of the American beavers inside their little enclosure, if nothing else. Acland had gallantly joined them. 'Have thrown buns to bears before,' he announced. 'Nothing to it,' before sending the keeper off to find him a third chair. As Simon strode away he could hear him recounting to his uninterested, but captive, audience a short history of the early days of the foundation of the Gardens.

Grinning to himself, Simon found his party standing before the wooden hut next to the bear pit where a stout lady in a mob cap was selling buns, fruit and nuts to a large assembly of interested spectators. Other apparently exhausted women had been provided with chairs where they might watch the animals in comfort.

Meg and the Devereux party were made of sterner stuff, however. They were already equipped with a supply of goodies and the bear up the pole was waiting for the buns to begin raining in his direction again. Little Harriet Vancourt was relieved to see that all the bears were in a pit which was surrounded by a tall iron fence, and their pole was far enough away from it to make it unlikely that the bear might vault the fence in order to eat her instead of a bun.

Meg, unaware that Simon had joined them, found herself between Peverel and a rather stern-looking woman who had a little boy by the hand.

'Have a bun?' Peverel invited her, oozing charm, only for Meg to say coolly,

'No, thank you, I have a supply of my own.'

'In the land of double meanings,' he announced, 'great play could be made of your reply.'

'Could it?' she replied, still cool. 'But we are not, are we? Harriet dear, throw this piece of bun towards the bear.'

She had heard the woman beside her stifle a laugh when she answered Peverel so cavalierly—not that that troubled him.

Fortunately Cass Devereux, who had been inspecting the goats, provided a diversion. She came strolling towards them, exclaiming when she saw the stern-looking woman, 'Oh, Stroody—I mean, Emma—what a delightful surprise, and Thomas, too,' and she gave the little boy a kiss. 'I had never thought to see you here. I suppose George is with you?' and she gave the stern woman an affectionate kiss.

'Oh, indeed, he has taken Johnny to see the kangaroos again. He cannot get enough of them. Every time he visits the gardens, he bounces about the house afterwards as though he were one himself!'

'And this, my dear Comtesse—' Cass swept on in her impulsive way to Meg '—is my oldest friend and former companion, Mrs George Dickson, who is married to my husband's oldest friend. Is that not convenient! And this, dearest Emma, is my new friend Marguerite, Comtesse de Vaux, from Paris, on whom you may practise your excellent French. Appearances to the contrary, she is as English as you are, but her accent is a miracle.'

'My lady—' began Mrs Dickson, only to have Meg say, for once as impulsive as Cass,

'Oh, pray call me Meg, we cannot be friends else.'

The look Cass gave her was a glowing one, and Mrs Dickson said quietly, 'Then I insist upon being Emma. If you are from Paris, I must ask you if you were acquainted with my oldest friend, the late Vicomtesse de Chavannes—we were at Miss Pinkerton's Academy together. She was a number of years ahead of me, but I remember with gratitude the many small kindnesses with which Léonie favoured me.'

'She was my aunt,' Meg replied, her face sad. 'And she was kind to me, too. But stern. I miss her greatly.'

'I'm sure that you do,' nodded Mrs Dickson. 'How strange to meet you here. I lost touch with her many years ago when she went to France.'

She did not say that, after her father died and she had descended into poverty, she had been compelled to earn her living by being a companion and governess to young girls of good birth—Cass being her last pupil—until she had married George Dickson.

No conversation in the Gardens could last for very long, for too much was going on. First Johnny Dickson ran up, or rather, jumped towards his mama, his amused father following him. After that came Peverel, Vancourt, Will Osborne, and Sir Thomas Acland, who had abandoned Jane and Caro to the beavers. Simon was a little way behind them, talking to Jack Devereux. Surrounding *them* were all the small fry.

Everyone was duly introduced to the Dicksons, upon whom Peverel turned his charm despite the fact that they were obviously low Cits in trade, and to whom Vancourt gave only a less than deep bow and a passing stare.

'I have made arrangements for a cold collation to be served at four of the clock, in the paddock where the moveable aviaries are situated,' Simon announced. 'As that time is almost upon us, I suggest that we adjourn there, after we have collected the Ladies Kenilworth and Vancourt and seen the beavers.'

He bowed to the Dicksons, 'You will, of course, do me the favour of joining us. There will be more than enough for a party twice the size, if my housekeeper and chef live up to their usual reputations!'

'Oh, famous,' cried little Johnny Dickson, imitating a kangaroo again in his excitement. 'An open-air picnic in the Gardens, what fun.'

'All food taken in the open air is referred to as a picnic, my love,' his mother informed him, 'and even kangaroos must be quiet when they eat, so I hope that you will imitate them.'

This half-reproof flew over Johnny's head, but set George and Ritchie Devereux laughing.

'Oh, Aunt Meg,' Harriet Vancourt complained. 'I'm too tired to walk to Mama.'

'No need to worry, chicken. I will carry you,' and Meg picked up the little girl, who was still clutching the rag doll which she had carried all the way from Vancourt House.

Simon, who could not keep his eyes off Meg—he had begun to worry if there were something wrong with him, she obsessed him so—was watching her as she lifted Harriet up. Astonishingly, the mere sight of Meg tenderly kissing the little girl's soft cheek as she settled her into her arms caused a strong surge of desire—or was it lust mixed with affection?—to sweep over him. So strong was it that it shocked him.

Always, in his dealings with women, as when he had proposed to Meg, he had kept the sensual side of his nature under firm control. Caro Kenilworth had complained once that he always kept something of himself in reserve even when he was love-making—an unusually perceptive remark for her to make, he now realised, as he was confronted with his inability to control his emotions when with Meg, or when thinking of her in her absence.

He became aware that Jack Devereux was speaking to him, asking when the Society's next scientific

lecture was being given, and he tried to answer him
sensibly whilst keeping a half-watch on Meg. It was
plain that Harriet was too heavy for her to be able
to carry the little girl any great distance. In the
middle of a sentence from Jack, without a word
other than, 'Pray excuse me, Devereux,' he walked
over to Meg and said, 'Allow me, Madame, to take
over your burden. She is too much for you.'

This came out so abruptly and so unloverlikely—
it was almost as though, Cass and Emma Dickson
agreed later, he was giving an order to a recalcitrant
underling—that Meg retaliated by saying firmly,
'No, indeed, I am stronger than I look.'

Simon gave a half-laugh, said, 'I know that, but
it is not right that you should carry Harriet when
there are gentlemen about who have no burden
at all.'

He then looked meaningfully at Peverel, who had
been walking beside Meg, unwilling to spoil his
appearance as a well-dressed dandy by carrying a
small child *à la* Jack Devereux.

Peverel chose to ignore him, saying instead,
'Quite true, Madame. If my cousin wishes to carry
your charge, then I suggest that you allow him to
do so. I suspect that he will only fall into the sulks
if you cross him, and you do not wish to spoil the
afternoon with *that*, do you?'

Meg's instant agreement to allow him to take
Harriet from her as a result of his cousin's insolent
comment did nothing to improve Simon's temper—
more erratic these days than he cared to acknowledge to himself. It was all Meg's fault, of course.
And if his own jealousy of any man who went near

her appalled him, then that was one more annoyance
to add to the tally of offences that she was unwittingly running up!

He stifled an angry response to Peverel's remark
for the sake of Harriet, who offered him her doll to
kiss, saying loudly, 'Next to Aunt Meg, I like you
best, Uncle Simon.' Simon was a frequent visitor to
Vancourt House, mostly out of pity for Jane, whom
he had known since she was a small girl, rather than
through any friendship with Vancourt. Flighty she
might be, but she had not deserved *him*.

What had also shocked him was that when he had
lifted Harriet from her aunt's arms and had touched
Meg only lightly, that light touch had served to rouse
him again, as it had at the Leominsters' party—
something which had never happened with any other
woman before. Truly, he was a driven fool!

What he did not know was that Meg had suffered—if that were the right word—the same
experience, with the same result. If Simon was
listening half-distractedly to Jack Devereux as a
result, then she was undergoing the same experience
with Peverel, who had insinuated himself between
her and Cass.

Gossiping and laughing, much of their true
thoughts being concealed by the mask of politeness,
the little party reached the spot where Jane and Caro
had been left, in order to collect them for lunch.
Caro, an expression of supreme boredom on her
face, was engaged in walking around the enclosure
where the American beavers played, leaving Jane to
sit in silence, contemplating all her many grievances
against her husband, who had put himself on Meg's

other side, and was rivalling Peverel in his attempts to charm her.

Harriet, she saw, was in Simon's arms, demanding to be set down so that she might run to Mama. It had not occurred to Jane, until that moment, that her faithless husband might take it into his head to pursue Meg, and the thought made her feel so ill that she could hardly pay proper attention to her introduction to the Dicksons.

Fortunately for everyone's good temper, by the time that they had returned to the aviaries' paddock, Simon's servants were already arriving, carrying chairs, hampers of food, plates, cutlery, damask napkins, and a large number of wine bottles and glasses.

'At last,' drawled Vancourt, seizing on a glass of good red wine and accepting a large beef and horseradish sandwich from a Darrow footman. He threw himself into a chair as soon as was decently possible, after all the women were seated. He dismissed young George, who tried to tell his Papa about the wondrous beasts he had seen, with a curt, 'Not now, boy,' so that George was compelled to tell Mrs Dickson all about them instead. With the innocent shrewdness of childhood, he had already grasped that she would be a more willing audience than his selfish Papa.

The sun had come out as Caro had prophesied, something which she insisted on telling the company in an insufferable, I told you so, voice which had them all wincing, while she loudly complained of her dissatisfaction at being deprived of her parasol earlier, and of the shade of the beavers' pond later.

More to create a diversion than anything else, and

in an attempt to start a hare which might put some of the party in a better humour, Meg said thoughtfully, on picking up a chicken sandwich—a dainty one, made especially for the ladies—'When I am observing the animals I sometimes have the oddest thought: that *their* behaviour may afford us insights into our own.'

Her audience reacted to this statement each in his, or her, own fashion.

'Very odd, indeed,' was wrenched from Jane who was frowning, not being sure how much Meg was encouraging Vancourt.

'Dear Madame,' exclaimed Will Osborne, his honest face earnest, 'there I must correct you. We have it on the best authority of all, that of God himself, that we humans most resemble the angels, rather than the animals. We are of a different kind and of a different creation, so that any likeness between us must be accidental—if it exists at all.'

Jack Devereux paused in his demolition of a ham and mustard sandwich to say in his dry, but straightforward, fashion, 'Those of us who have engaged in warfare, Madame, might echo your opinion rather than that of Osborne's—eh, Dickie?' This last to George Dickson, who rewarded it with a silent nod of the head.

Simon's response was an internal one, and devoted to a quite different point, being of the order of, What kind of life has Madame been living to give vent to such a sentiment? More evidence, if such were needed, to support the notion of her loose-living, amorous career since animals were notoriously lax in that department!

For his part Peverel merely offered negligently, 'Such a remark, Madame la Comtesse, whatever its truth, serves only to display the witty liveliness of the mind that provoked its utterance.'

So, dear cousin, Simon silently glowered, you hope to follow the example of the animals with Madame, and take your pleasure with her as carelessly and as often as possible. Jealousy almost had him choking over his cook's excellent Shrewsbury biscuits.

Cass and Mrs Dickson, by contrast, said nothing at all, merely contenting themselves with exchanging amused glances, which said, What a splendid friend we have gained in Marguerite de Vaux. We shall have some excellent *causeries* with her, to be sure, if that is a sample of her thinking.

'For my part,' announced Caro Kenilworth, 'I consider it to be demeaning to my sex that such a comparison should be made at all, and by a lady. . .I have not the slightest wish to be compared to any animal.'

Meg, amused by the furore which her remark had created, had the greatest difficulty in not retorting to Caro, Not even with an honest cow, Lady K.?

The discussion that she had initiated received its death blow after Sir Thomas Acland, a silent man who had rarely uttered once during the afternoon, said in grave and bishoplike tones, 'The great Goethe, himself, Madame, discussed the matter at length in similar terms to your own, and reached the conclusion that we are more similar to the animals than we care to think.'

He paused, portentously, and it was plain to all

assembled that he was going to make up for his previous reticence by giving them an informed lecture on the matter, except that Cass Devereux exclaimed happily, 'Oh, if the great Goethe has spoken on the matter, then we must all hold our tongues and pass on to lower things, or do I mean higher ones?'

A general laugh in which even Sir Thomas joined, ran round the party—only Cass Devereux could get away with such charming irreverence. Will Osborne could be heard whispering to Simon, 'Now, who the devil is the great Goethe?'

Naughty Simon, delighted to see off a rival, muttered to him, 'If you really wish to know, Osborne, then have a word with Acland; he will be sure to enlighten you.'

Which would serve to keep him away from Meg for the rest of the afternoon, was his private, gleeful thought—one rival despatched for the time being. He was suddenly aware of Meg's sharp eyes on him—if he were watching her, she was watching him and she knew perfectly well that he had just dished Will! His respect for Madame's acuteness grew.

To Meg, the whole afternoon had been a revelation as each member of the party seemed determined to reveal their true selves, good or bad, without knowing what they were doing. She immediately amended that; some knew quite well, Cass Devereux among them, and Simon also, who was surprising her by his sharp eye to the main chance where she was concerned. If only he had not overheard that wretched conversation with his cousin Peverel and misunderstood it

No use repining, though. Or crying over spilt milk, as her old nurse used to say—and Aunt Léonie, who had said the same thing in French with more Gallic wit. What was done was done, and the real damage had been done that day long ago when she had refused Simon. Or later, perhaps, when she had married André. . .

The bright afternoon seemed to turn cold. She shuddered a little. No, she would not think of that, not now, not here, with the shouting children about her, and Jack and Cass Devereux present to show that a happy marriage could be achieved between two people who appeared to be quite different.

Peverel saw the shudder, and leaned officiously over to murmur, 'You are cold, Madame. May I lend you my jacket?'

Meg instinctively distrusted this chivalrous offer. Recovering her previous light-heartedness, she wondered what Simon's reaction would be if he saw Peverel in his shirtsleeves, and his jacket around her shoulders.

'How very kind of you, but no, I am not really cold. A passing frisson, I assure you.'

Cass Devereux, who was on her left, murmured in her ear, 'I am a little warmer than I care for, Meg. Take the shawl I am wearing, I do not really need it.'

Meg allowed Cass to drape it around her shoulders. It would be churlish to refuse a kind offer which would cause her no such embarrassment as Peverel's would have done. Simon's judgemental eyes were on her again, and she was sure that he had heard Peverel's offer. Perhaps he would think of her a little more kindly now that she had refused it.

Vain hope! Unknown to her, Simon had already decided that he would have words with his cousin as soon as he could decently contrive an opportunity. One came when all the children decided that they wished to visit the bears again before they went home. All except Harriet, that was, to whom Aunt Meg had promised a visit to the pelicans instead.

He caught Peverel by the arm, saying curtly, 'A private word with you, if you please.'

'What, here?' exclaimed Peverel. 'I have come on pleasure, not to be rebuked, for I see by your expression that some sort of rebuke is intended.'

'Yes, here.' Simon's voice was dangerous. 'I am not about to spend valuable time chasing you around town when all I need to do is detain you for a few moments. You will do me the courtesy of agreeing.'

He did not use the words the 'honour of agreeing' for he thought, rightly, that his cousin possessed no honour.

'Oh, very well.' Peverel shrugged his shoulders. 'If you must, you must.' He watched the rest of the party disappear into the distance, Madame among them. Another opportunity lost, thanks to his interfering cousin.

'I feel compelled to ask you not to pursue Madame. I have reason to believe that your intentions towards her are not honourable.' Simon could be no more definite than that, seeing that he could not reveal that he had overheard the conversation where Meg had given Peverel money.

'Oh, you are quite mistaken about that, Sim. My

intentions are purely honourable. I mean to marry her.'

'Do not call me Sim—' Simon began saying, only to be interrupted by Peverel's careless laugh.

'Cousin, then—if that is what you prefer.'

'Not that either. I do not wish to be reminded that we are cousins—' only to be interrupted again.

'Don't you, by God? But we are cousins, and I am your heir—or had you forgotten?'

Simon did his best to rein in his temper, aware that he was allowing Peverel to sidestep the true subject of the conversation. 'I suppose,' he said, cool again, 'that you are after her for her fortune.'

'What a low opinion you have of the lady's attractions,' drawled his cousin. 'I admit that her wealth is an inducement, but not the only one, I assure you.'

'Oh, I do beg leave to doubt that. Meg and I have had little to do with one another of recent years, but I should not wish to see her married to someone with your reputation.'

Peverel began to laugh. 'My reputation! That's rich. The lady's reputation is such that she should be grateful that anyone wishes to marry her!'

Only with difficulty did Simon prevent himself from striking the grinning face of the man before him. He had heard whispered and indefinite slurs against Meg before, but nothing so apparently downright as this. He contained himself by saying between his teeth, 'Now what the devil do you mean by *that*?'

'You mean that you haven't heard?' Peverel mocked him. 'Oh, I always knew that you were strangely innocent, *cousin*, but I thought that even you knew how André de Vaux came to his death. Why, when I was in Paris, it was the one topic of conversation: that little Meg Ashe, now a Comtesse, was Talleyrand's latest mistress, that André was twitted over it, and consequently was compelled to fight the duel in which he was killed. Rumour said that she had other, nameless, lovers.' He paused, adding with a significant wink and grin, 'As I was in a position to know.'

Simon stared at him, stunned. Of all the things that Peverel might have told him, he had not expected this. Oh, he had known from the conversation that he had overheard at the Leominsters' that Meg must have had an *affaire* with Peverel.

But what he had just learned was worse than that, much worse. His once innocent Meg had been the mistress of an old man who had been one of the most notorious *roués* of the last forty years! A man whose notoriety as a skilled seducer was only equalled by his notoriety as a wily politician and diplomat, who had managed to keep his head on his shoulders through all the changes of regime in France since the Revolution of 1789!

So *that* accounted for Meg's polish, her self-control, her worldliness, her damned double-dealing appearance of injured innocence. She had been taught by a master. He seized on a straw. Peverel might be lying. He told him so, fiercely.

'Oh, believe that if you will. I was in Paris at the time. Of course, being such a man of honour yourself, so highly principled, *you* could not forgive her, or wish her for a wife, but I, why. . .I am happy to accept her for what she is, and marry her. A truly

Christian attitude to adopt under the circumstances, I think you will agree.'

What could he say? Not, My blessings on the pair of you, you are a splendid match for one another. To do so would reveal the depth of his feelings for a woman who had turned out to be totally unworthy, and would also give Peverel the triumph over him which his cousin had always wanted.

Instead, he was almost indifferent. 'Well, if that is how matters lie, then I withdraw my objections.' But he didn't mean what he said.

'And, of course,' Peverel pursued, 'the sooner we are married, the sooner Darrow Hall and Darrow lands will have an heir of the second generation. You, I believe, still have no intention to marry.'

Simon felt like retorting that he would marry a hag from Hell and get a child on her to save Darrow from falling to Peverel and any of *his* get. His own dignity and sense of fitness prevented him from saying any such thing. Which, he knew, meant that he would always be at a disadvantage when arguring with his unscrupulous cousin.

'Forgive me,' Peverel said into the silence that had followed his last words, 'but if that is all that you have to say to me, *cousin*, then I will join the others.' He bowed, and strolled off, happy in the knowledge that he had hurled a bombshell named Talleyrand at Simon, and for the time being had gained himself a respite from his advice and his reproaches.

As for the lady, well, whether the rumours were true or not, he didn't care a tinker's damn. As far as Peverel was concerned, she was merely a source of possible wealth—with the bonus that he had begun to care for her—so any lie, or innuendo, would serve to gain him a clear run at it.

Simon, for his part, spent the rest of the afternoon in an unhappy daze. As Peverel had guessed, almost more than the news of Meg's possible immorality was the revelation that one of her partners had been Talleyrand. He almost felt that he could have stomached a handsome young buck rather than the monster who had betrayed everyone in turn, man and woman.

Oh, damn everything, he was lying, he knew he was. He would have hated anyone with whom she had cared to be faithless. The very worst had happened. Of all inconvenient things, he knew beyond a doubt that, whatever he had felt for the youngest Miss Ashe all those years ago, he now loved her— as he must have done then, without knowing it.

Nothing to do but trudge after the others, thinking that, being a mindless bear, happy to climb a pole and catch buns, might be a better fate than being born Simon Darrow. Best of all was to try to do what he had originally suggested and avoid meeting Meg altogether.

In the meantime, he must try to enjoy the remainder of the visit to the Gardens as the others were doing and pretend, like Voltaire's Candide, that everything was for the best in the best of all possible worlds!

Chapter Six

A week after the visit to the Zoological Gardens, Simon met Jasper at Louis Fronsac's fencing academy. Meg's brother was improving his ability with the sabre, and told Simon of a piece of news about her that had him seething all over again, and immediately breaking his resolution to avoid her.

'Care to come with me and visit m'sister in her new home, Darrow?' Jasper offered as he towelled himself off between bouts. 'Time you made it up with her.'

Simon ignored the second statement, and seized on the first, surprise and indignation in his voice. 'New home? I thought that she was staying with the Vancourts whilst she was over here.'

Jasper eyed him, and his indignation, over his towel. 'Changed her mind. Staying longer. Something about settling her late husband's affairs in England. She's rented Templestowe's place off Piccadilly.' Alex, Lord Templestowe had recently been appointed Ambassador to Spain.

So, Madame wanted a nest of her own where she

could entertain whom she pleased, did she, without
being observed? Suddenly Simon wanted most desperately to see her again. Why, God alone knew,
because since Peverel's revelations about her loose
life in Paris, seeing her—even at a distance—set
him off into such a froth of anger and annoyance
that he could barely think straight. A phrase he had
not heard or used since the days when he had been
a small boy and possessed a nanny.

'Alone?' he managed. 'In that great barracks?'

'Not exactly,' said Jasper through his towel.
'She's offered me quarters there, and she's taken on
General Hollis's widow as a *dame de compagnie*,
chaperon, what you will. Meg has nicknamed her
my watchdog—which both ladies seem to think an
excellent joke.'

'Oh.' For some reason Simon felt quite deflated.
'I wouldn't have thought that Meg needed a watchdog. She seems well able to look after herself.'

Jasper peered curiously at him, before throwing
his towel down and picking up his sabre. There was
a virulence in Simon's comments about his sister
which was at odds with his normal equable self.
What in the world was the matter with the pair of
them? He had tried speaking of Simon to Meg as a
possible brother-in-law, only to have her say in her
most freezing French great-lady voice, 'Quite out of
the question, Jas. Apart from the fact that I have no
intention of marrying again, if I were to do so, Simon
Darrow is the last person whom I should choose.'

And then she had swept out of the room, ending
all further conversation.

'So you will come with me?' Jasper offered as carelessly as he could.

Simon could scarcely bring himself to speak, so he nodded instead. Light in the attic, fit for bedlam, a glutton for punishment, were all phrases which passed rapidly through his tormented mind.

He repeated them to himself all over again when he reached Templestowe House, for who should be there before him but Peverel!

He was not to know how little Meg wished to see his cousin, who had set about ingratiating himself from the moment he had walked through her drawing-room door and bowed over her hand, saying, 'You must know, my dear Madame, that I could not wait to visit you when I heard of your move. I have such happy memories of Templestowe House and the dear Countess.' He sighed sentimentally, offering Meg his most killing expression.

Meg was not killed by it. She had no wish to entertain Peverel, but had been unable to refuse him entry—he had cunningly arrived with Will Osborne in tow. He had obviously brought him along to confer respectability on himself, and his smiling near-impertinence told her that he knew that she was well aware of what he was doing. He was still treating poor Will in the same offhand fashion which he had used to him at the Devereux's party and at the Zoological Gardens.

Meg's only consolation was that, with Charlotte Hollis present, there was little untoward which Peverel could do or say to her. Like Will, he was dressed absolutely *à point* and was just as determined to please her.

'I have never met the Templestowes,' was Meg's cool reply. 'I rented the house from their man of business.'

She had a piece of canvaswork in her lap, showing a peacock in full display—an apt symbol, she thought, for the smirking man opposite to her, so sure of his charm.

For all his good looks and his wit she could not like him, knowing of his blackmailing of Jane and his proposed treatment of herself. This was merely the opening shot of his threatened campaign to win her, she was sure, and to do so he was concealing his villainy behind a mask of charm. Meg could not help contrasting his subtlety with Simon's blunt honesty.

What's more, she was also sure that he had bamboozled Will into bringing him along as a supporter of Will's courtship! Once arrived though, he was busy cutting Will out—in the most charming way, of course—so that Will could not take offence. There was only one thing for it.

'Charlotte,' she said to Mrs Hollis, who, in her early thirties, had turned out to be a much younger woman than Meg had expected—she had been the late General's second wife—'Charlotte, you might care to show Mr Darrow the new album of *Views of the Great Houses of Britain*, which is on the map table in the corner. I am sure that he would find it most interesting.'

Having, as she thought, dismissed Peverel successfully, she turned to Will who was gazing at her in mute adoration, and asked him about his new curricle, which he had christened in Hyde Park the day before.

She had reckoned without Peverel's impudence. He stood up, bowed in her direction, and said gaily, 'Mr Darrow, indeed! How can you speak to me so formally, my dear Madame? Why, your family and mine have been neighbours and friends for the last five generations, at least. And, although we were not childhood companions as you and my cousin Simon were, I think that you might do me the honour of calling me Peverel, in exchange for me being allowed to address you as Marguerite—or even, dare I say it, as Meg.'

He ended this remarkable speech by taking Meg's hand, and offering her a deep bow before kissing it.

It was at this inopportune moment that Jasper, who had told the butler not to trouble to announce them, walked in, followed by Simon, whose first sight of the female thorn in his flesh was of her being publicly saluted by his worthless cousin!

An unknown woman, the chaperon presumably, was certainly not doing her duty and protecting her mistress as she should. That unmitigated ass, Will Osborne, had apparently nothing better to do than to watch this pantomime, his jaw slightly dropped.

Meg refrained from withdrawing her hand hastily when Simon entered. She would not allow him to think that his opinion of her mattered in the least. Indeed, Simon's thunderous expression had the perverse effect of inciting her to encourage Peverel further. How dare Simon presume to judge her!

So she allowed Peverel to hold her hand a little longer than she should—he was undoubtedly baiting

Simon by clinging to it—but denied him what he had begged for.

'Alas, my name is only for my relatives—and those—' and she dropped her voice so that Simon should not hear her '—whom I can trust. May I now add you to that list?'

Meg saw that she had wrong-footed him slightly, but his recovery was rapid. 'Oh, I hope so, I do hope so,' he murmured but, even as he spoke, his eyes mocked her.

She was not Jane, to be over-awed and intimidated by him. During her marriage she had refused to be put down by a greater master of the devious arts than Peverel Darrow.

Instead, she moved over to her brother, offered him her cheek, which he duly kissed, before she turned her attention to Simon. He was glaring at her as though she were an unlovely cross between Jezebel and Messalina. Meg thought that it was fortunate for his friendship with her brother that, although Peverel could read Simon's expression, and was amused by it, Jasper could not.

'Sir Simon,' she said sweetly, acknowledging his bow, but not offering him the hand which Peverel had so recently kissed. Given everything, that might be going a step too far. 'I am delighted to see you here. I believe that you are not acquainted with my *dame de compagnie*, Mrs Hollis. She was recommended to me by one of your old friends, Lady Devereux.'

Well, that last fact ought to spike his guns and no mistake! Having wrong-footed one cousin, she had now done the same to the other. It was growing to be quite a habit, and a delightful one this time, since Simon could surely have no fault to find with such a paragon of perfection as Mrs Hollis was reputed to be.

'So pleased to make your acquaintance at last,' Simon told the lady, who was beginning to understand that being an Anglo-French Countess's watchdog was not going to be either as simple or as boring as she had at first thought.

'I met your late husband some years ago when I first entered Parliament. I was truly sorry to learn of his death. Madame la Comtesse could have no more proper or pleasing a companion.'

And so he told Meg a little later, after Jasper had suggested that he stay for supper, Peverel having left, spouting promises that he would visit again in a few days' time, when he proposed to escort Meg and Mrs Hollis to the theatre, Will Osborne also in attendance, of course. Peverel's contempt for Will was so great that he did not fear his competition for Meg's hand. He rightly judged that such a feeble ass could have no attraction for her.

Meg was unable to refuse this apparently kind offer out of hand without betraying her difficult situation *vis-à-vis* Peverel to Mrs Hollis. Her acquiescence earned her a glare from Simon.

Supper might have been an uncomfortable meal, but surprisingly was not. Jasper was in great form, teasing Charlotte Hollis about trying, unsuccessfully, to be his sister's dragon.

'When she told me that she was acquiring a companion,' he said, raising his wineglass to her, 'I naturally assumed that I was going to meet a dear little old lady with a mob cap, a large canvas bag, and an elderly smelly poodle, not someone who looks as though she needs a chaperon herself.'

Even for Jasper, this was a little extreme. He was a great man for the ladies, mostly those ladies who were kindly known as opera dancers, or bits of muslin for want of a better name. Charlotte Hollis with her gravely pretty face, her simply dressed brown hair and her modest toilette, was not one of his obvious targets.

'You will have to guard one another,' remarked Simon drily. 'Especially if you are to keep away such adventurers as my cousin Peverel,' he could not resist adding. 'A trip with him to the theatre is sure to cause comment about the particularity of his intentions, especially if repeated.'

'Mr Will Osborne will add respectability to the party,' offered Charlotte swiftly. She knew that Peverel's reputation was not good, although not bad enough to bar him from polite society. 'And I don't believe that either Madame or I wish to repeat the experience.'

Simon could say nothing further without appearing churlish, and the rest of the evening passed happily enough—even though both Charlotte and Jasper privately noted that the polite formality between Simon and Meg was excessive, to say the least.

Except that when Simon had left, Jasper—who was staying the night—walked into his sister's little sitting-room, adjacent to the large best bedroom, and sat down opposite her. Meg was reading before retiring. He said, quietly for him, 'What is wrong between you and Simon, Meg, that you are at such odds? The air is positively sulphurous when you are together these days.'

Meg decided to treat him to a little of the truth: not too much, for Simon and he were old and valued friends, and she did not wish to spoil their friendship.

'Oh, Jasper, do not refine overmuch on what I hope is only a passing thing. Simon has heard a little of the stupid gossip about me, I believe, and it is making him unhappy. After all, he did propose to me once, so I don't suppose he feels very pleased if someone tells him untruthful *on dits* about my life in France.'

'I suppose Peverel has been trying to queer his pitch with you,' remarked Jasper shrewdly. 'Want me to have a word with him? I could tell him something of the truth.'

'Of all things, no,' exclaimed Meg, showing agitation for once. 'The matter is trivial, seeing that he and I are merely acquaintances these days.'

'As you wish, sister, but I don't think that Simon quite views you in that light. I know a jealous man when I see one, but least said, soonest mended, I suppose. However, if you should need my help, then you merely have to speak. What are brothers for, but to protect their sisters?'

He rose. So did Meg. She walked impulsively over to him and kissed his cheek. 'You are a good fellow, Jasper, the best of brothers. Always remember that you may come to me, too, although I cannot imagine that you will ever need my help.'

She sat for a time after he had left, listening to the peacocks screeching on the terrace outside. She was thinking of Simon. He was seldom out of her thoughts. When Charlotte came in to bid her good-night, after her maid had dressed her for bed, she found Meg standing at the window, looking out into the darkness, as though trying to find something there.

'May I be of assistance, Madame?'

Meg turned, startled. She had been far away. She understood at once that Charlotte was referring to what had passed with the Darrow cousins and, like Jasper, was offering her aid and comfort.

'You are very kind, but I do not believe that any-one can help me. It is for me to help myself. What you may do is join me in discouraging Peverel Darrow without causing any form of scandal. Jasper twitted you with not being my dragon—perhaps you could be my dragonette instead!'

This set Charlotte laughing at the mere idea that she could be a baby dragon, and the moment passed. Only, as she made to leave, Meg said, 'Not Madame in future, but Meg. There are so few left to call me that.'

'In private,' agreed Charlotte. 'In public, it would not be proper.'

Meg considered saying, 'Oh, I am beyond pro-priety,' but kept the thought to herself. As with Jasper, she had to consider carefully how much of herself she gave away. It was growing harder and harder for her to be frank with anyone.

So matters stood throughout the summer that fol-lowed. Jasper's care for Meg took the form of constantly escorting her and Charlotte to all the events of the season. They visited Ranelagh, the theatre—only once with Peverel—boated on the Thames, went to the Opera, and all the balls, receptions, and ridottos that filled the lives of the cousinry who ruled Britain.

Once Meg went to the House of Commons with Jane and Charlotte to hear Simon make a short speech on Reform, of which he was an advocate, since he believed that only through careful and progressive change could a revolution be averted.

Polite formality continued to reign. On one thing she and Simon apparently agreed: not to waltz with one another. To do so would have meant a physical contact that neither of them could bear, for it immediately revived all the suppressed passion which lay between them.

Of the two, Meg was the more astonished by this. When she had known Simon at the time of his proposal, his touch had meant nothing to her, although the sight of him had excited her after a fashion which at the time she had not fully understood.

Marriage to André changed me, she thought one evening at a *bal masqué* given by Princess Lieven, as she watched Simon waltzing with Caro Kenilworth, who was still doggedly pursuing him with a view to marriage. If he taught me nothing else, he taught me what passion could mean. He awoke my sleeping senses. And that is why I feel such a pang when I see Simon with Caro. Are they going home together, I wonder? To. . . And if to think of *that* pains me so, what does it tell me about my feelings for him?

She was not to know that Simon's feelings for

her, when he saw her, lightly clasped in Will
Osborne's arms, circling the dance floor, were
equally strong, if not stronger. To the devil with him
and her, and Peverel, too! For his worthless cousin
always seemed to be hovering nearby.

Commonsense told him that Jasper Ashe's
constant hovering about Meg was proof of his intention to safeguard both her and her reputation—or
was it that Jasper was after the chaperon, despite
her difference from all the other women he had
pursued?

He taxed Jasper with this immediately. Simon's
only concession to the Princess's masquerade had
been to adopt a long dark cloak and a black bird
mask with a long beak. Jasper, however, was splen-
didly turned out as a Cossack, and not for the first
time Simon wondered where Jasper's money, to pay
for all the trappings of high life, came from.
Although he was a half-pay officer in peace time,
from a family which was notoriously poor, he
appeared as rich and improvident as the young heirs
to vast fortunes who were his friends.

'Tell me, Ashe,' he remarked, apparently carelessly, 'is your constant dancing in attendance on
Meg and her friend on behalf of your sister's
honour—or is the chaperon your true target?'

For once Jasper was not frank with him. 'Why
should it be for either reason? Can't a man have
a pretty woman on each arm without his friends
immediately consigning him to the duelling field or
the altar?'

Nevertheless, it was becoming increasingly clear
to Meg and Simon that Charlotte Hollis had suc-

ceeded in doing something which no other woman had done before—she had captured the heart of that fickle cavalier, Jasper Ashe.

For the Lievens' ball, she had adopted the pretty rustic clothing of a shepherdess, and its delightful simplicity had enchanted Jasper even further. That night it was obvious, by their manner to one another, that Charlotte was as attracted to Jasper as he was to her. Meg, dressed daringly as Cleopatra, and still alienated from Simon, had the dubious pleasure of watching their happiness. Fancy Jasper being caught at last, and by someone so good and modest: who would have believed it? The pity was that she was as poor as he was—thus proving the purity of his intentions, for there was no reason to believe that Charlotte's attraction for him was her fortune.

'But reformed rakes always marry good women,' explained Cass Devereux to Meg, as they sat pleasantly chatting to one another whilst watching the fun. 'Safer so. Jack says its always better to know that your sons are your own, and not someone else's.'

'Is that the only reason?' asked Meg, entertained, as usual, by Cass's witty down-to-earth conversation.

'Not entirely. Flighty women choose bad housekeepers, too, and a man prefers a comfortable home when he reaches mature years, rather than a trumpery love nest. Now here comes someone who has never wished for a trumpery love nest. Good evening, Sir Simon. Have you arrived to take my friend away so that I shall have no one left with whom to talk sense? I'm sure that you are determined to talk nonsense to her!'

'If she will allow me,' retorted Simon gravely, openly light-hearted for once. Perhaps it was the mask he was wearing—or was it that Cass Devereux could always disarm him? Meg thought enviously. Shall I ask her how she does it?

Instead, as Simon bowed and asked her to stand up in the quadrille with him, she accepted, putting out her hand for him to raise her to her feet. She was aware of Cass's shrewd eyes on them, so she was as gracious as she could be. So much so that Simon remarked, still retaining her hand in his so that her whole body quivered and silently sang, 'You are pleased to be at evens with me tonight.'

'I am always at evens with you,' riposted Meg tartly. 'It is you who are at odds with me.'

Normally she might have expected her dart to be thrown back at her as she came out with this, but for once it was no such thing, since he continued by saying, 'Jasper's presence seems to have sobered you, Madame, or is it the example of Mrs Hollis? My cousin Peverel appears to be in exile so far as you are concerned, which pleases me even if it does not please him.'

'I was not aware that my conduct ought to be arranged so as to please either of you,' was Meg's answer to that, immediately before they separated to bow at one another before the music began.

'Oh, our conduct ought always to be arranged so as to please our friends,' replied Simon as they passed one another in the dance.

Meg, on their next encounter, asked sweetly, 'And do I count as a friend so far as you are concerned,

Sir Simon? I was not aware that I had that honour.'

'Good God, Madame,' he said as he passed her again. 'I thought that we had been friends since you were in short skirts.'

'But not, apparently, when I wore long French ones. Unless you have changed your mind recently.'

Against his will, this set Simon laughing, but his face had regained its normal composure when next they met. This impelled Meg to remark, 'You are suddenly grave, Sir Simon. Is it French fashions that you object to? If so, I cannot promise to reform— English ones seem so dull.'

This should have annoyed him, served to confirm her frivolity, but this evening he could not be angry with her. The laxness which *bals masqués* invariably imposed on those who attended them was doing its work. Everyone knew everyone else, even though they were masked; but eyes glittering through slits and bodies wearing unfamiliar and exciting clothes had a strange effect on their wearers.

Simon's mask gave him the air of a predator, and he could convince himself that Meg's disguise as Cleopatra was a disguise and that she was quite unlike the free-living Egyptian queen, and so he was kinder to her than usual. Or was it, he thought afterwards, that he had a mind to lull her? Once the dance was over and they stood bowing, before he consigned her back to Cass again, instead of doing so he took her hand, and said, 'Come.'

Whether it was his bird mask which transformed him into an eagle ready to pounce on its prey, or whether it was the mere sight of Meg as Egypt's queen which caused him to lose all his stern resolve to keep their relationship distant, Simon never knew.

Using his considerable strength, he urged her through the milling crowds, through a glass door and, closing it firmly behind them, led her on to a terrace from where they could see London and its gas lamps below them.

Meg's initial wish to struggle rapidly disappeared. Easier to let him pull her gently along. In any case, without making a scene she could not refuse him— and did she wish to?

Once on the terrace, he released her. She thought that he was about to step back; indeed, he began to do so, but no, instead, he looked down at her, tense and silent. His eyes glittering through the mask were exactly like those of the eagle it was portraying. He stepped forward instead, saying hoarsely, 'Unfinished business, Madame,' and took her in his arms.

It would be true to say that Simon was as astonished as Meg by his actions. He had had no intention of doing any such thing. He had meant to speak to her carefully and seriously, to ask her to deny the rumours about her reputation that were running around society; to praise her, perhaps, for her recent circumspect behaviour.

Alas, all such good resolutions flew away when Meg stood before him, her lips parted, her eyes shining, her head a little thrown back, her whole beautiful body displayed to advantage in the trappings of the desert temptress!

Tempted he was. And fell.

Mouth met mouth. Body met body. Hands misbehaved. Simon said something hoarse and broken,

Meg echoed him. They clung together as though they were a stone nymph and satyr making love in the gardens below them.

An idyll out of time, Meg thought later, alone in her chaste bed. What would have happened had it been allowed to continue might have given a whole different course to their subsequent lives. But the door to the terrace opened, and a familiar voice said, mocking them, 'Ah, there you are, cousin. Enjoying the night, I see.'

It was Peverel Darrow. He must have seen them leave, and had followed them, giving them just sufficient time, Simon thought savagely, to begin to misbehave themselves. Slowly, reluctantly, they fell apart, their bodies protesting at joy denied.

'I believe, Madame,' Peverel said, grinning as he advanced towards them, wearing the trappings of the Devil—Mephistopheles in person, down to a small tail—'that you agreed to dance the cotillion with me, and the music is about to begin.'

It was true. Meg had so agreed, as much to keep him quiet, without conceding a lot to him, as for any other reason. She and Charlotte had agreed on such a ploy. Simon, however, thwarted, took matters differently.

'Oh, indeed,' he almost snarled. 'Dance with him, by all means, Madame. Please the Devil, if no one else.'

You might, thought Meg bitterly, have believed that in their recent encounter *she* had fallen on *him*, instead of the other way round.

'Oh, so I have your permission, Sir Simon,' she shot at him, Peverel grinning the while at Simon's discomfiture. He had been shocked to see them disappear, even more shocked to discover them in one another's arms: it was no part of his plans for Meg that she and Simon should become reconciled.

He held out his hand to her and, perforce, Meg took it. She could almost feel Simon seething behind her as they walked through the garden door and re-entered the ballroom. For a moment it had seemed to Meg that what lay between them had been forgotten, that they might take up where they had left off when she had so foolishly refused him.

But she had reckoned without Peverel, and it might be wise not to reckon without him again.

Chapter Seven

The blue skies of summer are frequently spoiled by the appearance of unexpected clouds. So, too, life may deceive the unwary into thinking that all may be well—and will remain well. Just as Meg had begun to hope that she and Simon might be coming to terms again, and that Jasper was at last prepared to settle down, dark clouds arrived to spoil her summer, which had begun to be a happier one.

Simon's friendliness to her had been destroyed by Peverel's breaking in on them at the Lievens' *bal masqué*, whilst Jasper, who had begun to spend more and more of his time with her and Charlotte, suddenly retreated into the wild life that he had led before coming to stay at Templestowe House. They rarely saw him during late June and early July, and Charlotte, whose cheeks had become rosy under Jasper's attentions, grew sallow again.

Better, thought Meg sadly, that he had never paid her any attentions at all, rather than show her such particularity and then withdraw. To make matters worse, Peverel and Will Osborne haunted them, or rather haunted Meg, for Charlotte, having lost her one devoted cavalier, now had no cavalier at all.

'I would wish,' Meg said brightly to Charlotte as they were busy with their canvaswork one afternoon, 'to visit Astley's Amphitheatre. I have never been there, but it would not be proper for us to go without a gentleman dancing attendance on us. I shall ask Jasper to take us, but I do wish that it were possible for ladies to look after themselves a little more than we are allowed to.'

Charlotte stitched on in silence, her head lowered, before she muttered, 'I do not think that Major Ashe cares for our company these days. We rarely see him, and I have no wish to impose on him. I would prefer you not to ask such a favour of him.'

'No!' Meg's answer was spirited. 'Why should it always be presumed that men may do exactly as they please whilst we are always condemned to please them? I do not greatly care what Jasper's wishes are. He should be prepared to sink his own wishes for once and oblige us. Besides, his recent conduct is most strange. He has always been a good and loving brother to me, particularly in the past when the rest of my family showed me little consideration.'

This surprised Charlotte and roused her from her apathy a little. Meg rarely talked of personal matters, and for the first time it occurred to her companion that perhaps her employer's life had not always been a bed of roses.

'That is true,' she said slowly, and then in a rush, 'Oh, do forgive me, Meg, but I have been so foolish. . .I had thought. . . No, no, I must not say it,' and she began to cry, wildly and loudly after a fashion quite unlike that of her usual equable self.

'No, Charlotte, no!' Meg threw down her stitchery, in order to cross to where Charlotte sat sobbing. She put her arms around her to comfort her.

'You were not foolish. I, too, thought that Jasper had a *tendre* for you, and it is most unlike him to play fast and loose with a good woman such as yourself. If you were deceived, so was I, so do not call yourself foolish. If he has really treated you so lightly then you may call him wicked for all that he is my brother.'

Charlotte's response was to cry even harder, so that Meg began to rock her, murmuring, 'There, there, cry for a little if you must, but then be brave and show the world a bold uncaring face.'

Even as I do, she thought sadly. Even as I do.

After a time Charlotte stopped weeping, pulled out a most inadequate handkerchief, mopped up her tears and blew her nose.

'I was a fool,' she muttered, 'to think that a sought-after and handsome man like your brother could care for a dowd past her last prayers such as I am. Who would want to marry a penniless widow when the world is full of well-dowered young girls?'

What to say? Nothing was best. Meg made comforting noises until Charlotte recovered herself and picked up her stitchery again, saying, 'Oh, dear, Meg, I have wet you through, and it is my duty to comfort you, not you me.'

All the same, decided Meg, after she had rung for the tea things to be brought in and life had resumed its normal tranquil way, I shall have a word with

Jasper. He had no right to raise Charlotte's hopes
as he did, and then drop her so unkindly. I shall try
to see him tonight, however late he returns home
and, as Cook said of a misbehaving kitchen boy, I
shall have it out with him. Best to do it when all
the world is safely asleep and none may overhear us.

Late it was. The clock in the drawing-room nearest
to the big front door was striking four before Meg
heard the noise and clatter attendant on Jasper's
return. She had decided not to speak to him immediately, but would allow him time to retire to his rooms
before she challenged him.

His progress up the grand staircase was slow.
He was obviously half-cut, and for a moment Meg
considered the wisdom of challenging him when he
was in such a state. The image of Charlotte's wan
face rose before her. No, she would not wait. If he
was not fit to talk to her, then he must tell her so.
He was by no means the first drunken man she had
had to cope with. . .

She knocked on his door. His valet, Tyler, had
passed her on the landing and had stopped to say,
'Madame, the Major is not himself. He will not
allow me to undress him. . .'

Whether or no he was shocked by Meg's riposte,
she did not stay to find out. 'I have no wish to
undress my brother, but I do need to speak to him.'
Afterwards, she was to ask herself what had driven
her to be so urgent and to thank God for it. At
the time she thought of nothing but knocking on
the door.

To hear Jasper call in a blurred voice, 'I told

you to leave me alone, Tyler. Go away.'

'It isn't Tyler knocking, Jas. It's Meg.'

'Doubly go away, then. You've no business with me tonight, or ever.'

He wasn't so overset that he could not answer her. Meg stared at the panelling. She made a decision.

'If you don't let me in, Jasper, I shall fetch the butler and a couple of footmen and have the door broken down. I don't think that Alex Templestowe would be too happy about that, do you?'

Silence. Meg stood, her heart beating rapidly. Something was wrong, she was sure of it. Jasper had been so unlike himself recently, and now he didn't resemble himself at all!

Please God, let him open the door, she prayed.

She heard footsteps. The door opened. Jasper stood there swaying a little, but somehow she thought that he was not very drunk. There was something else very wrong with him.

'Come in if you must,' he growled and retreated back to a small table in the middle of the room, sat down on the far side of it and stared at her.

'What is it, Jasper?' Meg said slowly. 'What's wrong? There is something dreadfully wrong, isn't there? I wouldn't have expected the Jasper I know to have treated Charlotte so unkindly.'

At the mention of Charlotte's name, her brother dropped his head into his hands. His shoulders heaved.

'Go away, Meg. Let me——' He stopped.

'Let you what, Jasper?' She advanced into the room as far as the table.

And saw on it a pistol.

She put her hand to her mouth, looking at her usually smartly dressed, self-controlled brother, who was hunched in a posture of complete abandon before a loaded pistol.

'Tell me, Jasper,' she said steadily. 'Tell me what is wrong. I once said that I would offer you help if you needed it, but I cannot do so if you will not tell me the truth.'

Jasper shuddered. He lifted his head to show her his ravaged face, his red eyes, the disarray of his clothing. 'You can't help me, Meg. I'm ruined.' He dropped his head again.

'Ruined, Jas? How ruined? Lift your head and tell me. At once.'

She had played this scene before, or one very like it, and Meg knew that she must be calm, be the voice of reason when all she wanted to do was shriek.

'I've lost everything. I. . .owe thousands—the moneylenders for my debts and to the people I played cards with when I tried to recoup my fortunes. I wanted to win enough so that Charlotte and I might marry—as well as pay my debts. I did win at first, and then I lost. . .I was plucked like the pigeon I am.

'In my position as heir, I pledged our parents' home, all that is left to them, as security for my debts—and now it is gone. My debts are being called in and I cannot pay them. Not only am I ruined, but so are they. All that is left to me, in honour, is that—' and he pointed to the pistol '—so go away.'

'Honour—? In that?' Meg's voice was icy. 'And how will killing yourself, here in my home may I remind you, save Mother and Father from being put

into the street? All that will do is save you from
suffering for your folly whilst leaving the rest of us
to pay for it. No, Jasper. That is not the answer.
How much do you owe?'

Bleary-eyed, he stared at her. 'Thousands, more
than I care to think of. Why?'

'How much?' she repeated.

Jasper told her. 'You fool,' she said calmly, 'to
lose so much, but if that is the sum of it—and you
must pledge your word, for what that is worth, that
it is—then I will pay your debts for you. But you
must promise me never to gamble again—or run up
debts of any kind.'

He shook his head. 'How can I promise to stay
out of debt? I am only a half-pay officer, for God's
sake, with no other source of income, and in peace-
time, no possibility of promotion, since I haven't
the money to purchase a commission. So, unless I
borrow money, I can't live.'

'Then resign your commission and be my agent
for the estate I am buying in Berkshire. If you wish,
and I think you do, to marry Charlotte, then you
may do so after a decent interval, providing you stay
away from London and the high life. You have told
me often that you love country living, and I know
that you are capable, when you are not busily
engaged in ruining yourself by living beyond
your paper.'

Her brother said, slowly and painfully, 'Are you
so rich, Meg? And so. . .hard-headed?'

'Both, Jasper, both—life has made me so. Say
yes, and we will go to Coutts Bank tomorrow and
arrange matters. I warn you that you must tell me

everything you owe, and sign a document that will commit you never to gamble in the future because, if you do. . .I shall not rescue you again.'

'Yes, yes, I understand you.' His voice was heavy. 'You must know that I can never repay you.'

'Only by living a good life in the country—and by the by, you will tell no one, not even Charlotte, that the estate is mine, until I am ready to acknowledge ownership. Let them think it is a friend's. So you see, I am not so hard-headed, after all, for I am giving you a second chance.'

'Oh, Meg,' he began, his voice husky, 'I promise you. . .'

'No, Jasper. Promise me nothing. I have had my fill of promises. . .and all of them broken. Just do as I ask. And if you truly love Charlotte, marry her.'

'Oh, indeed.' He was eager for the first time, more like his old self. 'I did it to gain her, you know. Because I could not afford to marry her. I have never gambled heavily before—I was always careful.'

'Then continue to be so.' Meg leaned forward, picked up the pistol and said, 'You will not be needing this.'

'No.' his voice broke. 'Meg. . .I can never thank you enough.'

'Thank me by doing as I ask. We shall visit Coutts in the morning. Goodnight.'

She was halfway down the grand staircase, holding the pistol away from her, before the irony of what had happened struck Meg. First Jane and now Jasper.

What next?

*   *   *

Peverel Darrow, wearing a Chinese dressing-gown, was drinking coffee at half past eleven in the morning in his rooms in the Albany. His valet, George Jackson, put his head around the door, and said in a disrespectful voice, 'There's that clerk fellow again, asking to see you. He says that his business is urgent.'

'Then take your Friday face away, and send him in, at once.'

Living as he did on the edge of ruin, one step ahead of a debtors' prison, Peverel had a number of dubious acquaintances and informants of whom his valet visibly disapproved. Well, damn him, let him disapprove away. Without them, and their information, Peverel could hardly have afforded a valet, and so he had told him more than once.

The clerk fellow? That was probably Lewis, a dogsbody at the moneylending house of Strauss and Sons. Now what particular useful titbit had brought him along this morning to earn a few pennies—or, if the information was important enough, perhaps a few guineas?

He was soon to find out. Lewis sidled in, his greasy top hat in his hand. Jackson had not deigned to dirty his hands by taking it from him. Peverel made no attempt to rise, saying brusquely, 'Well, what is it brings you here today?'

'Something I'll be bound you'll pay good money for, master,' whined Lewis.

'Fire away, then. And it had better be good, mark you, to be worth disturbing me at this hour.'

Lewis, whose day usually began at eight of the clock, nodded as though he, too, ate his breakfast at half-past ten, bowed his head and muttered, 'You said as how you wanted anything—rumour, gossip or facts—which I heard about the French Countess. Well, yesterday I had through my hands a draft from Coutts Bank, drawn on the account of Madame de Mortaine, to pay off a large debt which had been outstanding for some time. . .'

'How large?'

'Very large. To the tune of twenty thousand pounds, allowing for the original loans and accrued interest. It seems that Strauss bought up a lot of paper signed by the debtor.'

'Spit it out, man. Was it Madame's debt? And if so, for what? She's supposed to be as rich as Croesus, so it would be damned odd if she needed to borrow money—unless all the *on dits* are wrong.'

Lewis shook his head. 'That I don't know. Old Strauss keeps his business close to his chest. Only he knows who his clients are. I took the draft, with some others, to Coutts to be honoured. But my fellow clerk, Dickie Dobson, maintained that the debtor weren't Madame, by something Strauss said. It were a man, he thought, some nob.'

He made no apologies for breaching the confidential nature of either Coutts's business, or that of his employer. Poorly paid as he was, Lewis believed that he had the right to supplement his earnings in any way he could.

'But had he no notion of who she raised the money for? I'll give you a guinea for what you have told me, and I'll double it if you tell me the name of the man whom Madame was bailing out.'

A regretful shrug answered him. 'Nay, master.

I'm sorry to lose an extra guinea, but Dickie only knew that it must have been a man, nothing else. Besides, Strauss don't do business with women. Only takes their money if they clear a debt for some-one else.' Then, a sly expression on his face as he pocketed the coin which Peverel handed to him, he offered, 'Ain't it a possibility, master, that you might know who the lucky man is? Some lover, perhaps?'

Or her brother, thought Peverel, although he had heard no rumours to the effect that Jasper Ashe's pockets were to let. On the other hand, the Ashes were as poor as church mice, and Jasper wouldn't be receiving much from them in the way of an income to support his half-pay.

Knowledge being power, though, there must be some way in which he could use this infor-mation. 'Keep your eyes and ears open,' he told Lewis before he left, 'and there'll be more than a guinea for you.'

One piece of information that Lewis had passed over was worth as much as the knowledge of the banker's draft: that little Meg Ashe, turned French Countess, was even richer than he had thought that she might be. A prize worth winning, and by fair means or foul he would have a go at winning her! But first he would have to destroy his cousin Simon's chances. By her behaviour, it was plain that Madame had a *tendre* for him, even if the idiot wasn't aware of it.

On second thoughts, though, from what he had seen lately, cousin Simon had been busy destroying his chances himself.

*　　*　　*

He took this comforting thought with him when he drove to Hyde Park that afternoon to look for her. If he made the Comtesse his wife, then Simon could keep Darrow Hall, and the measly fortune which went with it. With Meg's money he would buy himself a palace.

The sun shone and there was a gentle breeze, when Peverel turned into the Park. As was customary, all the polite world was on parade there that afternoon. Cass Devereux was driving a perch-phaeton, her children and husband for once not with her.

She was wearing an outrageous habit based on a grenadier's uniform, something which only she could carry off. The Duke was there, Wellington himself, on horseback today, talking animatedly to Cass—twitting her on her turn-out, no doubt.

But where was Madame de Mortaine? Peverel looked about him and saw that his cousin Simon was present, but alone, thank God—he had feared that Meg might be with him. Simon was riding a powerful grey stallion, which only a strong man could tame sufficiently to make him behave in the over-crowded Park.

And there she was. She was neither on horseback, nor driving any kind of phaeton or gig. Instead, looking enchanting in the palest green, she was in a modest landaulet parked in the shade of a large tree. That plain prude Charlotte Hollis sat by her side. Meg looked so charming that Peverel was surprised all over again to discover that it was not only for her money that he wished to win her. Lust—or could it possibly be love?—was driving him, too.

So much so that, for once, sincerity rode on his face as he approached the landaulet. His pleasure at finding her was genuine. The other, baser, pleasure he felt was that, seated as she was, she could not avoid him, and what was even better, in Simon's absence there was no one to queer his pitch with her.

Meg had seen him coming, but she misread his expression, translating it as merely predatory. She muttered below her breath to Charlotte, 'We are finely trapped with no escape from him, but never mind, we may practice our politeness—and our indifference.'

Charlotte, who had been looking around for Jasper, who had promised to meet them there, nodded agreement. For all his good looks and his easy charm, she could not like Peverel. It was plain that he was chasing Meg for her fortune. Charlotte did not believe that he loved Meg: she believed that, like many men in society, he loved only himself.

'Good afternoon, ladies,' he said gaily. 'It is a fine one, is it not?'

Of such banalities was conversation in society made up, thought Meg acidly, but she gave him her cool agreement whilst looking around to see if Simon was anywhere near. She could not find him, but instead saw Jasper, who was riding a spirited chestnut, and was plainly making for her and Charlotte.

He had already begun to arrange his resignation from the Army, and was due to visit Meg's new property in Berkshire in the near future. Beside him was her sister Phoebe's husband, Fred Zealand, a discontented expression on his face.

Peverel had no objection to them joining Meg.
On the contrary, their willingness to be seen talking
to him proved that he was still acceptable in the best
society. Jasper was only interested in Charlotte, and
Zealand, happily married to Phoebe, could not
expect to attract Meg, even if he was attracted by her.

Which was nothing less than the truth. What
would have amused her with anyone but her sister's
husband, pained her when Zealand began to contend
with Peverel for her favour. Oh, the devil was in all
men. The one she wanted despised her, and she
despised all those who wanted her. Perhaps it was
life she was complaining of.

She thought so even more when Simon suddenly
appeared, flung himself off his magnificent grey and
walked over to join the party and add his mischief
to theirs.

'Well met, cousin,' Peverel taunted him. 'I had
not thought that you lent yourself to such frivolous
occasions as these.'

To Meg's fascination, Simon showed his cousin
his splendid teeth at once. 'Indeed? Then as usual,
sir, you are wrong!' He trod heavily on the word
'sir' to demonstrate his dislike at being addressed as
cousin, before he acknowledged Jasper and Zealand,
and after he had done his polite duties to Meg
and Charlotte.

Charlotte, indeed, not for the first time, thought
what a splendid specimen of manhood he was, putting even her beloved Jasper into the shade, and
making Peverel look effete.

Meg was busy thinking the same thing, as Simon
came out with, 'I had a mind to take the air this

afternoon. The House is sitting, but as it is not treating with any of my interests today, and as I am summoned to a meeting of the Zoological Society this evening, I have taken the opportunity of a little exercise. I shall grow fat if I do nothing but sit on the Commons' benches every afternoon.'

'If you were a member of the opposite sex, Sir Simon, you would be instantly accused of fishing for a compliment, but since you are not a female then I must assume that you are doing no such thing. I will simply assure you that you appear to be in no danger of rivalling Daniel Lambert.'

This reference to the man who was reputed to be the largest and fattest England had ever bred amused all Meg's hearers and even brought an unwilling smile to Simon's lips.

'Rightly rebuked,' he said.

'*Touché*, cousin,' came from Peverel, delighted to see the 'haughty baronet', as he privately thought of him, being put down for once.

'You are severe today, Meg,' Jasper put in, smiling affectionately at her, robbing his words of any possible sting. The gratitude that he felt for having saved him from ruin was so great that he knew that he could never thank her enough. He had said so on the day he had handed her draft to Strauss in his pokey office in the City.

But she had shaken her head and said simply, 'Don't try, Jas. Words mean nothing. Show me your gratitude by managing Monks Lovell for me and keeping out of trouble.

Well, he would try to do that, and his visit to the Park was in the nature of a farewell to his old life.

He would go to Berkshire, find out what being Meg's agent would mean and, after a suitable interval, he would return to ask Charlotte for her hand.

In the meantime, he was busy watching Simon, Peverel and, of all people, Zealand, dance around Meg. He had never thought of Phoebe's husband as a loose fish, and rumour had not touched him, as it had touched many others.

Meg, thinking the same thing, was equally surprised, particularly when, in a diversion created by a group of Jasper's fellow officers arriving, she was temporarily left to her own devices and Zealand leaned forward and muttered to her in an urgent voice, 'May I have your permission to call on you tomorrow, Madame? There is a matter of some import which I must discuss with you privately.'

Now what in the world can Zealand possibly have to say to me? was her immediate and private response after she had agreed to his request, but she was allowed no time to puzzle over the matter. Simon, who had overheard Zealand's question and her reply, immediately jumped to all the wrong conclusions.

So! Madame was up to her tricks again, was she?—and with her own sister's husband this time. Had she lost all sense of shame during her stay in Paris?

Meg looked up to see him glaring at her. Her heart sank—something which she had believed was a physical impossibility until she had met Simon again.

'Pray, Sir Simon,' she enquired sweetly, 'what wrong am I supposed to have committed now? For, by your expression, you plainly believe that I have done or said *something*.' Not even the presence of Charlotte sitting quietly beside her could prevent her from challenging him.

Nor did it prevent him from replying fiercely, 'You know perfectly well, Madame, what your offence is. No need for me to answer you in detail.'

'But if I have a desire to know, sir? What then?'

Simon opened his mouth to speak, to say something unforgivable, for he seemed to lose all sense of what was proper whenever he encountered Madame la Comtesse. He was stopped by the sudden knowledge that Peverel was now listening to them, and that Charlotte Hollis was staring at them both as they broke all the rules of polite conduct in public.

This would never do. He must speak to her privately, he must. Rage and desire, mixed in equal parts, swept over him. Meg had never looked more charming than when she had been having her half-private *tête-à-tête* with that. . .that. . . Adequate words to describe Zealand failed him.

He became aware that Peverel was also staring at him. He turned away, only for Peverel to touch him on the arm and say, 'I must have a word with you in private, cousin, before you leave. Pray walk over with me towards the tree where Cass Devereux is holding court.'

For a moment Simon hesitated before he decided against a refusal. He was in danger of making a raree-show of himself. 'Yes,' he replied stiffly. 'What have you to say to me which is so urgent?'

'This. I am troubled in my mind where Meg de Mortaine is concerned.'

Oh, the bare-faced hypocrisy of the swine, who had not only blackmailed Meg over her affair with him, but had also blown on her reputation to himself, and doubtless also to others! Peverel was not to know that he had overheard him taking Meg's money from her, and something kept him from telling the scaly swine so.

'Indeed, Peverel, and why should that be? More to the point, what is it that you think you know?'

'This. That she has been blackmailed once before, and now the rumour is all about town that she has been tricked into paying off the huge debts of one of her lovers. As we are all old friends from our childhood days, I do not like to think of her being up the River Tick where her fortune is concerned, nor barred from good society because of whispers about her reputation.'

Simon was not to know that there was not a word of truth in what his cousin was telling him. There were no rumours, and the ones about Meg's supposed wicked past, which Peverel had started on their way, had died the death in the face of the purity of her appearance and her behaviour.

As for the money supposedly paid over to a paramour—only Peverel knew of that through his bribing of Lewis, Strauss's double-dealing clerk. He saw Simon's face change and wondered again at the power of jealousy that left his cousin at his mercy.

'And I am to believe this?' enquired Simon glacially, for once refusing to credit Peverel's lies.

'Alas, I have it on the very best authority.' Peverel was solemn—so solemn, so grave, that Simon admitted with a pang that what he was saying might

be the truth. He looked away to where Meg was
now entertaining the Iron Duke himself, who had
driven over from one of society's known successes,
Cass Devereux, to one of the new ones.

Wellington had always had an eye for a pretty
woman, and there was no doubt that that eye was
now on Meg. The very sight of yet another besotted
roué pursuing her—even if he were the great Duke
himself—was enough to set him grinding his teeth
all over again.

Simon made a swift resolution. He would call on
Meg, this very day, before Zealand could visit her,
and try to help her out of the pit into which she had
fallen. Unwittingly Peverel had overdone things for,
whilst inciting Simon against Meg, he had also
spurred him on towards a confrontation with her in
which anything might happen.

Chapter Eight

'**Y**ou are sure that you do not wish me to remain with you this evening, Meg? If you are not feeling up to snuff, then I really should stay with you and give Lady Cowper's ball a miss.'

Charlotte and Meg were in the small drawing-room on the ground floor of Templestowe House. It was an exquisite miniature of all the other large rooms there. The portrait of an earlier Templestowe Countess hung above the fireplace.

Even the chairs and the sofa were more comfortable, more suited to the human body than those elsewhere, including one monster sofa, deep and wide. It was drawn up before a hearth that was filled with flowers and not with fire, since it was summer.

'Now that really would be beyond the call of duty, Charlotte. I know that Jasper wishes to escort you to one last London jaunt before he journeys to Monks Lovell, and I would be distressed to think that my slight malaise had deprived you of that. And since the Vancourts are calling at seven to take us there, my sister may act as your chaperon, and allow you to enjoy yourself without having to consider me.'

Charlotte could not prevent her pleasure at not losing the delight of one last evening with Jasper from showing on her face.

'But my duty—' she began.

Meg refused to let her finish her sentence. 'Oh, run along, my dear, at once, or you will not be ready when their carriage arrives. It would not do to keep Vancourt waiting—you know how uncertain his temper is these days.'

Charlotte needed no more pressing on the matter, and her and Jasper's pleasure in one another as they left for the ball was Meg's reward—if any were needed—for dispensing with Charlotte's company for the night.

Not that it was a sacrifice for her on this particular evening. She felt tired to the bone. Jousting with Simon gave her a perverse pleasure when she was engaged in it, but once away from him an enormous sadness overtook her at the realisation of the great gulf of misunderstanding which had opened between them. Explanation and reconciliation seemed alike impossible.

Neither her temper nor her mood had been improved by reading her mother's latest letter. Some busybody had apparently passed on some unpleasant gossip about her character and reputation, and the litany of complaint and reproach which always filled her mother's letters to her was worse than usual in her latest missive. Missile might have been a better description of it!

One might have thought, Meg mused sadly, that my having made such a splendid marriage, so splendid that I have been able to assist both her and father in their financial difficulties, would have changed her carping attitude towards me. But that was apparently fixed at my birth when I became merely another daughter instead of another son. All my title and wealth have done is to change the nature of mother's complaints, not silence them altogether.

She was minded to throw the letter in the fire, except that at the end of it her father had written a few kind words—all that he could manage now that his hands were crippled with a painful rheumatism.

Her sad and solitary reverie was broken by the butler who asked her if she was prepared to receive a visitor—Simon Darrow, no less.

For a moment, Meg contemplated the notion of snubbing Simon by sending him a message that she was receiving no one at this late hour. Something stopped her, and later she was to ask herself whether her subsequent life would have been better or worse if she had done so.

Instead, she nodded her head and remarked as indifferently as she could, 'Send him in and, James, do not allow anyone to interrupt us until I ring for you.'

She wondered afterwards what had impelled her to order any such thing. Perhaps she had thought that she and Simon might soon be at odds again, and did not want any servants as possible spectators of their differences which might mean gossip about them later. In any case, James seemed to find nothing odd about her instructions, and showed Simon in as impassively as ever.

Simon was obviously on his way to the Cowpers'

ball, by the splendour of his clothing. Meg rebuked herself for feeling overwhelmed at the sight of him. After all, he was scarcely the most handsome man in the world, and well dressed though he was, there were others in society far more dandified than he.

But no one else had such a superb and athletic physique, similar to the statues of the ancient Greeks which filled the houses of the cousinry. It was that which gave his clothes distinction, and not the other way around.

It was also that, perhaps, which made her feel so weak whenever she saw him, even before they began their verbal sparring. No other man, not even André when she had first met him, had succeeded in creating such a strange and immediate response in her.

But why had he come? Meg was soon to find out.

'I wished to speak to you,' he began after the politenesses were over. 'I had hoped to see you at Lady Cowper's, but when I arrived there, Mrs Hollis informed me that you were feeling a little under the weather and had decided not to attend. It is good of you to receive me, if you are not feeling A1 at Lloyds.'

A compliment! He had paid her a compliment. Wonders would never cease. Were there any more to come? Alas, apparently not, for he went on to add, looking earnestly at her, 'I hope you will forgive me for what I have to say to you, but please accept that I am only trying to play the part of a true friend and adviser to you.'

He paused, thinking perhaps that this might sound a trifle presumptuous, and attempted to placate her a little by adding, 'I have, after all, known you since you were a child, so pray overlook my apparent impertinence.'

Goodness, whatever could be coming? Meg answered him as cryptically as he had been addressing her, 'Until I hear what is is you have to say, Sir Simon, I am not in a position to determine whether it is impertinent or not.'

Simon had hoped that her answer might help him in what he now understood to be a difficult and tricky task. He tugged nervously at his perfectly tied cravat, of a kind known as a waterfall. Unfortunately, his tug was stronger than he had intended; it turned the waterfall into a positive torrent, which cascaded in a cloud of billowing white linen down his shirtfront and his black and white striped waistcoat.

Meg tried to repress a giggle, turned it into a cross between a blurred 'ahem' and a snort, but to no good purpose, since Simon had immediately realised that both his senatorial gravity and his self-possession had been destroyed. Nevertheless, he decided to plough on, but unfortunately it also became apparent that his tact had deserted him, too. Being alone with Meg was continuing to bring out the worst in him

'Is it,' he asked passionately, 'impossible these days for you not to conduct yourself in a manner which will draw censure upon you?'

Now what, in God's name, had made him say *that*? Whatever had provoked him into coming out with such a mealy-mouthed and impertinent question? He was not her husband, her father, nor her brother. It was really no business of his what the

Comtesse de Mortaine, once little Meg Ashe, did.

Apparently she thought so, too. Her voice was as stern as steel when she spoke. 'And who, Sir Simon Darrow, gave you leave to be the arbiter of my conduct?'

'Forgive me,' he began, which was acceptable, but what followed was not, 'but it hurts me to hear that you are busy dragging your good name through the dust.' Oh, hell and all the devils in it, what had his unlucky tongue come out with now?

Meg sprang to her feet and pointed to the door. 'Go,' she said, 'please go. You once asked me to marry you, but that gives you no right to speak to me after such a fashion. I do not know who has been spreading lies about me, but it is hurtful and demeaning to learn that you have hanged, drawn and quartered me without asking yourself whether any of the gossip about me is true before you came here to accuse me.'

How to rescue himself? He had only meant to help her, but his clumsy tongue had let him down again for the simple reason that he cared so much for her. Like all good men he had difficulty in articulating such delicate and involved sentiments.

Perhaps if he asked her one question, and one alone, she would answer him in such a way that he would be reassured that she was unchanged; that behind the mask of continental sophistication she was little Meg Ashe still. And then he might sleep again.

He said, attempting to make his tone more humble and placatory, but signally failing, 'I shall say nothing further, if you can assure me that the rumour, that you have paid out large sums of money to silence persons who have a hold on you by reason of your. . .conduct, is untrue. The *on dit* is that your latest transaction took place as recently as this week.'

Meg, now at the double doors, glared at him. 'I shall tell you nothing, for it is no business of yours. Now leave at once. I will ring for James to show you out—but if you refuse to leave, a pair of sturdy footmen might persuade you to change your mind.'

Whirling through her mind was the question: who has told him about the draft with which I paid off Jasper's debts? To clear myself in his eyes, I could tell him the truth: that the money was not for a lover, but for my brother. Alas, I am bound by my honour to say nothing, for I agreed with Jasper that only he, I and the moneylender should know the truth of the matter.

Simon stood stock-still. So, Madame had denied nothing, and, what was almost worse, she had threatened to have her footmen throw him from the door! She stood proudly before him in her pure white gown, with its high puritan collar, and its prim long sleeves. Her beautiful chestnut hair was severely dressed, giving her the air of an affronted vestal virgin.

How dare she? How dare she look so chaste, yet so desirable? And oh, by God, he desired her so much that it hurt. As on the night of the Leominsters' ball, one wicked thought pounded at the door of his honour, demanding that what others had enjoyed, he, who for his punishment loved her, might also share and enjoy.

Something in his expression and the set of his mouth frightened Meg as he strode towards her, pulling off his damned cravat as he did so, as though it were strangling him.

'No,' he said hoarsely, 'you shall not dismiss me. And I don't care if you have bedded every man in London and Paris, if you will only—' Before he had finished the sentence, he pressed her against the door and stole from her the kiss he now so desperately wanted.

Held prisoner, not by his arms but by the strong body which she had earlier admired, his mouth on hers—a treacherous mouth which opened itself to him, for she could resist him only so long as he did not touch her—Meg felt herself drowning in sensation.

A moment ago she had wanted to shriek at him, 'Oh, you wrong me, you cannot conceive how much you wrong me. And that being so, I never want to see you again.' But now, what did she wish to do *now*, now that his arms were around her—and her arms were so willingly stealing around him?

He lifted his mouth and his body from her, only to give her his mouth again, once they were apart. This time his touch was not violent, but tender, so that, had she wished to, Meg could have thrown him off. He cupped her face, oh so gently, in his two big hands, and when the kiss ended, murmured, 'So sweet, oh, so sweet.'

It was Meg, impatient for more of him, who put her arms around his neck and pulled his face down to hers, to resume where he had left off.

This time, when he pulled away, it was to lift her

in his arms and carry her over to the big sofa, whilst Meg, witless with desire, caring nothing at this moment for what he thought of her, but wanting him, and only him, made no effort to stop him.

Once there he took her on his knee and began to stroke and pet her, kissing her so gently, but so thoroughly, that Meg thought she would die of the delight of it. She felt like a flower being delicately ravaged by a bee, except that it was no bee who began to push her backwards and pull down the prim collar of her dress.

She had made no attempt to stop him, indeed, as Meg later ruefully conceded, at every turn she had encouraged him, rather than thrust him off. His cravat had gone long ago, his shirt followed it, and Meg knew that it would not be long before they were naked together in front of the summer flowers: as naked as father Adam and mother Eve.

But long before they reached that point, shortly before kissing became more passionate than tender, he had reared back a little, and said, his voice hoarse with emotion, 'Meg, I have no wish to force you. Much though it would pain me, I will stop now if you ask me to.'

Stop! Now? Whatever did he take her for? Regardless of the consequences, and whether her behaviour would convince him that she was the lightskirt she had been branded, and which he obviously took her for, she would offer the man she loved everything that was hers to offer. She knew that he would only take what she would freely give—and knowing this, she chose to give, even if it proved to be the only time that she would ever hold him in her arms.

'No,' she whispered, 'no, Simon, don't stop.' Even the prospect of a possible child could not deter her, for it would be his, and God knew, that whatever else André had done for and to her, he had left her rich enough to ensure that neither she nor the child would suffer. It would have a name, even if it were not hers or Simon's, and a place in society.

He was strangely gentle with her, as though to prove to himself, as well as her, that he was not taking anything from her, only accepting, and para-doxically that was more exciting to them both than if he had been roughly passionate.

His body respected her more than his mind did, Meg thought afterwards. And what a strange thing that was, when with most men it was the other way round. It was almost as though he were proving to her that, whatever she was, he would treat her as though she were the most precious thing he knew.

With the result that together they achieved a har-mony given to few, and if Simon found surcease from the pain and jealousy which had consumed him, Meg found peace from the misery that the knowledge that he was at odds with her had created.

No one came to disturb them, and afterwards, all passion spent, they lay in one another's arms in a tranquillity so perfect that it could not last. Nor did it. Once he was himself again, Simon was wracked, not by jealousy, but by regret, and by a remorse so strong that it drove every other thought away. Even his recent passion could not stand before it.

The clock striking eleven awoke him from a light

sleep and recalled him back to the world of consequence and consequences again. He knew one consequence at once. The fact that he and Meg had been closeted alone for several long hours would be the talk of the servants' hall.

As, indeed, it already was. One of the footmen, with whom Meg had threatened Simon, said knowingly to James as he began to put out the lamps in the servants' hall—the kitchen maids had long ago picked up their candles to light them to bed—'Be Sir Simon *still* alone with Madame? Whatever can they be at?' His sly expression betrayed perfectly well what he thought they were at.

James, the long candle snuffer in his hand, said equably, 'Nothing to do with you, George. Their business, not yours.'

'Oh, aye? Reading together, be they? Mighty int'resting book, no doubt.'

James brought the candle snuffer down on George's head. 'Nothing to do with you, I said. Off to bed with you.'

George, rubbing his head, was irrepressible. 'And who's to show him to the door, then—if he chooses not to stay the night, that is?'

'My business, not yours. You heard what I said. Do as you're bid, if you value your position here. You'll not easily get one as good without a reference.'

All the same, as he watched George go, chuckling, to his room in the attic, he could not resist a private grin at the thought that the gentry were at their games again. But a good servant did better in the end by being discreet than by having a gabbing tongue.

George, on the other hand, annoyed by being reprimanded, remembered something which one of his cronies from another establishment had told him— that Peverel Darrow was paying good money to anyone who would sell him information about the saucy French Countess and his cousin, Sir Simon. No need to have your pockets to let if someone was willing to fill them in payment for tonight's little titbit.

In the drawing-room, matters were little more harmonious. Simon, a sleeping Meg in his arms, discovered that he had gone beyond jealousy and desire fulfilled merely to achieve guilt! He had not meant to compromise her, only to lead her by gentle means into a better way of life.

And what had been the consequence of that? He had behaved with her exactly as all those who had gone before him had done. He was no better than they were: he was worse. For he knew how he ought to behave and they—the 'they' including his cousin Peverel—did not.

As an honourable man, there was only one thing left for him to do and, when she awoke, he would do it. This resolution pleased him so much that he had difficulty in not allowing that pleasure to lull him to sleep again, but common sense said no.

Whatever would Jasper and Charlotte Hollis think, if they were to return and find them here— like this? He looked down at his naked body, and at the clothes strewn around the floor, mute evidence of the passion of the pair who had recently worn them.

Meg stirred a little in his arms. He lifted them both into a sitting position and the movement, as he had intended, woke her up.

'Oh,' she said, her opening eyes starry. 'I see that I didn't dream this!'

Such a frivolous comment was hardly in tune with Simon's newly made determination that the pair of them would behave with stern rectitude and propriety, after having been so abandoned.

'My dear,' he said urgently, 'we must talk.'

'What, now? At this hour? What about?' and she cuddled closer to his warm body. The sensation which this produced in him nearly destroyed all Simon's good resolutions, but he clung determinedly on to what he saw as his honour and his duty.

So he stared sternly at her. Nothing but plain speaking would do. And with that resolution he sealed his immediate fate. He had quite forgotten how useless and unprofitable his plain speaking before their. . .recent encounter. . .had been.

'There is nothing for it,' he announced ungallantly. 'I have ruined you, and therefore we must marry as soon as I can obtain a special licence.'

Meg's high spirits, which had given her the sensation of floating among the clouds rather like the painted gods and goddesses on the ceiling in Templestowe House's great dining room, plummeted to earth again.

Nothing had changed. If Simon had lived among the clouds for a brief space, which she now begged leave to doubt, the aftermath of their love-making had restored him to the position of the cruel and stern arbiter of her fate. All that had changed was that he now wished to marry her; presumably in order to be able to reproach her more easily. She sat up, and became suddenly aware of her nakedness, which had the effect of making her feel more vulnerable than ever.

Simon said nothing further: doubtless waiting for an answer to his scurvily made offer. He deserved nothing for it, and she would give him nothing.

'What for?' she asked, her tone and posture defiant.

Simon stared at her even harder. He had the face of a hanging judge, not of a man who had pleasured, and been pleasured, twice, both times right royally. 'What for?' he echoed. 'And what, pray, does that mean?'

The dignity with which he posed this question was somewhat marred by his nudity. If ever Meg had doubted that clothing gave men and women consequence, formality, and gravity, she now knew that her doubts were idle.

Unclothed, Simon showed a majestic body, powerful, well proportioned, muscular; in short, exactly what she had expected. But dignity and gravitas, the traits of a Member from the British Parliament, were alike missing. He looked ready to perform in one of the Greek Olympiads rather than lay down the law in the grave surroundings of Westminster.

Once more she gave him the answer he deserved. 'It means what I said. Why should you offer me marriage? And why should I accept such an offer, made only to confer respectability on us, rather than as a consequence of the passion which we have just enjoyed? A passion that I thought was mutual, but which was evidently not, seeing that you appear to regret it—whilst I do not.

'You are offering me marriage as a duty, not because what we recently shared meant so much that marriage was the inevitable consequence of love expressed.' She paused and added, 'I will be your mistress, but I will not marry you on such terms.'

Meg had not meant to say this, but temper moved her so strongly that wisdom and caution had deserted her. Besides, if what Simon was offering her was the product of wisdom and caution, she did not want it.

'My good woman,' he began solemnly, obviously aghast at her suggestion that she should be his whore rather than his wife.

Meg leapt up, picked her discarded clothing from the floor and began to dress herself with more speed than precision.

'No,' she flung at him. 'Say no more. You do not consider me to be a good woman. Do not spoil for me the delight I felt during our love-making by passing judgment on me, yourself and the whole business which lies between men and women.'

This passionate speech was somewhat marred by the difficulty which she was experiencing in man-oeuvring herself into her elaborate clothing without the assistance of her maid. Simon was now off the sofa and was also attempting to dress himself, a task made difficult by his fashionably skintight clothing. Even with his valet's assistance, this was usually a lengthy task.

Meg, almost decent again, watched him cover what had so recently delighted her, and exclaimed with exasperation as he fumbled with buttons and fastenings. The aftermath of passion should never be ludicrous—but cold reality always took over once the business of pleasure was completed.

'Goodness,' she exclaimed. 'I never thought that men went through such a tohu-bohu in becoming clothed. Here, permit me to help you,' and before he could stop her, she was assisting him, as deftly as his missing valet, into tight breeches, by fastening buttons, and with tying his cravat, so that very shortly he was nearly as *à point* as usual, and more respectable than she was.

Once clothed, formality in them both did not seem nearly so comical to Meg. She was more prepared to listen to him, but no more prepared to accept him. If only he had once said, I love you. But, then, she had not said it to him. Three words, and that was all they were, words. She had given him her love with her body, and in reply he talked of marriage as a duty he was to perform to prevent her from being a fallen woman.

This thought excited her to more excesses. As he opened his mouth, doubtless to propose marriage again, she announced gaily, 'Do you know, Simon, I rather fancy I like being a fallen woman. No ties, no responsibilities. I'm surprised that you don't enjoy being a fallen man—but then, men don't fall, do they? On the contrary, they do the pushing. Comfort yourself with the thought that I don't feel exploited or depraved, but fulfilled.'

'Oh, Meg, Meg,' he cried hoarsely, showing

emotion for the first time since their mutual trans-
ports. 'Supposing there is a child?'

'Somewhat late to think about that, isn't it?' she
carolled. 'And it's my worry, not yours. You really
must go, Simon. Charlotte and Jasper won't want to
be late home tonight. He is off to Monks Lovell
tomorrow afternoon. Should you require me again,
you have only to write me a little note, or call in
person. But no more talk of marriage, please. The
notion does not attract, either with you—or with
anyone else.'

She had driven him mad, and now *she* was mad,
was Simon's mournful conclusion. He opened his
mouth to offer for her again, but she jumped back,
saying wildly, 'No more, tonight, please. Just go,
Simon. And if you must marry, pick a hymn-singing
Methodist, and then you may be proper together.'

Somehow he managed to leave Templestowe
House, his dignity in shreds, wondering how he had
come to make such an infernal cake of himself. He
fell into his lonely and comfortless bed, having
drunk so much port—in order to find oblivion—
that he could hardly walk to it.

But oblivion refused to oblige him. His buzzing
head once on the pillow, all that he could think of
was Meg in his arms on the sofa, the joy they had
shared, and his own folly in antagonising her all
over again.

He would never understand women, never. Why
should she be so insulted when all that he had wished
to do was make an honest woman of her?

As for Meg, she reached her room just before
Jasper and Charlotte returned, to sit on her bed, eyes

wide and smarting with unshed tears, too distressed to ring for her maid, to sleep, or even to cry. Was she a fool not to have accepted him on his terms?

And then she remembered that she had accepted André on his terms, and look what *that* had led to.

Chapter Nine

Meg was standing by the window, staring out at the magnificent formal gardens at the back of Templestowe House when her brother-in-law, Zealand, was announced the next morning. She was alone and, theoretically speaking, she should have rung for Charlotte to be present when she received him.

But she was suddenly tired of formality and conventions. Charlotte was enjoying a late breakfast in her room, having stayed at Lady Cowper's ball to the very end. Besides, she had the impression from Zealand's manner, when he had spoken to her the day before, that he might prefer to consult with her alone.

Her guess was correct. His manner to her when he came in was perfectly proper, but she thought that she detected relief in him when he looked around and noted that her companion was absent.

Once they were seated, he began without preamble, using her pet name to establish a family intimacy since it proved that he had called to discuss a family matter.

'Oh, Meg, Phoebe and I are greatly in need of your help. You are aware, I am sure, that when your father and mother come to town for the Season, they have always stayed with us. It has been their custom since Phoebe and I were married.'

Puzzled, Meg said cautiously, 'Yes, Fred, I was aware of that.'

'Well. . .' he swallowed and looked uncomfortable '. . .it's like this, my dear. You know that Phoebe and I have never been fortunate enough to have children. It is a matter of great grief to us. We both dearly want them, and not simply because I need an heir, but because we both—particularly Phoebe—love children.'

He stopped, and Meg nodded agreement—to what, she wasn't quite sure—but it seemed to encourage Fred to continue. Looking away from her, he began again.

'The trouble is. . .it's your mama. These last few Seasons, every time she comes she talks non-stop about all her grandchildren, and constantly seems to hint that it's somehow Phoebe's fault that we haven't given her any. Phoebe spends a large part of her visit crying in private. Two days ago, when your father's letter arrived with the dates of their proposed visit this year, she had a violent fit of the hysterics, took to her room and hasn't come out since. Most unlike her, as I am sure that you will agree.'

Meg nodded again. Yes, most unlike. Phoebe had been the equable, the placid sister, always cheerful and uncomplaining.

'Oh, Meg,' he said despairingly. 'What am I to
do? I know it's unfashionable, I know it's not quite
the thing, but I dearly love Phoebe, and it hurts me
to see her so distressed. I hardly like to write and
tell them not to come. Your mama would be sure
to take that amiss. Part of the problem is that our
place in Bruton Street isn't very large and there's no
easy way Phoebe can hide from your mama without
causing offence.'

Meg knew immediately how much Fred Zealand
was troubled, for only if he were in dire distress
would he have said such a personal thing to her.
But she knew her mother. Once she had an idea in
her head, she was like a dog worrying a bone which
it refused to give up. Worse, she always required a
whipping boy to vent her life's disappointments on,
and Meg had once been that boy. Now it seemed
that Phoebe was her mother's target.

A way out for Fred and Phoebe occurred to her.
It was not a happy one. It meant a considerable
sacrifice on her part, but so be it.

'I have a notion which might save Phoebe, Fred.
Suppose I were to write and ask my parents to stay
with me this summer? Templestowe House is large
enough for an army, and as I am a widow, Mama
cannot reproach me for not providing her with a
grandchild.'

'Would you, Meg? Would you really?' Even Fred
knew that Meg had never managed to please
her mama and that she would simply be a revived
target for her bad temper. He did not say, 'You are
making a great sacrifice', for it had been difficult
enough to confess the truth about Mrs Ashe and her

treatment of Phoebe without saying more.

And so it was settled.

And now I shall have Mother reproaching me as well as Simon, thought Meg with wry amusement. I shall surely achieve heavenly salvation, having endured so much on earth!

There was more for her to endure later that day. Charlotte was with her when Will Osborne was announced; Meg knew immediately why he had come, without Peverel in tow. He intended to propose to her. He had been working himself up to do so for the last few weeks.

Nevertheless, she was bound to see him. Nothing had happened between them which could justify her snubbing him. Perhaps, in the end, it would be better for both of them if he proposed to her sooner rather than later—at least it would be out of the way.

The trouble was that, as soon as he had asked to see her alone, and she had sent an agog Charlotte out of the room, she knew that her refusal of his proposal would be bound to hurt him. All his life everything he had wanted had fallen either into his lap, or his open mouth.

Without being unpleasantly spoiled, he yet considered that everything which Will Osborne wanted, he ought to get. Even the cavalier treatment that he received from Peverel could not daunt him, since he scarcely recognised it.

So here he was, not exactly on one knee, but charmingly bent before her, offering her himself, his future title, his vast fortune and approximately one-tenth of the entire acres of England, Wales and

Scotland. Surely she could not refuse *that*?

But she could.

And did. In the gentlest possible manner.

Will pulled himself slowly erect. It was plain that he was finding it difficult to believe what he had just heard.

'You have done me a great honour, sir,' Meg had said, 'by proposing to me. Alas, it is not an offer which I can accept, however. While I both like and esteem you, I do not love you, and I think that you deserve to receive the last sentiment from your future wife, as well as the first two.'

'Oh,' he said, bravely trying to conceal his chagrin by smiling kindly at her, 'I understand that many ladies' modesty is such that they find it difficult to accept a proposal from a gentleman at its first offering. I had flattered myself that matters between us were such that you would feel able to accept me immediately. I am, however, prepared to wait.'

Meg, appalled at the prospect of watching Will wind himself up all over again, said, 'I must emphasise that my "no" to you is unlikely to turn into a "yes", however long you wait. It is not my custom to say what I do not mean, particularly when to do so might raise false hopes. I would be happy to remain your friend, even if I do not intend to be your wife.'

It was plain that he could scarce take in what he was hearing. Somewhat bewildered, he came out with, 'You do understand that, if you marry me, you will be Lady Stanyon when my cousin goes to his last rest—surely a prospect which any woman might find difficult to refuse.'

Meg could hardly retort that she was already the Comtesse de Mortaine, owned a large part of France, and had not found that either fact had brought her much in the way of happiness. She doubted whether marrying a man she did not love in order to acquire yet another title would bring her any more.

Instead, she said gently, 'If I married you, sir, it would not be for your title, but because I loved you enough to wish to be your wife. Since I do not, however, I have no desire to be a party to a loveless marriage, for I have observed that such arrangements frequently end in misery.'

'But if you did marry me, I am sure that you would come to love me in the end,' he said eagerly. 'Reconsider your answer, I beg of you.'

'You must,' Meg returned, 'accept that I am unwilling to take that risk. Moreover, I do not yet feel prepared to venture into marriage again at all— even with someone whom I might love.'

She was thinking of Simon when she said this, and of how and why she had refused him. The burned child fears the fire. It was the notion of marriage itself which Meg found fearful, not the act of love. But she could hardly tell Will that, when he was prepared to prattle about female modesty to a woman who had been married to André, Comte de Mortaine.

Meg could see by his face, his whole posture, that he was attributing her refusal of him to female whims, the unaccountably flighty behaviour of her sex, which must be the only reason why she would not accept him: the most desirable catch of the Season.

She sighed. 'Come,' she said. 'Bite the bullet— if you will allow me to be so brusque—and accept that I am unlikely to change my mind. There are other young women, younger than I am, who would be only too happy to become Lady Stanyon.'

'But I don't want those other young women, I want you,' he told her mournfully. 'And I do believe that, if you think things over, you are likely to change your mind. So I will leave you to reconsider my offer, so that you may the sooner decide to do so.' Nothing which she could say would change *his* mind, and so she sadly told Charlotte when he had gone in a cloud of ill-conceived optimism. Fortune's favourite could not believe that he was not every woman's favourite, and that where he pitched his desires, there would not be a woman panting for him.

'Refused you, did she?' said Peverel Darrow when will told him his sad news. 'I could have told you that she would, if you had cared to consult me beforehand, and saved you the trouble of offering for her. She needs a seasoned man, not a boy, does Meg de Mortaine!'

For once Will neither ignored nor swallowed this insult. 'I don't care for your manner to me these days, Darrow. I believe that you are trying to deter me because you are after the lady yourself. I suppose that you consider yourself a seasoned man.'

Peverel stifled his inward amusement at Will's sudden discovery of what everyone in their circle had known for weeks—that he was after Meg de Mortaine, too. It would not do, though, to try Will's patience overmuch. To be one of his friends gave

Peverel access to social circles which he would have otherwise found it hard to enter, and the money he gained from cheating Will at cards was a useful bonus for a man always strapped for cash. He made sure never to fleece a victim so much as to rouse his suspicions.

'A cat may look at a queen,' he remarked carelessly. 'And the lady is there for the taking.'

'She told me that she had no mind to marry,' retorted Will, who was at last beginning to grow up and therefore be ready to throw off the patronage of such as Peverel. 'So there is no point in you spending your time making a leg at her, either!'

'True,' agreed Peverel, but despite that he was relieved to discover that he had seen off one rival for Meg in Will. Now, if he could only be sure that his cousin Simon was also *persona non grata* with Meg, his day would be made. He took no note of Meg saying that she had no wish to marry, for in his experience women frequently made such a claim, but rarely lived up to it.

He would be seeing Meg in a couple of days' time at a reception given by the French Ambassador. Her late husband had once been part of France's *Corps Diplomatique* shortly after the restoration, in 1815, of King Louis XVIII to the throne that his brother had lost nearly twenty-five years before. He had resigned immediately before he had married Meg, but she was still invited to all the Embassy thrashes.

It was said that the famous, or infamous, Monsieur de Talleyrand—according to the way you looked at him—was to be present. He was paying a short visit to London, and rumour had it that he was being considered as the next French Ambassador to the Court of St James.

But the rumour that Peverel was interested in was the one he had passed on to Simon, which said that Talleyrand had been Meg de Mortaine's lover, even though he had then been in his early seventies. He would dearly like to see his cousin Simon's face when the pair of them came face to face again, as they surely would. . .

It would be exactly the right time for him to propose to Meg himself; it would prove that he cared nothing for society's *on dits*, but only for her.

What Peverel could not know was that Meg was not entirely sure that she wished to meet Monsieur de Talleyrand again. Oh, it was not that she no longer liked him, or no longer wished to converse with a man of such intellect, wit and charm, to say nothing of his immense learning. No, it was the knowledge of the unpleasant gossip, which had painted his kind friendship in such ugly colours.

She had met Talleyrand at a time when her life was at a low ebb: when her marriage, which had once seemed to open before her a long road of love, offered instead only a cul-de-sac with a bleak wall at its end.

Astonishingly, since there was some fifty years between them, they had struck up a friendship based on mutual interests. Behind the mask of age, behind his monkey face which many had mocked, behind the devious mind which had enabled him to keep his head and his life through all France's turbulent changes of government since 1789, Meg had seen something of the bright and charming young man that he had once been before France's *ancien régime* had ended.

By his manner to her, she could only imagine that he saw her as the grown-up daughter whom he had never fathered. It was this last memory which persuaded her to meet him again. They had done nothing wrong, and she would not forgo the pleasure of his company.

She knew, as she walked up the grand staircase at the French Embassy with Charlotte Hollis and Fred and Phoebe Zealand by her side, that curious eyes and salacious whispers followed her slow progress.

She had dressed herself with particular care in a gown of the deepest topaz with the new lower waist. The neck of it was high, consisting of a straight slash from shoulder to shoulder, revealing little of the shapely bosom beneath it. Its sleeves were long, reaching to the wrist and ending in a small cream ruffle. The cream motif was repeated in the two flounces on her skirt.

Her jewellery was magnificently simple and consisted of a parure of topazes set about with pearls which André had given her as a wedding present. Her fan was a tiny one, as was her tiara.

Altogether she considered that her turn-out had given the gossips something to get their teeth into— something worth staring at, as well as her encounter with her supposed lover. She knew very well that they would watch her when she was presented to

Talleyrand to try to discover what their true relationship was.

They learned nothing. Simon, who was watching her, not jealously—for jealousy, oddly enough, seemed to have flown our of the window since their passionate encounter—but with the deepest interest, saw nothing but the cool politeness of old friends meeting again. To his astonishment, when he had seen her enter with the Zealands, he had discovered that jealousy had been replaced by a deeply protective feeling for her.

Because he feared that he had hurt her, he wanted no one else to do so. If only she would consent to be his wife, he would make sure that the scandal-mongers would never again have cause to look sideways at her.

Meg saw that Talleyrand had grown older, and more dependent on his friend, almost certainly his secret wife, Dorothea, the Duchess de Dino. For his part, Talleyrand could see at once that his good friend the Comtesse de Mortaine had not only grown more beautiful, but had gained more *savoir faire* than ever before.

'My dear Comtesse,' he said gravely to her in French, as she curtsied before him, 'you have grown up, and in the doing you have become an even more accomplished woman. If my companion—' and he looked at the Duchess de Dino '—will forgive me for saying so, were I fifty years younger, I would be storming your front door. Are all Englishmen bloodless, that you are not married yet?'

Meg smiled. 'Oh, Monseigneur—' for she could

never forget that he was a Prince '—I have no mind
to marry.'

'Now that, Madame, is a pity, for you were meant
to be the mother of prodigies. Besides, I do not
believe you. I think that you are particular, and that
only the right man will do for you. Meet him soon,
I beg of you.'

Given the formality of their circumstances, it was
her *congé*, and she moved on, after another curtsy,
pleased that the rapidity of their conversation meant
that few near them could have followed it. She wondered if Simon were present, and whether the sight
of her talking to her supposed elderly lover, had
fuelled his jealousy. She had not met him since she
had refused him, and was not sure whether she
wished to.

The person she did meet, almost immediately, was
Peverel. She always seemed to be encountering him
these days. He bowed to her companions, but it was
plain that Meg was his target.

'May I compliment you this evening, Madame?
Your turnout is superb. I wish you will do me the
honour of allowing me to take you into supper.'

As usual, without causing offence, it was difficult
to refuse him. He walked along with them, bowing
and nodding to their mutual aquaintances. Despite
the late war with France, everyone in society wished
to be seen at their Embassy.

Peverel was engaging in his greatest accomplish-
ment: light conversation. Behind it, his brain was
working furiously in order to use his recently learned
information to the best effect.

Earlier that day he had been standing in the mews

where his curricle and pair were kept, ruefully wondering how long it would be before the cost of maintaining them became so prohibitive that he would have to sell them again.

He had bought them after he had paid in Meg's bank draft, elated by the picture of himself driving into Hyde Park in a spanking carriage behind two prime specimens of horseflesh, at last the equal of those upon whom he preyed. But elation would not pay his mounting bills.

Even as he had been thinking this, he had become aware that a hovering presence was now directly approaching him. A respectable-looking young fellow of the servant class, his hat in his hand, bowed servilely at him, saying, 'Master, I have been told that you pay good money for information about my mistress, Madame de Mortaine. I have a little titbit which you might like to hear of,' and he held out his hand.

'Information first, money afterwards,' replied Peverel curtly. 'I like to know what I'm buying.'

'Oh, indeed, master. It's this. Your cousin, Sir Simon Darrow, visited my mistress late in the evening two nights ago.' He licked his lips and paused.

'And?'

'And stayed in the drawing-room alone with her for three hours, so he did. Mrs Hollis was out with friends. And she gave orders when he arrived that on no account was they to be disturbed while he was with her. . .' He paused again.

Peverel pulled a guinea out of his breeches pocket and held it out to his informant. 'That's for you when you've finished your story.'

The man bowed again, 'And a right generous fellow you are to be sure, master. James, the butler, told us to say nothing, it worn't our business, but the old girl who cleaned the room said as how all the evidence was that they'd been having a bit of. . .hanky-panky. . .if you take my meaning. She'd served in other houses and knew the signs.'

Peverel stared at him before handing his money over. 'You're quite sure of this?' He could scarcely imagine his upright cousin and Meg engaging in illicit. . .hanky-panky on a drawing-room sofa. Nothing he had seen of the pair of them together had suggested that any such behaviour was likely. Quite the contrary.

And then something which he had read at University came back to him—that the philosopher Aristotle had said that hate and love were two passions which were closely intertwined.

'Oh, yes. Quite sure. Or I wouldn't have troubled you, master. I'm an honest man He bowed and moved away again, pocketing his reward.

Peverel said after him, whilst savouring his informant's quaint understanding of honesty, 'There'll be more for you, mind, if you have more to tell me.'

And now here was Meg de Mortaine, walking along beside him as though butter wouldn't melt in her supposedly virtuous mouth.

And here came cousin Simon, the damned hypocrite, whose two-faced dealings rivalled those of the characters in Moliere's old play *Tartuffe* which some rich widow, whom he had vainly pursued, had made him sit through. They, too, pretended to virtue whilst practising vice. Hanky-panky indeed! It was all enough to make an honest man of the world choke.

But knowing what he knew was a bonus. He smiled engagingly at Simon.

Simon was not best pleased to see Peverel. He bowed stiffly at him and his companions. He tried not to look too hard at Meg. He had spent the day consumed by pointless remorse after they. . .he could think of no polite word for what he and Meg had done. . .after they had consummated their passion was the flowery, literary phrase for it, he supposed. For he was sure that, one way or another, he had dished himself with her for ever.

He could not imagine what had happened to the Simon Darrow who had once seen women, whether mistresses or wives, as part of the background of his life, not to be taken seriously by a serious man.

But Meg, and that one short bout of pleasure with her, had changed all that. Oh, he wanted more than a passing affair—he wanted her in his bed and his life, no matter what she had got up to in their years apart.

Without her, a long vista of loneliness opened up before him. He could not now imagine asking some characterless girl to be his wife. He also understood why he had never wanted Caro Kenilworth to become Lady Darrow. He could not imagine that, in either case, he would wish to hurry home to be with them.

He had considered going round to Templestowe House and asking to see Meg, to speak to her, to try to change her mind. But fear that she might turn him away kept him from doing so. Loving Meg had made a coward of him.

For the first time, he felt a bitter regret for what he now grasped was the careless way in which he had proposed to her, not once, but twice. What a jackass he had been to throw his pearl away so lightly—and all because he had not understood that she was his pearl.

He felt ill, but did not look it. Was Meg in the same case? This evening she was glowing. Was she, like him, suffering behind a cheerful exterior?

He was, without knowing it, looking at her so ardently and so hopelessly, that even Freddie Zealand noticed his unlikely state, and said in his cheerfully inconsequential way, 'You are alone, I see, Darrow. We are going in to supper. Why not join us? Phoebe told me once that you and the Ashe girls were playmates when you were children.'

This was the last thing which Peverel wanted— Simon to be one of their party, but he smiled his agreement all the same. As did Meg. Seeing Simon again, after an absence of nearly three days, was doing strange things to her, as it was to him. Desire took no heed of time or place, it just *was*, whatever the circumstances in which it manifested itself.

'Not exactly,' Simon found himself saying. 'Phoebe and I, yes. But Madame de Mortaine was a mere baby when Phoebe, Jasper and I considered ourselves fully grown.'

'But Madame is fully grown now,' put in Peverel slyly, trying to discomfit him, for he at least understood why Simon and Meg were so constrained in one another's presence. 'So there is no objection to you being play. . .I mean friends, now, is there?'

This extremely oblique *double entendre* affected both Meg and Simon, even if it passed straight over the heads of Fred and Phoebe.

That Peverel was in some way twitting them both was plain. But surely he could know nothing of their. . .joint contretemps. . .could he? Oh, but he could. The servants always knew everything about their masters, and one or more of them might have talked.

Silence, they both decided, was the best thing. Meg offered Peverel and the company an enigmatic smile.

Simon said, 'I saw you introduced to the great man, Madame.' He had decided to be formal with her in public to quieten doubts about their possible free and easy. . .intercourse, in private.

'He favoured me with a smile and a nod of the head which I suppose passed for a bow, but he was much less formal with you.'

'And all in French, too,' commented Phoebe, a trifle enviously, as they settled themselves around one of the tables laid out with food and drink, 'and so fast that no one could understand a word of what they were saying. You used not to be so accomplished a linguist, Meg.'

'Oh, eight years in France does wonders for one's command of the language,' Meg replied with a smile. 'And what we were saying was innocuous enough. Except that, as usual, I was twitted about not marrying again!'

She tried not to look at Simon as she said this. Or at Peverel. The latter muttered, half under his breath, 'And is there no one who might tempt you to do so, Meg?'

This somewhat daring personal remark had several members of the company showing disapproval. Meg took it in her stride whilst accepting a vol-au-vent from a large salver offered her by a white-gloved footman. 'Oh,' she said, carelessly, 'marriage, and whomsoever one might marry, is too serious a topic for discussion at an Embassy party.'

'Quite so,' uttered Charlotte Hollis repressively, playing the stern companion for once and shooting a glance of dislike in Peverel's direction. 'Might one enquire, Lady Zealand, if your mama and papa are to stay with you again this Season?' Unknown to her, this topic was no more a welcome one than that of Meg's marriage or her possible suitors.

'Not this year,' replied Phoebe a trifle stiffly. 'I believe that Meg has invited them to stay at Templestowe House.'

Now here was a facer for Simon and Peverel, who had both hoped for a clear field with Meg. Peverel was the more dismayed, seeing that Mrs Ashe had always favoured Simon's suit in the past, and would surely do so in the future. On the other hand, he consoled himself with the thought that if Simon had privately hoped for future entertainment either in Meg's bed or her sofa, he was scarcely like to find it with the Ashes hovering in the background.

As for Simon, he glumly considered that Mrs Ashe's favouring of him, far from encouraging Meg to accept him, would most likely achieve the opposite. Of such contrary stuff is life made up!

The training in perfect manners to which all

members of the supper party had been subjected saw them behaving as though there were no undercurrents to mar the equally perfect surface of social life on which they were all skating. Only the fact that Simon was drinking rather more than he ought betrayed that anything was wrong.

The sight of Peverel making even Charlotte Hollis laugh by retailing some pointless anecdote did his temper no good at all, since he had thought of Charlotte as an ally, and here she was, consorting with the enemy. He must speak to Meg privately, he must, to warn her yet again about Peverel although surely, after her experiences with him that had caused him to blackmail her, she ought to need no warning?

He was about to take another swig of the Embassy's good red wine when it occurred to him, a little belatedly, that perhaps getting himself blind drunk was not the way either to put himself in Meg's good books, or be able to give her the high-minded, disinterested advice which she so badly needed.

He leaned towards Fred Zealand and whispered urgently to him, 'Fred, be a good fellow, get rid of Peverel and the rest for me in such a fashion that I might have a word with Meg alone.'

Fred, catching firm hold of the wrong end of the stick, thought that this must mean that Simon wanted to propose to his sister-in-law, not read her a lecture, and was only too delighted to oblige.

'Of course, Darrow, at once, and good luck to you. Deserves a good husband, does Meg. She's not only a good catch, but a jolly good fellow. More sense than most men, as I have reason to know.'

Simon suppressed a sigh. 'I'm not about to propose, Zealand,' he said hastily, for he did not want that *on dit* flying round to dish him even further with Meg. 'It's a. . .' He cast about frantically for something to say, ended up by coming out with, 'It's a matter of business, merely.'

This seemed to satisfy Fred, although in similar case it wouldn't have satisfied Simon. 'Well, yes,' he beamed, 'even a clever woman like my sister-in-law needs a man's help in her business dealings. Leave it to me. Tact is everything in these matters.'

Fred's idea of tact consisted in taking Peverel by the arm and literally dragging him away, saying loudly, 'I have an old friend I would like you to meet, Darrow. He's over there, in the party around the Ambassador. Quick march, old fellow, or they'll send him off with the diplomatic bag or something equally mysterious, before I have a chance to introduce you.

'And you, Mrs Hollis, you, too. I know that Meg is already acquainted with Jack Fawcett, and she won't want to meet him again, I'm sure. Look after her for us, Darrow,' he continued remorselessly, dragging Phoebe—who was wondering what had got into her usually somewhat lethargic husband—along with him.

A trifle bemused, Meg watched them go. Short of actually frogmarching Peverel, Fred Zealand could scarcely have been more insistent on tearing him away from her. She turned to see Simon grinning after them. Her eyebrows rose.

'Oh,' she exclaimed, 'I suppose that I have you to thank for Fred's exceedingly odd behaviour. You put him up to this in order to be alone with me. Well, I will not be tricked in such a scurvy fashion. He'll be informing half of London by tomorrow morning that you and I are almost at the altar!'

She rose to go, but Simon put out a beseeching hand. 'Don't hurry away, Meg. I told Fred I wanted to speak to you on a matter of business, and that was not actually a lie. It's the business of asking you if you have considered my offer of marriage, and telling me what you have decided.' He had already forgotten, now that he was alone with her, that his original intention had been to warn her of Peverel's possible machinations.

His smiling impudence, heightened by the fact that, for once, he had drunk more than was good for him, almost overset Meg. The spectacle of him being impudent at all, smiling or not, was so surprising that she found herself unwillingly captivated by it.

His harsh face was softened. The smile which curved his mouth was a true one, for it had reached his eyes as well; they shone at her with earnest entreaty. Almost was she beguiled.

Only almost. Something, she knew not what, held Meg back. She said, and her voice was soft when she spoke, neither harsh nor angry, but sorrowful, rather, 'Oh, Simon, I gave you your answer the other night, and it was a refusal, as well you know. I also refused to promise to think the matter over, for I know my own mind. My yea is my yea, and my nay is my nay, and there it stands.'

She must be honest with him, but her heart almost failed her when she saw his face change, and the light in his eyes begin to die out. Desperation in her voice, she added, 'Oh, Simon, it is not you. It is marriage. I meant it when I said that I would rather be your mistress.'

'But I don't want you for a mistress, Meg. I want you for my wife.'

'No more,' Meg said, the tears not far away. 'I cannot bear this, Simon. I know that I am hurting you, and that I deeply regret. You have had your answer. Do not torment me any more.'

But he must. For he had really meant to warn her yet once more against Peverel. He opened his mouth to do so, but before he could utter a word she had picked up her fan from the table, and had arranged her face so that she presented a perfectly composed aspect to the world before she said, resuming her best great-lady manner, 'I really must rejoin the others, Simon. We shall cause unkind comment if we remain here alone. We are already being watched.'

He could not stop her, and then she was gone from him, leaving him to wonder what her marriage must have been like for her to reject the notion of marrying again with such horror that she was prepared to become his mistress, but never his wife.

Chapter Ten

Charlotte was writing a letter to Jasper. Meg was reading the accounts and documents relating to her estates both in France and England that her agent, George Paton, had presented to her that morning. L'Angelier, the steward who ran her French possessions for her, had come over from Paris a few days earlier, and he and George had spent the time since his arrival going over them together.

George was a middle-aged man, the younger son of a poor gentry family, and she had been recommended to hire him by Jasper, who knew his nephew. They had been fellow officers in the army. Meg had found George so useful that she had come to use him as a kind of secretary. His command of French was good, and he was pathetically grateful to her for employing him.

His previous post had been with an elderly Marquess whose profligate heir, on succeeding to the title, had dismissed him when he had tried to advise him not to throw his inheritance away on the gaming tables. He was shortly to leave for Berkshire to help Jasper in his new role as Meg's land agent there.

Meg sighed and closed the ledger she had been reading. Unlike many women in her position, she had taken the trouble to learn about the management of her vast possessions. George had been a trifle concerned that, in her ignorance, she might make decisions without properly consulting him, but she had shown a fund of good sense which had been sadly lacking in some of the men he had worked for.

He had queried the sums of money which had been paid over to Peverel and Jasper, but she had looked him in the eye and said coolly, 'An expense of a personal kind, George, which will not recur, I assure you—' words that she was to recollect somewhat wryly before very much time had passed.

She and Charlotte ate lunch early; a cold collation served on the small lawn behind the house, for the day was warm. It was while they were idling over the tea board after it that James, the butler, arrived.

'Your sister, Lady Wallasey, asks if you will receive her privately, Madame. I have put her in the small drawing-room after telling her that I would convey her wishes to you.' His bow was as grave and as formal as his words.

Being Comtesse, Meg thought rebelliously, inwardly reverting to the hoydenish youngest Miss Ashe again, meant that everyone spoke to her as though she were some sort of grand institution, not a woman at all. She was always wondering what James was really like when he was not treating her as though she were the Empress of China.

'In the small drawing-room, James? I will go to

her at once. I hope that she was offered tea.'

'Indeed, Madame, and cakes. But she declined them both. She seems a trifle agitated, if I may say so.'

Well, there was one good thing about James, he always warned her if anything seemed out of place, so that she might be prepared. As for Hetty seeming agitated; that was certainly not news. All her family appeared to be agitated these days, and she could only hope that her parents, when they came, were going to be an exception to this apparently general rule.

James had not been mistaken. Hetty was pacing up and down the room like one of the caged animals which Meg had seen so recently at the Zoological Gardens. She flung herself at Meg when she entered and gave her a distracted kiss.

Meg extricated herself from her suffocating embrace and cynically wondered what her sister wanted from her. She did not have long to find out after she had bidden Hetty to sit down, and had rung for tea which she at first declined, but then accepted when it arrived. Meg had refused to talk to her until she had composed herself.

'What is it, Hester? What is worrying you?'

'Oh, how clever you are these days, Meg, to see immediately how troubled I am! Oh, I am in deep water, indeed. So deep that I consulted Jasper...'

She paused, and Meg, who thought that only a blind fool would not have known immediately how distressed her sister was, could not resist saying, 'Oh, yes, a wise choice. Jasper knows all about deep water. How, exactly, did he advise you to swim out of it?'

'He told me to come to you for help. He said that he had needed assistance recently, and that you had been a tower of strength—although he refused to tell me why he needed help, only that he did.' She paused again, and began to cry—artistically and dramatically. Her distress might be real, but the fashion in which she coped with it was of the stuff of theatre.

'I cannot help you,' Meg said, 'unless you tell me what is wrong.'

Hetty dropped a lacy handkerchief to reveal a tear-stained face. 'Debts, my dear. Debts! Oh, I have been such a fool. I have plunged deep in play of all kind and I am at my wits' end. Wallasey does not know, of course. I should die if he ever found out, but I have not the slightest notion of how I am to pay my IOUs.'

'You know, of course,' remarked Meg conversationally, 'that there is no legal obligation to pay gambling debts. The law does not recognise them.'

'Oh!' Hetty was scandalised. 'Of course I must pay them. They are debts of honour, and those to whom I owe them would let the whole world know that I had defaulted. Where would my reputation be then? Besides, what would Wallasey say? He is always droning on about the need for retrenchment, complaining that when he inherited he had found the estates encumbered because his papa had lost thousands at the gaming tables. He never gambles, and I know that he would send me into the country forever if he knew that I had been doing so, particularly if he ever discovered how much I have lost.'

The youngest Miss Ashe looked at the sister who, before Meg had left England for France eight years ago, had always patronised her. Being only human, she decided that Hetty must pay a little for that.

'What exactly do you want from me, Hetty?'

Hetty disappeared into her handkerchief again. Her sobs grew louder and longer. 'I know that you have helped Jasper, and I have reason to believe that you have done the same for Jane and Phoebe, so why should you not help me?'

'I may be rich, Hetty, but I am not a money well. I take it that that *is* what you want from me? Money to pay for your folly.' She was being harder on Hetty than the others because Hetty had always despised her as the plain sister and had mocked her both publicly and privately. Oh, she would help her in the end, but a little decent gratitude from Hester would not come amiss before she was saved from the moneylenders and the duns.

The eyes which stared at her over the handkerchief were fearful. 'Oh, God, Meg, don't refuse me. I don't know what I shall do if you fail me.'

'Fail you!' Meg's laugh was short. She picked up one of the ledgers which George Paton had left behind. 'Allow me a few moments to examine my financial affairs to discover whether I have the wherewithal to aid you a little—'

'A little!' echoed Hetty.

Unknown to her sister, Meg's account books told a revealing tale of her wealth; not only did she have a vast fortune in what George called the 'immovables'—land, houses, and possessions which could not be sold—but also a tally of riches in cash, specie, stocks and shares which would have made Croesus—the old Greek king, reputed to be the master of untold wealth—jealous. Hetty's gaming debts were like to be a flea bite that would go unnoticed, except to George's shrewd eyes.

'How much, Hetty?' Meg was deliberately curt.

Hetty told her.

'Three thousand pounds. Oh, Meg, I shall love you for ever if you clear them for me.'

'Oh, I do doubt that, Hetty. Love me enough to pay me back, d'you think?'

Hetty began to sob again. 'Oh, Meg, don't be so hard. You must know what a short leash Wallasey keeps me on. I haven't a penny to call my own.'

'All the more reason not to gamble, then. Let me have a list of what you owe, and I will clear your debts for you—on one condition. That you do not play again, for if you do—and you lose—I shall not give you a penny more.'

'Anything, Meg, anything. Oh, you are the best of sisters,' and she made to embrace Meg again, but Meg dodged away. 'No, Hetty. No histrionics, please. Just give up gambling.'

Which, Meg thought, after Hetty had gone, promising to send her the details of her losses, and to whom payment must be made, was not very likely. And after this, who else from her family was left to throw herself on her mercy and demand rescue from Lady Bountiful?

All that was needed to complete the day, she thought wryly, was to have Simon arrive, pestering her to marry him again. After Hetty, she didn't think that she had the spirit left to stomach that.

But it wasn't Simon who arrived to pester her, but quite another pair of visitors: her father and mother, a day early.

'I knew that you would not mind if we arrived before times, Meg. Your father, contrary as usual, said that we should keep to our word, but stuff, I told him, no need to stand on ceremony with Meg.'

She stood back to see Meg the better. Meg was wearing a loose gown of the kind which Cass Devereux often wore about the house. Cass had seen an Indian lady wearing one. A sari, it was called, and Meg had liked it because being loose, she could be at ease in it.

Now her mother said critically, 'Don't you think that your turnout is a little *outré*, Meg, my dear?'

'No, Mother, I don't. Otherwise, I wouldn't be wearing it.'

This calm riposte took her mother aback. The Meg she had always known would have been stridently defiant in making such a statement, not coolly confident.

Oh,' she said. 'Indeed.' She looked about her. 'What in the world possessed you to rent such a barracks as this? You would have been much better off in a little place in Bruton Street.'

'Because I like space about me, mother. I grew accustomed to it in André's mansion in Paris, and I would feel cooped up in a little place in Bruton Street. As it is, here I shall be able to give you a suite of rooms where you and Papa may be privately happy on your own.'

Daunted for the first time in her life by one of

her children, who had now trumped her ace twice, Mrs Ashe looked at her husband. He was indulging in a small secret smile, which he was to repeat at frequent intervals when his hitherto domineering wife came up against her coolly masterful youngest daughter.

Meg smiled, and added, 'I will show you to your rooms; they have been made ready, and were only waiting for your arrival. They overlook the lawns at the back, and the view from the windows is excellent. I will order tea and a cold collation to be sent to you. If you would prefer something a little stronger, Papa, you will find an interesting selection of bottles and decanters on the sideboard in your drawing-room.'

In the face of such kind and carefully organised consideration, Mrs Ashe could find little to say. She did try for a parting shot as they reached the suite of rooms set aside for her and her husband, but her bow and arrow failed her yet again.

'My dear, I understand from one of my correspondents that you have been encouraging Peverel Darrow. That, I must say, I deplore. I do not understand what you are about. His cousin Simon ought surely to be your target. He would make you a most suitable husband and would save you from becoming the victim of gossiping tongues.'

'So he would, Mother. Except that I have not the slightest wish to marry. In any case, out of the frying pan into the fire would be the best description for marriage undertaken in such circumstances. Now, here we are at your rooms and Mrs Hutchings, my housekeeper, has tried to anticipate your every wish.

If she has not done so, pray ring for her, I beg of you.'

All her mother could say was, 'We seem to be a long way away from one another, my dear.'

Meg's parting shot was a deadly one. 'Oh, I thought that you would prefer that, Mother, seeing that so little I do pleases you. The less we see of one another, the happier your temper will be.'

Meg tried to avoid her father's eye as she swept out of the room, Madame la Comtesse de Mortaine in full fig and flower, mistress of all she surveyed. Why in the world had her mother frightened her so in the past? But of course, the youngest and power-less Miss Ashe had been the perfect target for a woman who battened on the fears of the weak.

A week later, seated in Templestowe House's li-brary, Meg was being shown its superb collection of early printed books—or incunabula, as the learned called them—by Templestowe's librarian, Mr Gore, who had stayed with the house, and whose employ-ment was part of her contract with the Earl's estate.

Her dress was a puritanical grey one with a broad white linen collar: over it she was wearing a plain brown holland apron, like those which the house-maids wore when cleaning.

Mr Gore had already complimented her discreetly on her commonsensical apparel. 'Most ladies,' he had said, 'insist on retaining their lightest and prettiest turnouts when they visit me. Most unsuit-able wear if one is examining old folios—they shed dust and their calf skin bindings are invariably dis-integrating with age.'

Meg wryly wondered how commonsensical Mr Gore would consider her if he were privy to her thoughts. For the past few days she had found herself secretly wondering why she had ever wished that Simon would not call on her. She had expected him to visit her once he knew that her parents were in town, but no. He was staying resolutely away.

She was missing him, there was no doubt about that. Was she regretting that she had refused his offer of marriage? Was she also disappointed that her courses had arrived on time so that there would be no inconvenient legacy of their abandoned evening on the sofa? Meg didn't know.

She only knew that his cousin Peverel, a constant visitor—much to her mother's annoyance, if not to say anger—was becoming less and less attractive to her, but to refuse to see him would create as much gossip as seeing him too often.

Think of someone and you conjure them up, her papa had once told her, so be careful of whom you think! Her lips were curling in a small smile when the ineffable James entered to inform her that Sir Simon Darrow had called and was asking if Madame would receive him.

'Yes, James. And James, show him into the library, not the drawing-room. He might like to inspect the Templestowes' incunabula.'

So, Papa had been right. Perhaps the only time in his life he had been wrong was when he had married her mother. The only explanation she could think of was that when her mother had been young she had been as pretty, but as stupid, as Hetty; and that age, and the disappointments of marrying a poor gentleman, had not improved her.

This was a strict judgement, indeed, and Meg reproached herself for making it, but a week spent listening to her mother's constant criticisms of everything in general, and herself in particular, had been a trying one.

She tried to compose herself whilst waiting for Simon. It would not do to let him know that the mere thought of him excited her, and worse than that, he must never suspect that, since that fatal evening, he had nightly walked through her dreams.

His splendid appearance no longer surprised her. Was it that which made her heart beat faster when James announced him, and he crossed the library to take her hand and bow over it?

He straightened up, and looked about him at the walls lined with oak shelving, at the two tall break-front walnut bookcases, at the marble busts of Roman Emperors that stood along the room's cornices, and the giant Van Dyck over the hearth, showing the Templestowe family in all its seventeenth-century glory.

'How like you, Meg, to receive me here in the library. I have often longed to inspect Templestowe's superb collection, but he has been either abroad or in the country during my time in London. And now you have granted my wish.' The smile which he gave her was one of pure pleasure.

No reproaches, no sulks, no scowls. Instead, he was pouring over her the kind of diplomatic honey which six years of being an MP must have conferred on him. Meg found herself charmed by him, and responded in kind. 'I'm delighted to learn that I have allowed you to achieve an ambition, Simon.'

Perhaps it was because she was wondering whether he would ever have gone into Parliament if she had married him, that the 'Simon' slipped out so easily. It was as though they were back in those last two years before his proposal when he had taught her to ride, shown her about his home farm, and had advised her on what to read. Before she had changed from a child into a woman, and all the world had changed, too.

With a wife and children he might have been content to be a country farmer all his life. Knowing the success he had achieved as an MP, that would have been a waste.

Now, Meg, she told herself sternly, you are imagining that you had far more power over his life and ambitions than you actually possessed. But the thought haunted Meg a little when Mr Gore came over to show them an early Caxton, with its splendid woodcuts and black letter printing.

A footman arrived with tea for Mr Gore, who retreated to his little study-cum-office off the library to drink it, tactfully leaving them alone.

'I had thought,' Simon began, 'to find you with your mother. I came to pay my respects to your parents—as well as to see you, of course.'

The look he gave her as he said this was a glowing one. The constraints under which their class lived meant that members of the opposite sex could have little time alone together without causing scandal.

Meg gave a short laugh. 'Alas,' she told him ruefully, 'my mother and I are like oil and water these days, I fear. You must remember that when I was a child I never pleased her. Once I thought that, when I grew up, that would change. But no, I fear I please her less than ever.'

'I know.' Simon nodded, and said no more on that, other than, 'On the contrary, though, now you please me more than ever.'

Meg sparked at him almost without thinking. 'Now, sir, you are not to flirt with me. A library is not a suitable place for flirtation.'

'Then tell me which room *is* suitable and let us repair there, for I have a mind to behave as frivolously as I should have done ten years ago and never did. I have a further wish that you would forget your new-found severity and join me in the exercise.' His eyes, his whole bearing, challenged her. Oh, yes, he burned for her as she burned for him. To be near to one another was temptation itself.

And why should she not accept his challenge? Had she not told him that she was prepared to be his mistress? Was he about to accept her offer? And, if he did, if he surrendered to her wishes, would she be glad or sorry? The thought of what being Simon's mistress would mean brought colour to her cheeks.

He noticed this at once. He put both his hands flat on the table between them, and leaned forward until their faces were almost touching. 'You are looking very well today, Madame la Comtesse. Are you well?'

Meg's reply was sturdy. 'Very well. And you may take that to mean, sir, that there will be no legacy of our. . .folly.'

'And would you marry me, Meg—if there were?'

This was plain speaking with a vengeance! But she was equal to it.

'Now that question, sir, I could not answer until there were such a legacy. Until then, the matter being hypothetical, I cannot make an informed judgement.'

'Then you really meant what you said, Meg—that you would be my mistress?'

Although this came out softly, and the door to Mr Gore's study was half-closed, Meg looked guiltily across at it. He had left them alone. Had he heard anything? Were they being talked of?

Simon saw the glance and interpreted it correctly. Was Madame, then, so used to this game of *double entendres* and secret assignations? The thought depressed him. He had not meant to behave as though he were about to take up her offer of an affair, for he still hoped to make her his wife, but he was finding this game of illicit love exciting, to the point of arousing him—even if he were only engaged in the pretence that he might make her his mistress.

But was it pretence? Having shared such delight with Meg, did he want to do so again even without achieving his greatest desire—to marry her? And if he did, if he accepted her offer, would he still not be content until she married him?

Yet if he were the man of honour he thought he was, then should he not refuse all intercourse with her, other than that sanctioned by marriage? And why was this making his head ache, as well as another, vital, part of his body? Were mind and body so intertwined that merely thinking about Meg in his arms could send him into a cold sweat of desire?

Was the naughty madam aware of what she was doing to him? Had Talleyrand, even in old age, been able to teach her the erotic secrets with which rumour said he had enchanted every woman with whom he had ever lain?

And would he kindly stop asking himself questions, which had apparently taken him no time at all, for now his mouth was descending towards Meg's until it was the only part of their bodies which were touching—and across a supposedly chaste library table at that!

Meg savoured the kiss. Was this conquest—or surrender? And who was conquering and who was surrendering? Oh, why was life so full of questions? Wouldn't it be better just to enjoy sensation?

Being so separate, yet so intimately one at the same time, and in this haven where love was usually only words on paper, was strangely erotic, both parties were beginning to find.

An intimate part of Simon's body was beginning to strain against his breeches, whilst Meg was wishing that she was not wearing such a puritanical high-collared gown. Both were cursing their nearness to Mr Gore; and their distance from anything which might be described as a comfortable place to lie down.

What ended the overpowering kiss was the farcical nature of life itself. A woman's voice was heard crying, 'Oh, no, James, I do not need announcing simply to enter the library in order to greet my daughter and her long-time friend. Pray leave me. I am sure that you have other urgent duties to perform.'

It was Mrs Ashe, about to break in on them. Simon, to his astonishment, found that he was quite equal to the saving ploys of the game of illicit love, played out in the wrong place where detection was always imminent. Aware of his betraying condition, he hastily retreated behind a tall lectern where it might not be seen. Meg seated herself again and began to read the noble work of Juliana of Norwich with the most rapt attention.

Mr Gore, who had also heard Mrs Ashe's fortunately noisy approach, discreetly left his study in order to be found on his knees before a tall bookcase not far from the would-be guilty pair. Thus, when Mrs Ashe entered the library, still hectoring James, all was most proper and scholarly—Simon's head being deep in a learned treatise by Isaac Newton.

'So, there you are!' Mrs Ashe advanced on Simon, who, by now respectable again, overt desire having been quenched by her interruption, came from behind the lectern to bow over her hand.

As usual, she could not forbear to criticise Meg. 'What a strange place to receive Simon, my dear. I suggest that we repair to the large drawing-room. I vow that I am beginning to acquire your *penchant* for space.'

Simon looked surprised at this remark. Meg blushed. James, hovering in the doorway, privately relieved that all was decorous, obeyed his mistress's order to arrange for tea to be served in the large drawing-room. That should surely placate her mother.

But it didn't. She roared relentlessly on. 'What in the world has come over you, Meg, to choose such an odd turn-out? You will not credit this, Simon, but the day we arrived here she was wearing some outlandish Indian costume, while today she is disguised as a housemaid. What is the use of your being a Comtesse received at the French court, if all you can do is dress like a servant?'

'What in the world, indeed, Mother? May I point out that you are going the wrong way if the drawing-room is your destination? You are following James, who is making for the kitchens. Knowing you, I cannot imagine that that is where you wish to take tea.'

Meg was not surprised to notice that Simon looked astonished at her shrewish outburst, but after a week of silence, enduring such reproaches, she could not help herself.

He was even more astounded when her mother, blinking back tears, said to him pathetically, in a voice most unlike her usual one, but rather resembling the whining tone which Hetty had adopted when begging for help, 'You see how it is with me these days, Simon. There is no pleasing her. Who would be a mother? Why, if it were not for her father and I, she would never have gone to Paris and married poor André. There is no gratitude in children. None!'

Simon nodded gravely, and remarked as neutrally as he could, 'I suppose that we all disappoint our parents. I know that mine were disappointed in me when I said that I had no wish for the Parliamentary career that they had planned for me. It is one of life's ironies, I suppose, that now that I have achieved it, they are no longer here to enjoy my success.'

This interesting sidelight on Simon's past flew over Mrs Ashe's head, for she began most vigorously to contradict him. 'Oh, no, Simon dear. Both your parents were always very proud of you, I know that for a fact. Meg, though, was always a disappointment until she married André.'

By now they had reached the large drawing-room. Mrs Ashe, seated in its most comfortable chair, droned domineeringly on whilst James and a footman brought tea and Mr Ashe arrived, blinking from the delights of a comfortable afternoon nap taken in his noisy wife's absence.

Mrs Ashe, still discoursing loudly on Meg's failings, leaned forward to say to Simon in what was doubtless intended as a confidential voice, but of which both Mr Ashe and Meg could hear every word—nay, every syllable, 'Of course, my dear Simon, it was always my fondest wish that you and Meg would marry, but the silly child had nothing better to do than marry herself to a Frenchman—and we all know what they are. I suppose that his only saving grace was his wealth!'

To her astonishment, Meg found herself defending her late and unlamented husband, something which she had never thought to do. To such a pass had her mother's stupid spite brought her.

Before the embarrassed Simon could say anything, she remarked dangerously, 'Indeed, Mother, I am not sure that I do know what they are. Frenchmen, I mean. Perhaps you might care to enlighten me.'

Mr Ashe turned a stifled laugh into a cough as Mrs Ashe, for once, struggled to find a suitable put-down for her daughter. At last, 'You know very well what I mean, Meg. You really are impossible these days. Mr Ashe, pray tell your daughter that she is impossible.'

'I had rather not, my dear, seeing that we are living on her generous bounty, both in our own home and in this splendid palace to which she has so kindly invited us. Thanks, rather than criticism, I believe, ought to be directed towards her late husband for leaving her so magnificently endowed. If I, at least, can forgive him for being a Frenchman, surely you must be able to do the same.'

Meg saw both Simon's and her mother's faces change as her father revealed that he and her mother were her pensioners, something which none of the rest of her family knew, for she had asked her father for secrecy in the matter. Annoyed by her mother's baiting of her, he had forgotten his promise.

Even this revelation could not affect Mrs Ashe. After a moment she came out, somewhat sullenly, with, 'Oh, I am sure, Mr Ashe, that I am properly grateful for a daughter doing what, after all, is nothing but her duty. But that does not mean that I am unable to speak my mind when such speech is needed. Speak the truth and shame the devil, *I* always say.'

For the first time Simon was being made aware of the unpleasant spite with which her mother had always treated Meg. He said gently, for he was also suddenly aware of how much Meg must have suffered—and was still suffering—at her mother's hands, 'Oh, I agree that we should always try to be truthful, Mrs Ashe, but my time in Parliament has convinced me that it is sometimes wiser and kinder to be silent. In that fashion, one avoids the unpleasant without perjuring one's self.'

Meg, near to tears, threw him a look of such gratitude that his heart swelled at it. Fortunately, Simon's diplomatic reply had been so carefully couched that Mrs Ashe was uncertain whether he had meant it as a reproach or as praise of what she had said.

So she nodded vigorously, and their later conversation, to Meg's relief, was conducted in all the clichés of polite society.

Before he left, Simon took the opportunity to have a short private word with her. 'My dear,' he said kindly, 'do not take me amiss, but is it not possible for one of your sisters to entertain your mother and father? I have not observed that she is as. . .harsh with them as she is with you.'

Meg's laughter at this was a little strained. 'Pray forgive me, Simon. The subject is not really a matter for mirth, but you must understand that I am only entertaining them at all because Fred Zealand begged me to help them out—my mother's visits to them were putting Phoebe's health at risk. I had forgotten. . .' She bit her lip for she did not want to criticise her mother publicly—not even to Simon.

She started again. 'I mistakenly thought that I could manage to let it ride over my head—and now here I am in the boughs. And there are a pair of metaphors fit only for a bad play at Drury Lane.' She gave another sad little laugh as she finished.

'I see.' Simon stood there helpless, knowing at last how true his love for Meg was, since he wanted, more than anything in the world, to protect her from that world's despite. He was beginning to understand a little why she had refused him eight years ago: that it might have been a reaction against her mother's bullying her to marry him. The thought made him unhappier than ever.

Lust for Meg had temporarily deserted him in the face of her distress. He would dearly have loved to say, 'Marry me, my darling, and I will see that she never hurts you again.' But that would be blackmail of a kind which, because she had been so wounded, Meg would reject. What he did not yet know was that Meg possessed other wounds, which only time and patience would heal.

Meg saw him hesitate and ponder. She wanted to say more, but she had the dreadful belief that, if she lingered any longer with Simon, her mother would follow them and say something so outrageous that the rapport which was slowly growing between herself and the man whom she loved might be damaged by her own behaviour.

She laid her hand on his sleeve, and murmured, 'You must go, Simon. Do not worry overmuch. I think that I am strong enough to bear my mother's presence during the Season. After all, poor Phoebe has had ten years of her, and this is only her first visit to me! I must be strong, for all our sakes.'

What could he say to that? Nothing, only bow over her hand and kiss it, his eyes speaking for him. Meg watched him leave before returning to the drawing-room to find her mother somewhat subdued, and her father looking stern.

It occurred to her for the first time that if her father had been more concerned to care for his children, rather than retreating from his wife's presence to live a quiet life away from her, the history of the Ashe family might have been somewhat different.

But Mrs Ashe did not stay subdued for long. Even before Meg had time to sit down, she resumed her attack on her. 'I am sure that I do not know what has come over you all these days, Meg. Nothing I say or do seems to please. Even Simon's manner to me was a trifle odd. It really is most hurtful when all I am trying to do is promote the happiness of those around me.'

These last words of her mother before she retreated to her suite of rooms left Meg not knowing whether to laugh or to cry. What did remain with her, though, was the look of kind compassion on Simon's face when he had been comforting her.

Chapter Eleven

The ruin which Peverel Darrow had staved off ever since he had left University was suddenly staring him in the face: the moneylenders were threatening to send the bailiffs in. All that was left to him was either a debtor's prison, or flight to the Continent to live a straitened life in Calais, as the late George Brummell had done when his creditors had closed in on him.

One thing, and one thing only could save him: marriage. Marriage to an heiress would solve all his problems at a stroke. The duns would retreat, secure in the knowledge that, once the ceremony was over, they would receive their money back with interest.

Desperate, he had proposed twice in the last week. Once to a young girl of good fortune who would at least be bearable in bed, and then when she had refused him to the fat widow of a filthy rich India merchant who had laughed in his face.

'No title,' Mrs Skinner had jeered at him. 'My poor Thomas left me enough to buy a Viscount at least, and what have you to offer me? Not even a broken-down mansion and a few barren acres!'

'I'm Sir Simon Darrow's heir,' he had protested
feebly. 'He is a man of good fortune and large
estates, a confirmed bachelor, and—'

'And stuff and nonsense,' she had told him
robustly. 'I know all that. Why, he's younger than
you are, so even if he never marries you're like to
die before him. No, I want a title and lands and I
want them now. Money I already have.'

So the low bitch had had him investigated. If that
wasn't the outside of enough! All that was left to
him was to propose to little Meg Ashe, now the
Comtesse de Mortaine. If only she hadn't been told
by her bitch of a sister about his blackmailing of
her, she might now be his wife. He was sure that,
without that hanging over him, he could have
won her.

Even so, he might yet succeed. And what a prize
she was! Not only because of her money, but
because, dammit, he liked her. She would make him
a good wife, to whom he would be able to talk,
unlike Mrs Skinner, and Charlotte. . .thing. He had
already forgotten the young girl's second name.

But if she refused him, what then? Well, desperate
men had to employ desperate remedies. He could
always try to succeed where Edward Gibbon
Wakefield had failed a year ago, and attempt to
kidnap and marry her. Wakefield had been caught
after he had married his heiress, had been sent to
Newgate prison for three years and the marriage had
been annulled.

If he could only get her to Gretna Green and
marry her, he was sure that the Ashes and his cousin

Simon would not set the law on him, for none of them would—he hoped—wish to see the son of old family friends sent to Botany Bay for marrying an heiress against her will.

He didn't ask himself whether, if he succeeded in getting Meg to Gretna Green, she would agree to marry him—even with the threat of social ruin hanging over her if she didn't. Like many another man, he could not see the indomitable spirit behind her charming exterior. Only his cousin Simon was beginning to understand that Meg de Mortaine had a will as strong as any man's.

Oh, Goddamn everything, that he should be driven to contemplate committing such a crime! But it might not be necessary. Meg might accept him.

She certainly didn't seem to want to marry Simon, although rumour had it that *he* now wished to marry her, which was another potent reason for spiriting Meg away. If Simon should persuade her to marry him, he would surely get the heir who would condemn Peverel to be the permanent poor relation. He would never be Darrow of Darrow Hall.

His meditations were interrupted by his man-of-all-work, Ham Fenton, whom he had sent out earlier with orders to bring back with him George, the footman at Templestowe House, from whom he hoped to gain some more useful information about Meg's life.

'Money for you,' he said abruptly, when George at last stood before him, 'if you can tell me how Madame la Comtesse orders her day and any details about her life.'

George appeared only too willing to oblige. He had already run several small errands for Peverel, and regularly brought him news about Meg's visitors. The latest titbit he had to lay at Peverel's feet was about Simon's latest meeting with her. Part of Peverel's desperation lay in the knowledge that Simon and Meg had spent time together recently— and to learn that they had been alone in the library of all places was a bitter blow.

'Well, almost alone,' George admitted, 'only that half-blind librarian with 'em, James said, and he wouldn't see any hanky-panky, not him. Only half a man.'

'Anything else which might interest me?'

George hesitated, then came out with something which he had overheard James say to the housekeeper. 'Only that that family of hers are like leeches. If any of them want any help from her, she always comes arunning to settle things for 'em, does Madame. Pays their debts, has that 'orrible ma of hers in the house cos no one else wants her, James says.'

Peverel was thoughtful. 'Does she, indeed?' He remembered that Meg had paid him the money to buy Jane's letters back without any demur. *She always comes arunning*, does she, if any of her family are in trouble?

Now he came to think of it, the word was that Jasper Ashe had suddenly paid off his debts, resigned his commission and was working as a land agent somewhere in the country. So who else but Meg could have done that for him? Could this knowledge provide him with the means to trap Meg if she refused his proposal? He questioned George a little more before he handed him his bribe and let him go. A mighty useful traitor in Meg's camp was young George!

What Peverel did not know was that, as he walked back to Templestowe House, young George was feeling the first pangs of awakening conscience. Mr Darrow's money was useful, no doubt of that, but what was he planning for Madame that he needed to know so much about her?

Only that morning Madame had spoken kindly to him, and all the servants were agreed that they had never served a more considerate mistress. He made a private resolution that would hurt his pocket, but never mind that: this was the last time that he would sell information about her to Mr Peverel Darrow. . .

'So you see, my dear, having been such good friends this Season, I thought that I ought to tell you that Jack and I are off to Coverham at the weekend. He says that he has done his duty in the Lords, and is tired of London. Too large, too dirty and the life here too trivial. I most particularly did not wish you to learn the news from anyone else.'

Cass Devereux was seated with Meg on the lawn at the back of Templestowe House. She had brought her children with her, for she was that most unfashionable thing, a loving mother who was rarely parted from her offspring.

'And you are happy to go?'

'Of course. I have to say that I agree with Jack, not just because he is my husband, you understand, but because I, too, love country life. Until I was twelve I lived deep in the Yorkshire countryside, and although Coverham is in Hertfordshire, and the landscape is soft, not wild and rocky, I still prefer it to the town. Jack sends word that he wishes you to visit us when you are tired of London. He believes that you are a country girl at heart.'

Now this was shrewd of Jack, for Meg had said nothing overt to him of her passion for the country life, nor had she told anyone but Jasper of her Berkshire estate. Even her father believed that Jasper's post had been found for him by Meg, not that he was working for her.

Soon she intended to leave London herself and retire to live among her horses and cows. She would have done so before, had it not been for looking after her father and mother on the Zealands' behalf.

'Of course, I shall visit you. I can think of nothing better.' She watched Cass's little son flying his kite so happily and for the first time consciously wished for a family of her own who would run round shouting and laughing, and calling for Mama to look at them. Yes, she thoroughly approved of Cass's attitude towards her children.

'Come soon,' Cass said, shortly before she left. 'The autumn is beautiful at Coverham, full of mellow fruitfulness, as the poet says.'

So Cass liked Keats, too—another bond between them. She would miss her lively, unorthodox presence in the staid ballrooms of the grand and the conventional who made up the bulk of London society. She was faithful to her husband as well, something of which Meg approved.

'I shall leave London as soon as my parents wish to go home. I hope that day will not be long delayed. We are having a grand reunion for the Ashe family before the weekend, at which all of them here in London will be present. Even Jasper is coming up from Berkshire, and Simon Darrow is hoping to look in during the early evening.'

She glanced over to where Charlotte was helping the children to fly the kite, and whispered confidentially to Cass, 'I am hoping that Jasper will soon propose to my companion. He has settled in well in his new position, I understand. I shall be sorry to lose her, but she will be the kind of steadying influence on him that he needs.'

Cass and her children gone, Meg sat down to read the latest novel by the author of *Sophia*. She had only managed half a chapter when James announced that Mr Peverel Darrow wished to speak to her privately. It was really quite odd. Everyone wished to speak to her privately these days.

She had little doubt as to what lay behind Peverel's request. He had come to propose. She had been avoiding him for the last few weeks; with Jasper gone, he had had little excuse to visit her.

Well, he would have to be satisfied with her present turnout—a hoydenish one, because she had dressed to enjoy herself with Cass's children. She was wearing a simple muslin gown, and her hair was loose. With any luck, her informality might dampen his enthusiasm a little.

It didn't. Peverel, staring at Meg's glowing face, at the graceful line of her body, and at her proud carriage, saw nothing of what she was wearing. He saw one thing only, that Meg de Mortaine was a prize worth winning—and not simply for her

money. In that moment, he fell genuinely in love
with her—he who had never loved anyone before.

To his astonishment, he found that this unlooked-
for event made his task of proposing to Meg more,
not less, difficult. He was so locked into the habit
of charming insincerity that the revelation that he
loved her had him almost stuttering as he began
to speak.

For the first time, his despair at the notion that
she might refuse him was linked to his loss of her,
not of her fortune. And sincerity was a trait which
he had not practised for years; his tongue stammered
over unaccustomed words. Besides, all the words
in his vocabulary were shop-soiled by his previous
misuse of them.

He had intended to throw himself immediately at
her feet in order to display his overpowering desire
to marry her. But this ploy now seemed fustian,
mere Drury Lane heroics that she would surely
despise. How to begin?

Inspiration struck. He would go gently at first.
'Have you had news of Jasper lately? I would dearly
like to know how he is coping with country life and
country quiet? And for whom is he working?'

This anxious questioning about her brother had
the effect of wrong-footing Meg. Knowing Peverel,
she had anticipated from him a proposal employing
exactly the kind of histrionics that he was so carefully avoiding. Indeed, he was behaving in such a
subdued fashion that it did not seem likely that he
was about to make one at all.

'Oh, I assure you that Jasper is a happy man. He
is working hard, he says, and is finding that he

enjoys the rural life. Which is not surprising, after all, seeing that until he joined the Army he was a country lad himself.' She avoided answering Peverel's question about the name of his employer.

Once Peverel would have jumped on that omission, but in the flurry of emotion which his new understanding of his feelings towards Meg had created, he missed it. For several minutes he was reduced to banal chitchat of the kind in which he never normally indulged. The question of how to phrase a proposal that might be successful held him in such thrall that he was quite unable to begin making it!

Meg, indeed, was beginning to wonder exactly what it was that Peverel wished to say to her that he had demanded the privilege of saying it in private. Ten minutes into their meeting, he had said nothing which could not have been heard by Charlotte Hollis.

She decided to broach the question herself, driven, she afterwards concluded, by an intense curiosity as to what the wretched man was about.

She waited until Peverel ended a lengthy and boring disquisition on their recent visit to the Zoological Gardens with the statement that he wished he might be able to afford to join the Zoological Society himself, but alas, his circumstances forbade such a decision.

He cursed himself as soon as he had said this, because it was no part of his plan to dwell on his relative poverty. On the contrary, he was intent on presenting himself as a man of reasonable means. But alas again, an inconvenient truthfulness, usually alien to him, was suddenly breaking out in all directions.

'I understood,' Meg said as he halted to an end, 'that you wished to see me on a private matter. Perhaps my butler was mistaken.'

'Oh, no.' Peverel seized on Meg's statement with avidity seeing that it allowed him a useful and tactful opening to the meat of this interview so far as he was concerned. 'I have a matter of the utmost importance to raise with you.'

Having come out with this, he fell into an unaccustomed silence.

Puzzled, Meg decided to help him out. 'Which is?'

Peverel hesitated, then plunged. 'Oh, Meg,' he exclaimed, falling on to one knee as he spoke, an action not contrived, but coming from the depths of his heart. 'I have fallen madly in love with you. Please marry me,' and he clutched at her hand and began to shower kisses on it.

Unknown to him, it was alas again. He had shown two faces to the world for so long that Meg did not believe a word of this truly impassioned and heart-felt plea. She jumped back, dragging her hand from his, saying briskly, 'Oh, Peverel, do get up, there's a good fellow. You know that you don't believe a word you're saying, so you surely don't expect me to. It's my money you want, not me.'

Peverel was in agony. 'No, no,' he exclaimed, 'not at all. It's you I want, not your money. I love everything about you.' He was dismally aware that even to his own ears every word he said rang with insincerity, however truthful his intent. He had not meant to fling himself on to his knees before her, but the long habit of dissimulation had destroyed in him the ability to speak and act sincerely.

'And if I had no money, Peverel, would you then propose to me?'

Now Peverel knew as well as Meg that this was a question phrased in such a way as to expect the answer no. Peverel's newly found truthfulness where she was concerned plunged him into a further dilemma. Because, even though he loved her, his circumstances were such that, were she penniless, he would never have thrown himself into her way, and would never have learned to love her.

Meg, watching him, was surprised by the varying emotions that chased one another across his usually smilingly placid and carefree face. He wished to tell the truth, but he also needed to win her for two overpowering reasons—one of which was that he needed to save himself from ruin.

He hesitated, and his hesitation told its own tale. 'But I love you, Meg,' burst from him when he saw by her sad dismissive face that his suit had failed. 'Oh, I do, I really do. What do I have to do to make you believe me?'

'Accept,' Meg said, 'that even if I thought you honest in your declaration, I would not agree to marry you. I do not love you, Peverel. Indeed, I do not know whether I can love any man enough to marry him. If you love me, walk away from me without reproaches and without useless words of regret.'

He had failed, and although he still loved her, dissimulation was Peverel's master again. It had to be if he were to survive. Had she accepted him, and they had married, he told himself that he would never have had need to cheat again: that he might have enjoyed the luxury of being an honest man.

But she had not, and he was already beginning to make his plans. The dreadful thing was that the love he felt for her was to drive him on the harder to marry her by any means, fair or foul.

And since fair had failed, foul would have to do.

So he smiled, and smiled. He rose gracefully to his feet, said all the right things, told Meg how sorry he was, and tried to convince her that they could continue as friends—unless, of course, she were to change her mind. . .

But it was plain that she was implacable: there was no likelihood that she would ever willingly accept him. And whatever she had said about never marrying, it was his cousin Simon whom she loved. Simon, who had everything: the title, Darrow Hall, his membership of Parliament, his friends and patrons in high places, the promise of office—and would soon have Meg and her fortune, although, unlike himself, he had no real need of either.

Well, to the devil with Sir Simon Darrow. Whether she willed it or no, she would be Peverel Darrow's bride—and soon.

Chapter Twelve

'You may ask me, Charlotte, why Peverel Darrow wished to speak to me privately. I cannot believe that you are not all agog.'

There was no outward sign that Meg was disturbed by the scene which had just passed, but she had an overpowering desire to discuss it with her companion. Charlotte, who was now seated before the glass doors overlooking the lawn, and engaged in stitching a canvaswork bell-pull, smiled at Meg.

'I am supposing,' she said, serenely stitching on, 'that it was yet another proposal.'

'Indeed it was, and an odd one.'

'Oh, and what was odd about it? It cannot have been a surprise, surely? He is up the River Tick, or so rumour says, and doubtless thinks your fortune would help him to paddle out of it.'

'True, and strangely enough, I am relieved to hear that you consider that it was the charm of my money rather than my own charms which drove him on. Which made it all the more surprising when I heard him declare so frantically that he was passionately in love with me. I hardly knew him, he seemed so changed.

'And then, after I had refused him, he changed completely again. He said quite calmly that he accepted my refusal, and hoped that we might still be friends. Friends! Never. There is a reason why we could never be friends. But. . .' and Meg fell silent.

'Sentences beginning with "but" which then break off,' remarked Charlotte serenely, 'always intrigue me.'

'But why do I feel that there was something wrong about the way it ended? Oh, I fear that I am growing fanciful these days. Perfectly behaved though he was, I felt threatened. That was the odd thing.'

Charlotte put down her stitchery. 'Yes, that is odd. One usually feels threatened by bad, not by good, behaviour. Odder still when one contemplates the interesting fact that Mr Peverel Darrow always goes out of his way to be charming to all the ladies.'

Meg was suddenly restless. 'Oh, I must be starting a megrim. I shall be supposing that every bush is a bear, as Shakespeare said. I think it was Shakespeare. . .

'I had better retire to my room to lie down a little before we go to Lady Granville's reception this evening. The party is small, and when I am with her I always feel that I must be very up to the mark, and up to the minute. She may be good fun, and she is always very shrewd. I came to know her well when her husband was the British Ambassador in Paris.'

Charlotte's expression was thoughtful as she watched Meg leave. It was not like her to be so distracted. She might have been describing herself when she spoke of Harriet Granville. If she thought that there had been something strange about Peverel Darrow, then she had probably been correct. The only problem was in what the strangeness might consist.

She shook her head. Speculation was catching and, indulged in overmuch, decidedly led to the megrims—which was possibly what was wrong with Madame la Comtesse de Mortaine, who was usually so practical and down to earth.

A description of both Meg and Harriet Granville, with which Simon Darrow would certainly have agreed. He thought that Meg looked particularly lovely when she entered the Granvilles' large reception room later that evening, to find that Monsieur de Talleyrand was holding court.

Simon had spoken to him briefly and had decided that although he was certainly a monster, he was a charming monster. Had he been monster enough to seduce Meg? That was the question which ran round Simon's brain like a squirrel trapped in a cage.

Meg had dressed herself in the palest green. She was talking to Lady Granville, a woman with a face full of wit and character, but completely lacking in beauty. After a few moments, Meg walked away and Simon could not prevent himself from watching her every move. Being truly in love for the first time, not knowing whether or not that his love would ever be returned, was like living in a kind of hell.

So distracted was he that when Harriet Granville spoke to him about the debate in the Commons that afternoon—she knew that Simon admired her hus-

band's coolly sensible views about the necessity for
constitutional reform in order to avoid revolution—
he was hard put to give her a sensible answer.

'Oh, it was the usual nonsense,' he managed to
say. 'Both sides of the House catcalling, the one at
the other. There are times when I wonder how we
manage to govern sensibly at all!'

He had said the right thing, for she smiled approv-
ingly at him. 'That was what Granville said when
he was an MP. He thought that men of sense ought
to get together to agree on policy, not hurl abuse at
one another. Imagine a battleship, he said, or a regiment which ran things the same way—nothing
would ever get done, and we should lose every
battle.'

Simon laughed, and agreed with her. 'True, Lord
Melbourne always says that the less Parliament does,
the better. It has no business to meddle with the
activities of men of sense.'

'And you are a man of sense, I hope, Sir Simon.'
Did her eyes turn to look meaningfully at Meg when
she said this, or was he seeing subtleties where none
existed?

'I hope so, m'lady.'

Apropos of completely nothing she remarked,
apparently idly, 'You should not believe all the *on
dits* that flow from Paris, dear sir, about the habits
of those in good society. Monsieur de Talleyrand,
for example, is credited with a reputation that, if the
rumours were true, would have a man of his age in
his grave in no time. True, he likes to talk to clever
young women—as does Granville. But these days,
it is invariably only talk. And he also likes to bring

cheer to clever young women who are unhappy.'

She was looking at Meg again as she spoke, no doubt of it. And what had she just told him in her clever, guarded way? That the rumours about Meg were untrue—something which he had already begun to believe—and that her relationship with Talleyrand was innocent. More, she had also told him that Meg's marriage had been unhappy, for he had no doubt that Meg was the unhappy and clever young woman of whom she had spoken.

He bowed to her, and said. 'They told me that you were witty, Lady Granville, but they did not tell me that you were kind.'

'I will return the compliment, sir. They told me that you were a sound and honest man, much to be relied on. They did not tell me that you were shrewd. I wish you well in all your endeavours, Sir Simon Darrow.' And yes, she *was* looking at Meg, no doubt of it.

It was also his *congé*, for she was moving on to speak to her other guests, leaving him free to approach Meg. He thought that she looked flushed, a trifle feverish perhaps, but her eyes sparkled and shone the more for it. What was better was that they were sparkling and shining at him.

What a strange mixture of emotions consumed him! Love, lust, a desire to protect her, a desire to share his life with her. And fear that he might never be able to indulge—nay, fulfil was a better word—all these emotions.

'You are in looks tonight, Madame,' he told her. 'You have enjoyed a happy day, perhaps?'

The word 'happy' flew out as an echo of what

Lady Granville had so guardedly told him. Meg looked at his smiling face. Some instinct, she knew not from whence it came, had her telling him of his cousin's proposal that afternoon.

'Which was not exactly a happy moment for either of us, except now that he has had his answer I hope that he will no longer haunt me, for I made my refusal as firm as I possibly could.' She paused and said almost below her breath, 'I tell you this because I know that my association with him made you unhappy.'

Hope stirred in him. 'And you are disturbed by the thought that *I* might be unhappy?'

Meg lowered her eyes as though to examine the fan which she was carrying. 'Yes.'

Hope did more than stir in him. It grew and burgeoned. The desire to hold her, an impossible one to fulfil in a room full of the best society, also grew in him. His eyes were glittering now.

'You are thinking of what I asked you?'

'Yes.'

'And you are ready to give me an answer?'

'Not yet. You must give me time. I have made so many mistakes in my life, you must understand. I have no great wish to make another.'

Hope began to shrivel again. But she had not given him an outright refusal as she had done before—as she had done to Peverel. Hope revived a little, and a savage glee at the thought of Peverel's discomfiture was hope's dark companion. And perhaps he should expect her to hesitate, given what Lady Granville had hinted to him about her marriage.

'We may be friends until you decide—and afterwards, too, I pray.'

'You will always be my friend, Simon, whatever answer I give you.'

Why was she half-encouraging him? Meg did not know. Perhaps with Peverel out of the way, and his suspicions of her dispelled, it might be that they could meet on level terms at last. But always there was that residue of fear about marrying again, which her life with André had left with her.

They were walking along as they spoke, bowing to some acquaintances, smiling at others. More than one man who had become aware that Simon Darrow was in full chase after the Anglo-French Comtesse determined to place their bets when next at their club that they would marry before the Season was over.

Peverel was not present to see his discomfiture completed—Lady Granville rarely invited such as he—but another hopeful lover was. Caro Kenilworth came towards them. She had neither seen nor spoken to Simon since the visit to the Zoological Gardens.

She bowed to them both before looking around the room in order to say sneeringly to Meg, 'I see that your *cavalier servant* is not here tonight.'

'If you mean Mr Peverel Darrow, then pray say so,' retorted Meg coolly.

'Oh, do you have others, Madame, that you need them distinguishing?' Caro's spite was naked. She showed it further by adding, 'You must know that you have lost one of them. Mr Will Osborne proposed to me yesterday, and I have accepted him.

The announcement will be in the public prints tomorrow.'

'Then my congratulations to you both. He is not present tonight, I believe, so you may inform him of my good wishes.' Meg did not let her surprise show, not only because of the disparity in age between Caro and Will, but also because it was so soon after his failed proposal to her.

'No, indeed. Tonight he is informing his cousin, Lord Stanyon, you know, of our happy news. His cousin was most urgent for Will to marry and my name was one of the highest on his list.'

'But why?' Meg asked Simon, genuinely bewildered, after Caro had left, bestowing extreme unction on all about her. 'She is ten years older than he is, and I have rarely seen him speak to her.'

Simon shrugged. 'Stanyon wanted it, I believe. After all, she is not only filthy rich, but owns half of Derbyshire. His lands and hers added together will mean that Will can press for the earldom to be raised to a marquessate, which was always Stanyon's dearest dream. If he couldn't achieve it, then the next best thing is that Will may do so.'

Meg could not prevent a shudder. 'What a dreadful reason for marriage. Oh, I know that our kind do it all the time, but still. . . There was never a sign that he even liked her.'

'Don't you wish to know who was the first heiress on Stanyon's list?' Simon could not prevent himself from saying.

'Who?' And then she knew who it must be. 'Oh! You mean that *I* was?'

'Oh, yes, indeed. You are even more of a prize

in that department than Caro. I will do Will Osborne
the honour of believing that he cared for you, but I
doubt that he would have chased you so hard if you
had been penniless.'

'Which is what I told Peverel,' Meg said, without
thinking. 'Oh, dear, I should not have said that.' Her
voice was rueful. She looked up at him. Their eyes
met, and passion suddenly held them in its thrall.

Simon spoke to break the tension. 'Believe me. . .I
would marry you if you possessed not a halfpenny
and were in rags. Indeed, I would prefer you in rags.
Or in nothing at all.'

And this in a public room surrounded by the
cream of society. Bishops, Cabinet Ministers, a
Prince—Talleyrand—and two Royal Dukes. To say
nothing of assorted dignitaries of every kind. There
was even an Admiral present, and the Duke of
Wellington, Lady Granville's especial friend, was
expected any moment.

Best to pretend that she had not heard his last
sentence. 'Well, I do possess more than a halfpenny,
sir. Like most present here tonight, I believe.'

'Rumour has it that the Granvilles themselves are
not too flush though, particularly after refurbishing
the Paris Embassy to their liking,' Simon offered.

'Now, Sir Simon, you are sufficiently a man of
the world to know that if Lady Granville is the late
Duke of Devonshire's daughter, and Lord
Granville's brother is married to the richest and most
powerful woman in Scotland, then in their case,
shortage of money is no drawback!'

Both of them were seized by the same thought:
that Peverel Darrow was not high enough in

society's hierarchy for his poverty not to matter. A
thought which must have struck Peverel himself
more than once.

Meg determinedly changed the subject, as much
to show Simon that her slight move in his direction
over the question of marriage was a real one. 'I hope
that, like me, you are looking forward to the family
party I have arranged for tomorrow afternoon. Jasper
is coming up from Berkshire and will be pleased to
see you, I know.'

'And will you be pleased to see me, Madame la
Comtesse?'

She looked up at him, her eyes glowing again.
'You know I will, Simon.'

What heartened him most was that she had
dropped the Sir from his name. They stood for a
moment, face to face.

'I believe you,' he said abruptly.

Puzzled, Meg said, 'About what, Simon?'

'About Talleyrand. About everything. I believe
that you were telling me the truth when you protested your innocence. I even doubt the nature of
your involvement with my cousin, despite what I
overheard. I believed you even before Lady
Granville virtually told me that the rumours circulat-
ing London about your life in Paris are false. You
will forgive me for thinking otherwise.'

If that did not change the nature of the relationship
between them, nothing would. To Simon's astonishment, Meg stood silent while two tears, tears like
pearls, ran slowly down her face, to be followed by
no others.

They were not touching, and yet, in the truest

sense of all, it was as though they were heart to heart. Not only that, it was as though they were alone. The noise of the reception died away. Time stood still

Meg spoke at last. 'Yes, I forgive you. Though why you should. . .?' She ran down.

'Change my mind? I have watched you these last weeks, and the woman I have been seeing is not a woman who would play fast and loose with her husband. Or with any man or woman.'

And all that Meg could find to say to that was a simple, 'Thank you.'

Time began to run again. They were no longer alone. The noise of the crowded room returned. They both knew that they ought to separate. They had been together for far too long.

Simon bowed and took her hand to kiss it in farewell. 'I cannot wait to see you again tomorrow,' were his parting words. Meg put the hand he had kissed to her lips for a brief moment—and then returned to the mundane world where she must do her duty, see and be seen, and revert to being the serene Madame la Comtesse de Mortaine, that great lady who bore no outward resemblance to the youngest Miss Ashe.

But, inwardly, she had never felt more like her younger self. Except that this time, if Sir Simon Darrow came a-courting on the morrow, he would receive a different answer from the one which she had given him eight long years ago.

'You're sure that you know exactly what you are to do, Fenton, and when to do it? Make a mistake and, at the best, we shall sail in irons to Botany Bay or, at the worst, dance on Tyburn Tree.'

Peverel Darrow had made all his preparations. Usually idle, he had begun a fevered campaign to ensure that he married Meg de Mortaine and saved himself from his creditors even before Meg had turned him down.

He had hoped never to have to put it into operation, but now speed was essential because the bailiffs might be knocking on his door at any moment. He was going to use against her her own generosity towards her family, even though he felt himself to be a cur as he set about doing so.

After all, he loved her and, once they were safely married, he would treat her kindly. Or so he told himself. It was not as though he were going to abduct her solely for her money.

'Trust me, master. Done this before, ain't I?' was Ham Fenton's response. Well, that was true enough, Peverel acknowledged, but Ham's previous piece of villainy had merely concerned his assistance of a minor squire's daughter and the young man whom she wanted to marry, but of whom her parents didn't approve.

Rather than have a scandal, the Squire had glumly accepted the young man and the marriage after the guilty pair, with Fenton's help, had successfully reached Gretna Green and tied the knot, as Fenton always put it.

But this was a different case, was it not? Meg was a great lady, and she was certainly not going to connive at her own abduction. Failure might literally mean death.

'I trust, Fenton, that you have found a reliable lad to deliver this letter for me and who will then disappear, as well as a suitable person to play at being a footman. After that, make sure that the chaise I have hired will be ready to take me to the mews at the back of Sackville Street.'

'Aye, all's ready, master, never fear,' Ham announced reassuringly, before departing to make the final arrangements for Meg's abduction. If this desperate throw succeeded, then he would be in clover as well as his master. If it didn't. . .why, then Ham Fenton had places to hide which neither Peverel nor the law knew of. . .

'You seemed to find Sir Simon Darrow's company pleasing last night, Meg,' remarked Charlotte Hollis the following morning. She had been writing letters and was now busy sealing them.

Meg was contemplating a long list of arrangements that she had just passed on to the housekeeper and to James, all to do with the afternoon party. Her mother and father had not yet come down from their suite of rooms, and she was enjoying a brief respite from her mother's constant complaints.

'I did, didn't I?' was her quiet response, which warned Charlotte that here was a subject on which she chose not to speak. Taking the seat at the bureau which Charlotte had just vacated, Meg began to write a letter to an old friend in Paris.

Her labours were interrupted by the arrival of James, carrying a silver salver which he offered to her. 'A letter, Madame, hand-delivered by a respectable-looking young lad. He said that he could not wait for an answer.'

'A letter?' Meg took it from the salver, broke its seal and opened it. Her name was written on the front in a hand which looked familiar.

It was familiar. The letter was from Jane, and had obviously been written whilst she had been greatly distressed.

'Pray, dear Meg,' she had written, 'of your kindness, I beg you to help me again as you did once before. Oh, I have been such a fool. I cannot speak of this to you this afternoon with all the family present, and tomorrow will be too late. I must see you at once, privately. A friend has generously allowed me to use her home at 4, Sackville Street for a rendezvous with you this morning. Say nothing to anyone, for I fear Vancourt's temper. Come at once, is the sad request of your foolish sister, Jane.'

What in the world could Jane have been doing to lead her to this? Meg stared at the tear-blotted letter, her hand quivering. She looked over at Charlotte, who was now placidly reading. Should she tell her? *Say nothing to anyone*, Jane had pleaded, so she would not. Was it Peverel who was troubling her again? Had he kept back one of the letters?

Meg rose to her feet. She would keep faith with her sister. 'Charlotte, my dear. My letter is from an old friend who has fallen on hard times and wishes to see me urgently before she leaves town.' She looked across at the French clock on the mantelpiece, regretting that she was compelled to lie to Charlotte—but something had to be said to explain her sudden departure.

'I cannot believe that she will keep me long. I am sure to be back well before the family is due to arrive at three.' She looked down at her plain morning dress. 'I need to change into something a little more suitable. Will you kindly arrange for the small chaise to be harnessed and brought round to the front door? No footmen, please, just Jem as my driver. I don't wish to flaunt my consequence.'

Well, the bit about being not kept long would be true enough, for Jane would not wish to explain a long absence from home, she thought wryly as Jem drove her to Sackville Street. She wondered which one of Jane's friends had been ready to oblige her at such short notice.

Jem helped her down—a ragged youth had eagerly run up to hold the horses' heads for him in order to gain a small tip. 'Drive round to the mews at the back,' Meg told him, 'and wait for me, I shall not be long.'

She walked up a few steps to the front door and banged its big iron knocker in the shape of a wreath as vigorously as she could.

The footman who opened it indicated that she should follow him. 'Lady Vancourt is expecting you, Madame,' he told her, polite formality itself.

Meg never quite remembered what happened immediately afterwards. One moment she was walking along a wide entrance hall towards a drawing-room door, the footman before her. The next something dark and heavy was thrown over her head and she was dragged along by a man who was holding her in a cruelly tight grip.

She tried to cry out, but the blanket—she was

sure it was a blanket—muffled her voice, and when she attempted to struggle her captor announced gruffly, 'None of that, now. We don't want to hurt you.'

We? Who could we be? And where was Jane, or the woman who had allowed her to use the house? Surely *Jane* could have nothing to do with this, was her last thought before she was bundled through what must be the kitchen door and the blanket was removed.

Yes, it was the kitchen she had arrived in, but it was empty of all furniture but a grimy table, a broken stool—and Peverel Darrow, sitting in a battered high-backed Windsor armchair before a blackened, long uncleaned, hearth. His expression could best be described as hangdog. A pair of pistols lay on the table before him. The supposed footman had disappeared, and the man who had thrown the blanket over her head turned out to be a servant of Peverel's whom she had seen once or twice before.

Meg fought off the unreasoning panicked fear which was threatening to overwhelm her. She smoothed down her dress, held her head as high as she could, and assumed her most dominant great-lady voice in order to say, 'What in the world are you doing here, Peverel? And where is Jane? Surely she is not waiting for me in what I now take to be an uninhabited house? Is this some kind of strange and unkind joke? And if so, why play it on me?'

She turned towards the kitchen door before which Peverel's servant stood, enjoying her discomfiture, no doubt, and gave him an order. 'Kindly allow me to pass so that I may summon my driver to take me home at once.'

Peverel clapped his hands together in genuine admiration. 'Bravo, my dear. You are, indeed, the nonpareil I thought you. But, alas, I cannot allow Fenton to call your carriage. No, no, I have quite other plans for you.' He rose to his feet and walked towards Meg who stood frozen in sheer disbelief at what was happening to her.

'Oh, Meg, my darling,' he said sorrowfully. 'Why did you not accept my proposal of marriage? We could, I am sure, have dealt so well together, and now. . .'

Dealt so well together. He could not have said anything more calculated to cause Meg to turn away from him, her head still high, her gloved hands closed tightly over her reticule. Even in the midst of the confusion which this untoward turn of events had caused, she remembered only too well who had first said them to her.

Simon.

Simon, who was undoubtedly coming to propose to her this afternoon. Simon, whom she now knew that she loved, and who loved her. And here she was, Peverel's prisoner. By what he had already said, she was sure of his intentions towards her: abduction, and an attempt at forced marriage. And if he succeeded, she and Simon would be parted forever.

Never, no, never. She would never allow it. How, she did not know, but she would think of something. He was still speaking. She must listen to him.

'. . .and now you have compelled me to undertake

this desperate enterprise in order to make you my wife. Oh, Meg, believe me when I say that I truly love you, most passionately love you, but since you will not marry me willingly, then you must do so unwillingly. Although I still hope that you will soon forgive me and come to love me as I love you when you understand what desperate remedies your refusal has forced on me.'

It was true. He was prepared to abduct her—and at the same time had the impudence to declare that he loved her passionately!

Meg flung back her head, and taking the hand which he had extended towards her, she flung that back, too. 'Oh, really, Peverel, this is the outside of enough. You speak as though it is my fault that you are doing this dreadful thing. You have forged a letter purporting to be from Jane in order to bring me here. Your servant has manhandled me, and now you propose—correct me if I am wrong—to drag me to Gretna Green and marry me.

'Well, you are quite mistaken. I shall do no such thing. I will wait for you to come to your senses and send me home. Do so, and I shall tell no one of this fit of madness. I shall go nowhere with you.' She sat down on the broken stool, put her reticule on her lap, and defied him.

All that this achieved was to make him admire her the more for her indomitable spirit—but it could not change his mind. To do so would mean ruin. He felt a cur, and worse than a cur. He was not cut out for this kind of thing. A true villain would have threatened her cruelly, he knew. But he could not do as she asked. Time was wasting. They must be on their way.

'Oh, my dear,' he said sadly, 'my very dear. It is useless. I wish that I could do your bidding, but I cannot. Accept that I mean what I say and come with me, without making an undue fuss.' He picked up one of the pistols. 'I have no wish to threaten you, and I don't want to order Fenton to carry you out to your chaise so that we may all drive north, but I must.'

'And Jem? Is he one of your conspirators, too?'

'No, we have disposed of him, but not harmed him,' and Peverel smiled another sad smile.

Oh, the hypocrisy of him, was Meg's fierce reaction. She folded her arms, and told him, 'I shall walk nowhere with you, you may be sure of that.'

'So be it. But I do not want this—you are compelling me to do exactly what I have no wish to do. Fenton, put the scarf around her mouth, tie her hands, and carry her to the mews.'

'My fault again that you are maltreating me, I suppose,' Meg accused him scornfully before Fenton gagged her and carried her to her own chaise, Peverel following him. Once in, with Fenton as coachman, they drove out of the mews, then out of London to take the road north.

Meg's abduction having been accomplished, the false footman drove Peverel's chaise back to the stables from where Fenton had hired it.

Once they were safely away, Peverel put a tender arm around Meg's shoulders, ignoring the fierce eyes which stared at him over her gag. 'I will remove it,' he said, 'as soon as we are out of London, but if you try to call out or attract attention I shall restore it.'

So far so good, he thought thankfully. And now for Gretna Green.

That morning Jem Potter enjoyed himself at first. But later. . .no such thing. After seeing Madame safely into the house, he had scarcely had time to drive her chaise into the mews, where another already stood in the yard, before a footman came to him brandishing a sovereign. A sovereign!

'It's from Madame,' he explained. 'She will stay longer here than she thought so she has sent you this so that you may get something inside you in comfort, rather than sit out here. There's an inn round the corner. She says be sure to be back in an hour, and not overdo things.' This last was accompanied by a knowing wink.

Well, Madame was a kind soul to be sure. But all the servants knew that, so Jem made certain that he arrived back at the mews when the hour was up. But, Lord, what a turn-up! For on his return he found that both chaises had disappeared, and when he entered the house to find what was up, he discovered it to be empty of both people and furniture.

But worse than that, when, bewildered, and wondering where the deuce Madame and the chaise had gone to without him, he opened the drawing-room door, someone gave him a dirty great blow on the head which knocked him senseless.

He came to with a spinning head and the knowledge that he had the painful task of making

his way back to Templestowe House to tell them
his dismal story: that not only had he lost a chaise
and pair, but Madame as well!

Chapter Thirteen

'**Y**ou say that Meg left the house at half-eleven of the clock this morning to visit an old friend, and has *still* not returned? How exceedingly inconsiderate of her! But hardly surprising, seeing that she appears to think of no one but herself these days. Even so, I would have expected her to be present to receive her guests.'

Mrs Ashe was at her most dominatingly shrill. Before Charlotte could answer her, she continued in a voice which had the rest of her family wincing, 'And where, pray, did she go? I suppose she had the goodness to inform you of her destination!'

'Well, no,' Charlotte admitted. 'Only that she would be visiting an old friend and would not be gone long.'

'Not gone long!' Mrs Ashe threw up disapproving hands. 'And you have no notion of where she can be. What a way to run a household!'

Jasper came to Charlotte's rescue. 'That will be quite enough, Mama. It is not Charlotte's fault. Nor may it be Meg's. Something must have gone amiss.

What, I cannot imagine, but we ought to send for
the head groom, in order to find out how many
footmen went with her and who was driving her.'

'Oh, I can tell you that,' said Charlotte eagerly.
'She took the smallest chaise and one driver, Jem
Potter. She expressly said that she needed no
footmen.'

'Stranger and stranger,' sniffed Mrs Ashe who,
whilst apparently not liking her daughter, liked the
consequence which marriage and wealth had
given her.

The head groom, when sent for, confirmed
Charlotte's story. 'And young Potter's a highly
responsible lad—but who knows, they might have
had an accident, but if we don't know where
Madame went, then where do we look? The only
suggestion that I can make is that we send out as
many lads as possible to look for her.'

But where to look? London was so large. Jasper
and his three brothers-in-law went into a small
huddle with the head groom to discuss ways and
means, as a result of which he went to the stables
to begin to carry out their plans. Phoebe, always the
emotional sister, began to cry at this open admission
that Meg might be in trouble, only for her mother
to roar at her, 'Kindly stop sniffling, Phoebe. It does
not help matters'.

'True enough,' snorted Fred Zealand at his
mother-in-law, defying her for the first time. 'And
it doesn't help to rail at poor Phoebe, either, so hold
your horses for once, pray do.'

What scolding response Mrs Ashe might have
made to *that* was forestalled by James announcing

Sir Simon Darrow, whom he had already informed that the mistress had been gone for nigh on four hours, and no one knew where she was.

'Is this true?' Simon began, before looking at everyone's disturbed faces and hearing Phoebe's stifled sobs. 'Yes, I see it is. No search has been made for her, then?' His own voice betrayed his agitation. How could Meg be missing? He had come here determined to propose to her whenever the occasion presented itself, and instead he was being informed that his love had disappeared—had gone no one knew where.

He swung on Charlotte Hollis and asked her a question which, in their agitation, no one else had thought of.

'You say that she went to visit an old friend suddenly. Did someone bring her a message—or had she arranged the visit beforehand?'

'A boy brought her a letter,' Charlotte told him. 'He didn't wait for an answer. Meg read it and said that it was from an old friend who was in trouble and that the matter was urgent. She left at once, saying that she would not be gone long.'

'A letter,' said Simon, with Jasper echoing him. 'Did she take it with her? Or did she leave it behind? And if so, where would she leave it?'

It was typical of Simon, more than one of his hearers thought, that as soon as he arrived he probed straight to the heart of the matter. Charlotte went to the bureau that Meg had been using shortly before she had left.

'She was in a hurry,' she explained as she unlocked and opened it. 'I suppose that there is a chance that she might have left it behind. Yes, I do believe that this is it,' and she handed a piece of crumpled paper to Simon.

Watched anxiously by the whole party, Simon read the letter in silence. Fred Zealand, whose sole contribution so far had been to rebuke Mrs Ashe and murmur 'Good man,' at Simon during his inquisition of Charlotte Hollis, saw his face change as he finished it.

'What is it, Darrow, what's wrong? There is something wrong, I collect by your manner.'

'Very wrong,' said Simon heavily. 'I will have to read it aloud to discover how wrong,' and he did so, beginning, 'This is dated today from an address in Sackville Street. It is as follows.'

For a moment when he ended there was a dead silence, then everyone began to talk at once. Jane sprang to her feet, exclaiming, 'No, I never wrote that. I couldn't have written that. I was never at Sackville Street today. Vancourt will tell you that I never left home until I did so to come here,' and she burst into tears.

Mrs Ashe said angrily, 'This is all some kind of hum, I am sure. And it was very wrong of Meg to rush off on the very morning that she had arranged a family party, even if Jane did write her a letter. She was always an inconsiderate child.'

The dam burst. Jane, drying her eyes, swung on her mother, crying, 'Oh, how can you talk such nonsense, Mother? Did I not just tell you that I never wrote that letter? And Meg inconsiderate! What a story! Were it not for Meg I should be in Queer Street, and so, I believe, would my brother and my sisters.' She waved a hand at them to encourage them to support her. 'Is not that so?'

Even Jane might have been surprised at the chorus of support she was granted. Simon certainly was. Jane, looking her husband in the eye, bravely confessed, 'What's more, I believe that I know who wrote that letter. You see, Vancourt, I made a bit of an ass of myself with Peverel Darrow earlier this year and wrote him some silly letters. He threatened to send them to you unless I gave him money.

'If it hadn't been for Meg, I don't know what I should have done. But she bought him off for me. Now, since both Meg and I agreed to keep the matter quiet, and since Peverel certainly wouldn't have told anyone else about his wickedness, who else could have known about it? And who more likely to be able to forge my handwriting?'

She flung herself down beside Vancourt, crying, 'And now she may be in desperate trouble because she believed that I needed help again.'

Simon stood turned to stone as the true meaning of the conversation between Peverel and Meg, which he had so unfortunately overheard, was at last revealed to him. Oh, dear God, how cruelly he had misunderstood her. In that, as in everything.

He scarcely heard Jasper saying brokenly, 'She has also paid my debts, and has given me the hope of a happy future with my dear Charlotte. I know that she has done as much for Hetty and Phoebe, so no more reproaches for her, Mother, ever again.'

'Hear, hear, Jasper,' said his father. 'I should have silenced you long ago, my dear, where Meg was concerned.'

Nevertheless, still undaunted, Mrs Ashe opened her mouth to say something scathing about Meg, but caught Fred Zealand's stern eye on her and closed it again. Simple, honest Fred had succeeded where cleverer men had failed: he had been the first to reveal that, firmly treated, she could be silenced.

Simon ignored all this, ignored Mrs Ashe's stricken face, and started for the door, crying hoarsely, 'We waste time. To the devil with my cousin, for that is all he deserves. I am sure that he has abducted Meg to marry her and pay his debts. He has had the impudence to tell me that he loves her. He has several hours start, but I shall go after him at once.'

'Hold on,' exclaimed Jasper. 'I wish to find her, too, but how can we be absolutely sure that it is Peverel who has carried her off—or even if someone has?'

Even as he spoke, James burst through the door, his honest face anxious. 'Sir Simon, Potter is back, injured. He has a strange story to tell. George Newman also says that he has something to confess which might help us, but he will only speak to Sir Simon.'

Potter and Newman's stories confirmed that someone had made away with Meg, although neither of them had any direct knowledge of Peverel's involvement. Added, though, to the evidence of the letter, the likelihood that, as a last desperate throw, he had abducted her was very strong.

Newman was almost the more distressed of the two. 'I never thought he meant her harm,' he said brokenly. 'All he wanted was bits of gossip.' He turned his face away before confessing, 'Particularly about you and Madame. He hated the notion that you and she were friendly. I thought I could earn myself a bit of money for nothing. I suppose I shall be turned away now,' he ended mournfully.

'That will be for Madame to say,' Simon told him, almost absently. He only had one idea in his head. If Peverel had kidnapped Meg in order to marry her he would need to take the Great North Road to York. And Simon would follow him up that road. He would drive to Hell itself in order to rescue Meg.

By far the easiest and safest way for Peverel to take would be the road to Ware, which legend said Dick Turpin had followed, joining the main York Road some forty miles later at Huntingdon. The disadvantage of the mail coach route, which ran via Barnet and Edmonton was that it was so crowded that it carried the risk of his being seen by some friend also travelling north.

If Peverel had gone by Barnet after all, then no matter, Simon would simply have to drive on to Huntingdon in the hope of catching him there.

How fortunate it was that he had come in his two-horse curricle, which would enable him to pick up some of the time already lost. He would be travelling at a greater speed than the chaise—for he had no doubt that Peverel had made off with Meg's carriage.

It was also agreed that Jasper would follow the other route to Huntingdon, in case Simon's guess was wrong. There was to be no mass hue and cry.

'For,' Simon said, 'the less noise we make about this business, the better. If either of us can overtake them and take her to a place of safety before she has been in Peverel's company overnight, then we can save her reputation, otherwise. . .'

'Otherwise,' Jasper said heavily, 'she is ruined.'

'Not completely,' Simon said, 'for today I came to ask her to be my wife, and had hopes that she would agree. If we can thwart Peverel then, come what may, I shall marry her.'

Tigerless, not dressed for a possible long ride north, Simon set off in pursuit of his lost love, privately cursing the Fates who again seemed intent on preventing him from marrying her.

'Have you given any thought, Peverel,' Meg enquired sweetly, 'as to how you are going to manoeuvre me in and out of inns, without my making an unseemly fuss about my abduction, at every place we stop at overnight on the way north?'

Peverel was beginning to think that, even to get hold of her money, marrying Meg would be a great sacrifice on his part. After he had taken off her gag she had never stopped nagging and questioning him in a sweetly reasonable voice, which was unsettling him more than loud recriminations would have done.

'I see no problem there,' he told her stiffly. 'It is in your own interest to draw as little attention as possible to yourself if you are to avoid scandal and social ruin. The sooner we are married, the better for us both—as I am sure you will agree.'

Meg contemplated the passing scenery. They had made very slow time since leaving Sackville Street and the West End behind. Every drover in England seemed to be running their flocks of sheep and cows along the road to Huntingdon via Ware. Several times the chaise had come to a complete stop for some time, and Fenton's leaning down and cursing the offending countrymen seemed to have had no other effect than to slow them down even further. Their final humiliation had come when they had reached Edmonton, a mere seven miles out of London, when geese, ducks, and fowls had not only stopped them, but had almost driven Fenton from his seat, the fowls apparently mistaking the chaise for a suitable place to roost.

'Oh, I don't agree at all,' she informed him cheerfully. 'Social disgrace, so far as I am concerned, is immaterial. I intend to retire into the country as soon as this Season is over.'

'Indeed, you won't.' Peverel gave her an angry glare. 'When you are my wife, I intend to spend the entire Season in London every year—indeed, more than the Season. I detest the country.'

'Which is no more than I would have expected.' Meg put her head on one side in order to stare at him the harder. 'You have the air of exactly the kind of popinjay who considers that the whole of society revolves round him. Now, Simon, on the other hand. . .'

'Damn you, woman, hold your tongue,' he shouted at her angrily. 'I am heartily sick of hearing you prate about Cousin Simon and his perfections. I have had nearly twenty slow miles of it, and enough is enough.'

'Oh, but I like to talk about him. He's such a

noble contrast to your good self. I like that phrase, don't you? It's one the lawyers use. Oh dear, it doesn't really apply to you, though, does it? Not to a would-be felon already half way to Botany Bay!'

Peverel's face purpled. Meg thought that she might have gone too far in her campaign to unsettle him so thoroughly that she might make for herself an opportunity to escape him. She thought that he was more weak than wicked and intended to exploit his weakness. He opened his mouth to say something, but at that moment the coach gave a great lurch and Meg was thrown forward to land on top of Peverel. They had stopped yet again.

This time it was, or so Fenton told them once they had untangled themselves, because a lad had run in front of the horses and had been knocked unconscious. He was now lying on the roadside, being tended by one of the drovers. Another was holding the horses for him. It seemed that the rustics among whom they had been travelling had accused him of going too fast for safety, and there was talk of reporting them to the local magistrates.

'I am sure,' Meg's voice was impossibly virtuous, as she regained her seat, 'that Simon would never have gone so fast in such a mob. *He* would have had more sense.'

'I shall gag you again if you don't stop chattering about him, be damned if I won't,' roared Peverel, before instructing Fenton to get in the chaise and see that she didn't run off, whilst he went outside to try to quell what seemed to be turning into a riot.

Five minutes later he was back—to find that Fenton had pinned Meg back against her seat and had one grimy hand over her mouth. Only her eyes stared defiance at them both.

'Niver met such a troublesome and noisy doxy in all my born days,' Fenton told Peverel. 'What with trying to lean out the winder to scream for help and then offering me money to let her go, she niver stopped talking until I made her. I 'opes as how she's got enough tin to make up for the caterwauling. We shan't git to bloody Huntingdon at this rate, niver mind Gretna Green.'

Meg rewarded him for that by kicking at his calves, and only Peverel's presence stopped him from giving the troublesome doxy such a backhander as she'd not forget in a hurry.

'You're right about not getting to Huntingdon.' Peverel was bitter. 'To satisfy the yokels outside, I've promised to stop at the Fox and Hounds at Ware to find and pay for a doctor for the silly lad we hit, in order to quieten them. I propose that we remain there for the night and leave early before the road becomes filled with traffic.'

Fenton shook his head. 'Best press on, master, in case anyone twigs what we're a-doing and comes after us. We ain't gone very far yet.'

'No likelihood of that. Besides, I'm tired. Stop now and we can order a good dinner. It's been a hard day.'

Meg, her mouth now freed from Fenton's constraining hand, offered him no consolation. 'And several more hard days to come, I assure you, before we reach Gretna. Really, Peverel, is all this discomfort worthwhile, even to get hold of my fortune?'

The look he gave her was one of hate. Contemplating this journey, he had seen himself charming her into acquiescence on it—once she had realised that her case was hopeless. Instead, she had turned into as big a nag as her mother—and even more nonstop. Only the thought of the fortune he was going to enjoy once he had married her, sustained him.

Meg looked out of the window as they inched slowly towards Ware. On the edge of the small town, they came to a crossroads where a signpost informed them that one of the by-roads ran to Coverham. Coverham—was not that where the Devereuxs had their home? She had a fleeting memory of laughing and talking with Cass in happier times.

No time to think of that now. She pondered instead on how to convince the landlord of the Fox and Hounds, when they arrived there, that she was a wronged and abducted woman. Alas, Peverel wisely gave her no chance to do any such thing. Before they even drove into the inn yard he replaced the gag, tied her hands and feet together, and wrapped a large counterpane around her, so that her face was hidden, before bidding Fenton to carry her in.

Loudly shouting, 'Make way, make way, my mistress is taken ill and needs a bed straightway,' he bore her upstairs, an agitated landlady walking in front of them.

Trying to struggle in Fenton's iron grip, Meg found, was useless. Once he had dismissed the landlady, he threw her carelessly on to the bed, leaving it to Peverel to free her from her bonds when he arrived.

Meg, dishevelled and sore, her dignity hurt, as well as her feelings, shot at him, 'I cannot imagine what Simon will do to you when I tell him of this.'

'Too late, my dear. We shall be safely wed before you see him again. I have ordered a good meal for Fenton and myself. For you, gruel—it is all that you deserve and will cool your proud spirit a little. I shall bring it upstairs before we eat. In the meantime, I shall lock you in the bedroom. I do not advise you to call for help. I have told the landlord that your illness has made you delirious—so do not think that anyone will come to rescue you.'

He grinned at her. 'You see, I have thought of everything.'

'Not quite everything. When he catches us up, wed or not, particularly if we're wed, Simon is like to kill you,' Meg told him rebelliously before Peverel left her, locking the door behind him. He had laughed at the notion of Simon, the law-abiding, killing anyone!

Meg was not so sure. She knew of the hidden fires which Simon masked so successfully. She was not, however, prepared to wait for a rescue that might never come. She looked around the room after trying the door. Its lock was flimsy enough, but there was no way that she could break it.

Opposite to the bed was a window. Through it she could see fields stretching to the far horizon in what she assumed was the direction of Coverham. She opened it and leaned out, to see that a small lawn with beds of summer flowers lay below her. At the far end of the lawn was a hedge, and a gate that led on to the fields beyond.

Thoughtfully, Meg closed the window and sat down on the bed to think. The nearness of Coverham had given her an idea. If she could somehow escape from the inn, she might find refuge there with Cass and Jack, even if she had to tramp across the fields to reach them.

She was still plotting when Peverel came back with a tray on which stood a bowl of soup and a large slice of bread. He even knocked at the door before unlocking it, using as much circumspection with her this time as though she were an honoured guest. He had obviously decided to change tactics with her, since threats were unable to silence her.

'You are not feeling too overset, I hope?' he asked her kindly. 'I do regret having to treat you so roughly, but I am sure that you understand that it is necessary.'

'Do not think that you will win me round by being pleasant. I am here as your prisoner, not as your guest. Your absence will be more pleasing to me than your presence,' and Meg turned her back on him.

He placed the tray on the small table before the window. 'Oh, come, my dear. You must know that, despite all, I care greatly for you, even though you have behaved so shrewishly all the way here.'

Meg jumped to her feet. 'Pray forgive me, do. But I regret that I have never been instructed on the correct etiquette to be observed by a lady who has been abducted, has seen her own carriage stolen in order to carry out the abduction, who has been gagged, tied up and carried to her bedroom like a bundle of washing ready for the launderers. The devil take you and your so-called love for me, if this is how you express it. If you truly love me, you will take me home at once.'

She said this as loudly and shrilly as she could, so that Peverel winced at the sound. 'But you must know why I can't do that, Meg. I have crossed the Rubicon. . .'

'And the die is cast, I see. Pray do not speak to me again, I beg of you. Your very voice is hateful to me.'

Nothing was going as he had expected it. He had hoped to win her round with honeyed words, as he had done with other women to gain his way with them. But she had behaved like a fishwife from the very moment that she had found herself in the carriage going north.

Indeed, so noisy was she that he feared that someone might hear them and come to enquire whether anything was wrong, although he had tried to forestall that by telling the landlord and his wife that his own unfortunate spouse was not only sick in body, but in mind.

He had been so charmingly distressed, his luggage which Fenton had carried in was so gentlemanly, and the chaise and its appointments were so luxurious, that neither of them thought to question what he was saying—such a rich and fine gentleman as he undoubtedly was.

What he could do was keep her quiet by leaving her alone while he ate and drank in the inn's diningroom. He had made a point of asking for quarters away from the rest of the guests so that she might not be disturbed. He would put off the task of trying to placate her until the time came when she was so compromised that she could not hope for rescue.

He bowed his way out, determined not to allow her to provoke him into losing his temper again. A good meal, and better drink, awaited him downstairs. The Fox and Hounds' cellars were famous, as all travellers on the Great North Road were well aware.

As for Fenton's dooming that they ought not to have stopped, but should have travelled on into the night to gain an invaluable lead over any pursuers— why in the world should he think that there would be any, given all his careful planning?

Dusk. She needed dusk. Meg had drunk her soup and eaten her bread, surprised to find how hungry she was. Then, remembering the famous coloured print which showed a young woman leaving her upstairs bedroom in order to run away with her lover by climbing down a rope of bedsheets knotted together, she had imitated her, and sat waiting for dusk to arrive.

She was sure that Peverel would not soon return to the bedroom. Food and drink would keep him in the inn's dining-room until she was asleep. For all his faults, she was of the opinion that he would not try to force her—she shied from using the word rape—although, had she proved willing to enjoy his embraces, he would probably have urged her to spend the night with him.

Which was why she had behaved so noisily and shrewishly—to convince him that such a belief was groundless. She opened the window and put her head out. The little garden, as she had hoped, was empty.

She had already fastened one end of the rope to one of the bedposts, and now she paid it out of the window, to find that it was still well above the ground. Giving a great sigh she pulled it back, and finished it off by adding the bolster case to it.

Oh, famous. It now almost reached the ground. Next she must climb onto the window sill and begin to lower herself down—as she had once done on the trees she had climbed in the gardens at home when she had been a hoydenish girl. It was as though the years had fallen away and she was little Meg Ashe again.

She thanked God that she was still slight, and had not become puddingy with the years, so that she reached the ground safely, and scampered, her skirts held up, across the grass and through the gate.

Where, the good Lord be thanked, there was a lane and a small sign beside it with an arrow, dimly scored, and the magic words, *Footpath to Coverham*. No mileage was given, but what of that. Better to be on her way to safety—and eventually to Simon—than waiting to be bundled to Gretna by Peverel and his odious man.

The only drawback was that a wind had risen, and there was rain in it, but one could not have everything.

Simon set a spanking pace on his way north. He stopped at several posthouses on the road to Ware, once to change horses—he had no intention of ruining his good cattle by driving them too hard for too long—but also to enquire whether anyone resembling Peverel and Meg had gone through.

Running through his head was the memory of
Meg. Meg laughing up at him; Meg teasing him;
Meg, his pretty bird as he had come to think of her,
flying free, her own mistress. Oh, if he married her
he would never cage her, he would allow her to fly
free, sure that she would always return to him, for
she was both faithful and true—to herself and those
who depended on her, as her family had borne wit-
ness. Why had he ever doubted her honour?

Marry her! He had yet to rescue her and, if he
were mistaken about Peverel's plans, and his cousin
got clean away with her, then that marriage might
never be.

Like Meg, on drawing near to Ware, he noticed
that he was passing by the road to Coverham,
although at the time he thought little of that. Knowing that Peverel liked ease and comfort he was sure
that he would stop at Ware.

Sure enough, when he reached the Fox and
Hounds and questioned the ostler who came up to
serve the highflyer with the splendid curricle, he
learned that, yes, a gentleman, answering to
Peverel's description, and a lady had arrived in a
chaise some hours ago. But the lady had been ill
and unable to walk and had been carried in by the
gentleman's servant. The gentleman had dined alone
and was in the taproom at this very minute.

Simon threw money at him, bade him care for his
horses and carriage and set off at the double for the
taproom to discover whether his quarry was there.

He was. Peverel sat before the flaming hearth, his
booted feet up on a small table, a cigar in his hand,
a glass of port by his side: the very picture of suc-

cessful indolence. He did not see Simon until that
gentleman gave a roar, and hurled himself at Peverel
to send chair, table, cigar and drink flying.

'Damn you, where is she? What the devil have
you done with her, you cur? I'll kill you for this!'

All thought of discretion, of smothering scandal
for Meg's sake, had flown out of Simon's head. All
that he wanted to do was beat his worthless cousin
to a pulp. He had him by his lapels, had thrust a
face into Peverel's which was so leonine and threatening that Peverel quailed before him.

'I've not harmed her. I'd never harm her. I
love her.'

'You lie, damn you. You lie,' and Simon shook
his cousin as a terrier might shake a rat so that
Peverel's teeth chattered and tears came into
his eyes.

'I say, sir,' quavered a young gentleman, standing
by the bar. 'Hold on, there. What's to do that you're
in such a pother?' He appealed to the landlord.
'Ought we not to fetch the constable?'

Still holding Peverel in a vice-like grip, Simon
bellowed at the youth. 'Who the devil asked you to
interfere in a private quarrel? If I want a constable,
I'll send for one myself. I'll deal with this cur—
privately. Landlord! Is there a room I can use to
question this malefactor and decide whether to start
him on his way to Botany Bay?'

Peverel knew that the game was well and truly
up. He had never seen Simon behave after such an
abandoned and ferocious fashion before. Here was
a man he had never met. And he remembered Meg's
prescient words: 'Simon is like to kill you.' He had

laughed at them, and how wrong he had been to do so.

'I want no trouble in my house,' said the landlord sturdily. 'Will the gent you're aholding so cruelly agree to speak to you privately, though?'

'He'll agree to anything I ask of him, won't you, Peverel?' Simon snarled at him. Unable to speak through a combination of fright and shock, Peverel was only able to nod his head in the landlord's direction.

'There, you see!' Simon was triumphant. He twisted Peverel round, bent his arm up behind his back and shoved him into the room off the snug, indicated by the landlord, where he flung Peverel into a chair.

'Now. Don't lie to me, damn you. I'm prepared to let you go to save scandal if you'll tell me where she is.'

'Upstairs. She's upstairs,' quavered Peverel. 'I haven't hurt her. I swear I haven't. I love her.'

'And a damned odd way you have of showing it.' Simon bared his teeth, before saying, 'Now lead the way. Take me to her room. Try to trick me and I swear to God I'll have your blood.'

If Peverel did not know his cousin, Simon scarcely knew himself. From the moment that he was certain that Peverel had made off with Meg he had had only one idea in his head. To find her and give Peverel the beating of his life.

They had reached the bedroom. 'L-l-let go of me,' Peverel stuttered at Simon, 'and I'll unlock the door. I swear to you that she's safe and sound—asleep by now, probably.'

Only she wasn't. The room was empty. Rain was beating in through the open window, drenching the sheets which Meg had used to make her escape. Simon's pretty bird had flown.

Chapter Fourteen

'Safe, is she? Damn you, Peverel, you couldn't even abduct a helpless young woman without making a botch of it.'

Beside himself with rage, hope having been succeeded by fear, and the knowledge that Meg was somewhere out there in the rapidly darkening night, caught in the pouring rain, Simon dealt Peverel such a fierce blow that he was thrown backward over the bed, stunned.

He leaned forward to seize his cousin again by the lapels of his smart coat. 'I've a mind to beat you insensible, here and now, except that I haven't the time. I have a duty to find my poor darling, who has escaped you only to be caught in a storm. But I warn you, if she's harmed in any way when I find her, you'll pay a heavy price.'

And then he was gone, storming down the stairs to try to find his lost love. Peverel followed him, feebly crying, 'Only let me come with you. Oh, dear God. I never meant this to happen.'

Simon had reached the front of the inn and was

making for the lawn at the side before Peverel caught him. Fenton, alerted by his master's shouts, ran out of the room where the ostlers, grooms and postillions had been drinking, in time to see Simon, whose arm Peverel was now pulling on, turn and give him a mighty blow which had him reeling, but still hanging grimly on.

'What the devil's up, master?' cried Fenton, putting up his fists preparatory to attacking Simon. 'Let him go, damn you.'

This inapposite statement had Simon turning on Fenton, shouting, 'Damn you for a fool. *He*'s hanging on to me.' When Fenton struck at him, Simon, hampered by Peverel, swung his booted foot at him to catch him cruelly above the knee and below his midriff.

Fenton fell to his knees, screaming, 'Damn you, you've ruined me.' At the same time, Simon, beginning to be secretly surprised by his own violence, freed himself from Peverel, whom he threw to the ground to join Fenton. That done, he ran through the streaming rain towards the lawn which Meg must have crossed to leave the inn. Common sense told him that she could have gone no other way for fear of being seen. What more likely than that she had left through the gate?

Like her, once through the gate he saw the signpost saying Coverham—and the green lane which led to it. No doubt she thought that safety lay that way, but what she could not know was that the big house where Jack and Cass Devereux lived was over five miles away.

What to do? He could still not be sure that she

had fled in that direction, although the likelihood was strong. He stood for a moment, debating the matter, then Peverel caught up with him.

They stood face to face, water streaming from them both. The savage expression on Simon's face frightened Peverel into crying out in a vain attempt at mitigation or justification, 'Only let me help. Let me try to find her, too. I never meant this to happen. I swear. I never thought that Meg would be so daring, so rash as to put herself in danger.'

Simon was minded to strike him again, to roar at him that *he* had put Meg in danger, but in this desperate pass only common sense could help.

'Dare I trust you?' he asked grimly. 'If I take the path to Coverham, thinking that she has gone that way—will you scour Ware to find her? And if you do, may I have your worthless word that you will return her to the inn until I come back to claim her? If you try to abduct her again, I'll see you hanged or transported, on the word of the Darrows whose name you have shamed today, even if I have to follow you to Hell to catch you.'

Numbly, all his usual easy bravado gone, his face bearing the marks of Simon's fists, Peverel muttered, 'I promise. Dear God, what a mess, what an unseemly mess. What have I done?' He hung his head until Simon roared at him again.

'Be off with you. On a night like this, we've no time to lose. I'm for Coverham, and you, you do as I bid you.'

He stayed a moment to watch Peverel make off in the direction of the front of the inn before starting on his own long walk. There was no driving a curricle or, indeed, any other form of carriage, along the narrow track. Pray God he found her before long—or before anyone else did.

Meg, wet through, shivering, her teeth chattering involuntarily from time to time, was huddled in the lee of a hedge. The rain, which had not been heavy when she had left the inn, had grown more and more so as she walked along the track. The wind had got up, too, and she was walking into it, which made her progress slow.

Tired, weak through lack of food, and soaked to the skin, her light dress clinging to her so that walking was difficult, she had finally given in to exhaustion when the track became a mud bath and she had lost one of her light shoes. She had no idea how far she had walked, and there was no sign that she was drawing near to either Coverham village or the big house just outside of it. Either place would be sanctuary.

Lightning, which lit up the whole landscape to reveal that she was still out in the open with no houses near, was followed by a crack of thunder. The walk to Coverham, which had seemed to offer her salvation, had turned into something quite different. It might even have been wiser to have remained Peverel's prisoner.

Just as she was beginning to stand up, in order to trudge a little further in the hope that she might find a barn or a hut to shelter in, Meg saw a man walking up the lane towards her. Mixed emotions ran through her. Another human being might offer her assistance—or he might offer her something worse. She moved further into the lee of the hedge to hide herself until he had passed, but even as he did so she was overwhelmed by an almighty sneeze.

The man heard her, and turned his face in her direction so that she saw it for the first time. It was Simon! By what miracle had he arrived here? At the very moment that she recognised him, Simon called, 'Meg? Is that you, Meg?' and ran towards her.

It would not be exaggerating to say that they flew into one another's arms as recognition was followed by relief. Wet through, water running from his hair, Simon was kissing and caressing Meg, and she was kissing him back. 'Oh, my little love,' he exclaimed brokenly, whilst stroking and comforting her. 'Thank God that I have found you. Say that you are not hurt?' His loving attentions caused Meg to burst into tears for the first time on that dreadful day.

She muttered through her tears, 'I am quite wet enough without crying as well, to make matters worse. Apart from that, I don't think that there's very much wrong with me—although I do feel very strange. But how in the world have you managed to find me?'

'No time for that now, my darling. Later. Now we must try to find immediate shelter, and then. . .' he looked around him '. . .failing that, either return to Ware or press on to Coverham.'

Even in the circle of his arms the rain seemed to be able to find her. Meg shivered. 'How far are we from Coverham? I thought to find sanctuary there, but I seem to be no nearer to it than when I started out.'

Simon was making calculations in his head. He reckoned that they were slightly nearer to Ware than to Coverham, but to return her to Ware would risk courting the leers of the crowd in the Fox and Hounds and creating a scandal which would hurt her—the innocent party—the most.

On the other hand, to take the slightly longer route to Coverham would mean that they would not only find the sanctuary Meg had hoped for, but discretion and sympathy. Coverham it must be, and so he told her.

'Do you think that you are able to walk so far, Meg—over two and a half miles?'

What would she have done if he had not found her? Meg's shiverings were fuelled by that thought as well as by the cold and the rain. Without him she might have been unable to go on—and so she told him.

'Never!' Simon was robust. 'I know your gallant heart.'

'The worst thing is that I have lost one of my shoes, which will slow us down, I fear. It is difficult walking with only one.' Meg was trying hard not to sound stupidly complaining, but the resolution which had sustained her all day was being watered down by the relentless rain.

'Then take it off, my darling. I know the path is muddy, but it is soft and not stony, and it will make walking easier. Do you remember taking off your shoes when you were a little girl? And on being reprimanded, you always said that you preferred walking without them!'

Meg was struck by this. It called up memories of the hoyden which she had once been and one in particular, which she had sternly repressed ever since she had left England to become a French *grande dame*. 'So I did. I had quite forgot. What a nodcock I am.'

Walking without shoes was odd, she found, now that she was a grown woman, but more comfortable than with only one. Simon slowed his usual rapid pace, and together they progressed slowly towards the warmth and shelter of Coverham, like a wet Adam and Eve trying to find Paradise, not leave it behind.

Back in Ware, Peverel scoured the town and the roads leading out of it for any sign or news of Meg. He stopped the few people still about, continuing to use what was now a useful fiction to save her reputation: that she was his disturbed and ailing wife, who had run away from him and must be found. Like Simon and Meg, he was soon wet through.

Constantly with him was the knowledge that he, and he alone, had brought them all to this pass. Misery and remorse—new sensations for him— warred in his breast. Even his impending financial ruin seemed a faraway thing, of little note beside the dreadful knowledge of what he had done, and of what he now knew he was: a criminal and a coward who had hurt the one person whom he had professed to love.

Not professed! No, never, he *did* love her, and that one fact alone brought him face to face with the reality of himself and his life. And what he saw was shocking him into a long-belated penitence.

They were not far from Coverham when Meg began to flag. She had been walking more and more slowly, saying nothing to Simon of how ill she was beginning to feel, how exhausted. He constantly asked her if she wished to rest, but she always told him no. She was not sure that, if she stopped, she would ever be able to go on again.

The rain had ceased, which was a boon, and the moon had come from behind the clouds—to reveal that they were almost at the great gates which opened on to the gravelled drive which led to Coverham House. To their right was the road which led to Coverham village. It was at that point, with refuge almost in sight, that Meg's overtaxed mind and body gave way.

She suddenly clutched at Simon's hand, heaved a great sigh, and muttered, 'Oh, Simon, I feel so strange.'

Alarmed by the weakness of her voice, which had previously sounded so strong, Simon stopped, and put an arm around her. 'What is it, my darling?'

'I don't think that I can walk any more.' The gates and great house in the distance wavered before her; the very ground beneath her poor muddy feet seemed unstable. Finally everything, gates, house, ground and feet disappeared into the dark, and only Simon's sustaining arms saved Meg from falling unconscious into the mud.

He lifted her up to carry her: his precious burden. He kissed her white face with the great blue smudges under her eyes, and stroked her wet hair, loose and streaming down her back. He would carry her to the ends of the earth to save her, let alone to the doors of Coverham which drew ever nearer.

She was even lighter than he had thought, a frail vessel to contain such a dauntless spirit. Only the elements had conspired to prevent her from completing the journey herself.

Panting, dog weary, but sustained by the knowledge that Jasper Ashe had been decorated for carrying his wounded lieutenant to safety far further than this, and in worse conditions, Simon walked at a smart pace until he reached the gravelled sweep before the house.

At the bottom of the steps leading up to the huge front doors, Meg opened her eyes again, and began to try to struggle out of his arms. She had no notion of how far he had carried her, but, 'Set me down,' she croaked at him. 'You cannot carry me all the way to Coverham.'

His answer was to hold her to him even more lovingly. 'Oh, but I can—and have. See, we are here. I am going to set you down for a moment, so that I may knock on the door and try to wake the house.' He gently laid her on the top step before stripping off his sodden jacket—his caped greatcoat had been left with his curricle—and rolling it to make a pillow for her head.

Meg, now beyond anything but lying still, watched him hammer on the door again and again with a giant knocker in the shape of an imp before it opened and a querulous voice demanded to know, 'Who the devil is making such a damnable noise when all decent folk are readying themselves for bed!'

They had reached sanctuary.

Chapter Fifteen

'How is she? Tell me how she is?' Simon was frantically accosting the doctor outside Meg's room on the following morning.

Welcomed by Cass Devereux the previous night—her husband was visiting Woburn for a few days to discuss country matters with the Duke of Bedford—Meg had been put to bed immediately, and Simon's wet clothes had been exchanged for some of Jack's country wear.

After that, Cass had arranged for him to be fed, saying briskly when he demurred a little, 'Jack always says that the mark of a good officer is to see that his men have an excellent meal after battle or hardship. I can't feed Meg, but I can feed you, and then, and not before, you may tell me why and how you have arrived here.'

He did feel better when he had eaten, and then the whole sorry story came tumbling out. 'I thought that to bring Meg here might cut scandal off at the knees. No *on dits*, you see, if she has been staying with you. As for hubble-bubble at a posting inn in

Ware—who's to tell? Both Peverel and that criminal of a man of his risk transportation or worse if the true story came out.

'No, we are both your guests, and since you tell me that you have no others here, your servants may talk among themselves, but that is all. Your own reputation, m'lady, is spotless, so your word will not be questioned.'

'Call me Cass, pray do. And yes, I believe that you have done the sensible thing by coming to Coverham. But what of your cousin? Is it right that he should go scot-free after what he has done?'

'No, but consider the alternative and the damage to my poor, innocent Meg if the true story became known. It would cling to her always, and there would be those who would put their finger by their nose, and say, "No smoke without fire." Besides, I have given Peverel the fright of his life.

'He may not, in any case, remain long in England. The duns and the bailiffs are after him. Calais is his destination. Had he not done this to Meg, I might have helped him, but now. . .' and he shook his head. 'He has punished himself.'

'True. And we must both hope that Meg is better in the morning.'

She did not tell him that Coverham's doctor, roused from his comfortable bed in the West Wing, had privately told her that he thought Madame was suffering from more than exhaustion. 'She has a fever, I fear. But we shall know more in the morning.'

She must let Simon have a night's rest after his

labours—and trust that daylight might find Meg better.

But alas, she was not. And so the doctor informed Simon as kindly as he could, 'Madame's fever is worse. She does not know herself, nor where she is. I have given her opium to help her to sleep. Only time and cooling draughts will help her. If she grows worse, I shall bleed her to bring the fever down.'

'By no means,' Simon exclaimed. 'It has been my experience with both men and horses that bleeding does indeed bring the fever down, but weakens the patient to such a degree that they are unable to fight the illness and frequently die in consequence. Only if her life is in immediate danger will I agree to her being bled.'

'Pray who are you, sir, to make such a decision for her which goes against all medical practice?' The doctor was a trifle frosty at having his authority challenged.

'The man who hopes to become her husband when she is recovered—which I trust will be soon.'

But Meg grew no better. As she lay on her bed, she knew nothing of what was happening in the world outside, that Peverel had come to Coverham to discover whether Simon and Meg had reached there.

Despite what he had said to Cass, Peverel had looked so miserable and was so unlike his usual conceited arrogant self that Simon had arranged to give him a little money to make his forced flight to the Continent more comfortable. Peverel's servant was to go with him, relieved that he was not on his way to Botany Bay.

Jasper Ashe had finally arrived at Coverham after

a fruitless journey to Huntingdon, after which he had backtracked to Ware to hear from a bemused landlord of Simon's arrival and departure, and Meg's flight. Coverham, Jasper had thought, was their destination. He had been allowed in to see Meg before returning to London with the news of all that had happened.

Jack Devereux had come home in the meantime; and Simon was camped outside her room, suffering with her, refusing to leave to take up his life in London until she was well again.

He had been allowed in once to look at her. She lay silent and semi-conscious in the great bed, her face whiter than its sheets. He had wanted to stay with her, but both propriety and the doctor forebade it. A chair in the corridor was his place, vacated only when Cass insisted that he dine with her and Jack, lest he fall ill himself.

Not only were she and Jack surprised by his behaviour, but Simon himself could only wonder hazily what had come over him. Where had the coldly impassive, the almost stolid man he had always been, gone to? He had scarcely known himself from the moment that Meg had been in danger. He had helped to save her. And now she was in worse danger than ever, and from that he was powerless to save her.

On the next day she took a turn for the worse. Her fever had risen and she was delirious. Simon could hear her from his post in the corridor. The doctor was sent for, and came from her room, looking grave.

Distraught, Simon seized him by his lapels, much

as he had seized Peverel. 'How is she?' And then,
'She is in danger, is she not? You must let me in,
I must see her. Immediately.'

The doctor tried to struggle free, saying loftily,
'It would be neither wise nor seemly. You would
only endanger yourself, and all for nothing. She
knows nobody.'

Their raised voices frightened the servants who
were nursing Meg. One of them ran to fetch Cass.
Simon saw her coming, released the doctor and
cried, 'I must see her, Cass. Tell him to let me see
her. I don't care whether I endanger myself, or
breach the proprieties. If she is so ill that she is
despaired of, all the more reason for me to see her.'

'Let him in,' Cass told the doctor quietly. 'If she
is so ill, then it would be the greatest kindness to
allow Sir Simon to be with the woman he intends
to marry.'

The doctor shrugged his shoulders. 'Very well,
m'lady, but on your head and his be it. I cannot take
responsibility if my orders are countermanded.'

Simon stayed no longer. He was in Meg's room,
on his knees, her hand in his. Her eyes, brilliant
with fever, were turned on him, but she did not know
him. She was speaking, but not to him. She was in
the past, with the man she had married, and what
she was saying to him came nigh to breaking
Simon's heart.

He kissed the hot hand he held and tried to
reassure her. It was most plain that she was reliving
a life which had been desperately unhappy. For a
moment she seemed to be soothed by the sound
of his voice—and then she was in the past again,

reliving the troubled years of her marriage.

In her delirium, Meg was back in de Mortaine's chateau. Her husband was with her, telling her that he had married her because she was a stranger to his country, who had no one but her aunt in Paris to whom to turn, to tell of the long agony of her life with him. Of life with a man who thought only of himself, and condemned his wife to a living hell.

To try to soothe her, to quieten her, for she grew more and more agitated, Simon used his voice exactly as he would have done if he were trying to gentle a horse—and it seemed to work. He kissed her hot hand—only for her to withdraw it.

She tried to sit up, so he took her in his arms, her hot body burning against his cool one. One of the servants brought her lemonade and he held the glass for her to drink from it. She thanked him prettily—but still had no notion of who he was, only that he was being kind.

The doctor came in and said sourly, 'If the fever breaks, which I doubt, she will sleep and recover. If not. . .' and he shrugged his shoulders. Simon took no notice of him. All he knew was that he was with Meg, that he loved her, that she had suffered, and that if she lived he would make it his business never to let her suffer again.

Later, in the evening, he had his reward. Meg was still in his arms, the sweat pouring down her face and body, but suddenly she reared away from him, and said in the most melancholy voice, 'If only I had married Simon! How stupid I was not to realise that it was him I loved, not some imaginary Prince

Charming. I behaved like a child, and as a child is punished, so am I being.'

'No, no,' he told her earnestly—although he knew that she could not hear him.

'It was I who was wrong. I was careless in my manner to you when I proposed because I did not then understand how much I loved you. I don't think that I understood what love was. All I could think of was that I wanted a wife and that you were convenient. It was only when you refused me and I had lost you that I realised what I had done, and how much the youngest Miss Ashe had meant to me.'

After that she seemed to recover a little, as though, somehow, through the mists of the fever, she had grasped what he had said, although her hair and body were still as wet as they had been on her long walk through the rain to Coverham. Simon laid her down, but still held her hand in his: the contact seemed to comfort her. Later, when Cass came in to suggest that he rest a little after his long vigil, he shook his head at her.

As night fell, so Meg fell silent. She turned her head away from him, and began to sleep. The hand in his grew cooler, and her breathing, which had been noisy, quietened.

For a brief time Simon was afraid that the doctor's gloom had been justified, and that she might be dying but, as the night wore on, he lost his fears and, tired out with watching, fell asleep in his chair. Cass, looking in on them again, refrained from disturbing him lest she disturb Meg; they both looked so peaceful together.

*   *   *

In the morning when he awoke, Meg was awake, too, and fully conscious. Her first words to him were puzzled ones. 'Is this Coverham, Simon? And why are you sleeping in a chair by my bed?' Her voice was weak, but clear, and it was plain that she had no memory of her long days of suffering. Later, she was to tell him that her last recollection was of falling against him almost at the end of the green lane, at the first sight of Coverham.

The nurse, who had come in earlier, ran to fetch the doctor, to tell him that Madame's fever had broken, that she was conscious and was recovering. Simon bent over Meg to kiss her gently on the brow. 'You have been very ill, my darling. We almost despaired of you.'

Meg looked up at him. 'And how long have you been here, Simon?' she asked him, for she could see the stubble on his face, the growth of beard the result of his long watch, and the shadows under his eyes, which told of weariness and worry.

'They only let me in to be with you yesterday, and that because you were so ill, and I made such a fuss. Oh, Meg, my darling, we all feared for you, but I do believe that you are over the worst.'

The eyes on him were bright, but no longer with fever. 'Did I dream that Peverel kidnapped me, that I ran away from him, and that you came to save me?'

'No dream, my darling, but that is all over. Now you must get better.'

She turned her head to kiss the loving hand which held hers. 'Oh, Simon, when I was a little girl I always dreamed that one day a brave knight would come along to rescue me—from what I could never imagine. It was the rescuing which was important, not the reason. And now I have my brave knight, who rescued me and brought me safe to Coverham.' Her voice ran out from very weakness.

'Dear Meg, I was a very belated knight. For you had rescued yourself before I reached Ware. Did you ever imagine doing such a daring thing when you were the little girl, whom I now know I have always loved?'

There, he had said it to her in tones so tender that Meg could not doubt him. All the way along the green lane before he had arrived to help her Meg had been regretting one thing, and one thing only: that she had refused him again. In her delirium, she had relived her time with André and had run from him, trying to find a saviour—whom she now knew was Simon. They had found one another—and this time she would not refuse him if he were to renew his offer.

'But I would never have reached Coverham on my own,' she told him tenderly.

He kissed her for saying so. 'You were my brave girl, forever and always. And what is even better: you are my generous girl who secretly helped the family which had always scorned her—and asked no thanks for it.'

Meg shook her head at him. 'Oh, I was not really brave. I think that I was only able to escape because Peverel was not really a villain—only weak and stupid. A true villain would have treated me even more harshly and made sure that I would never have had the opportunity to escape.' She made no answer to his words about her generosity—she had no wish

to discuss it, and Simon respected her the more
for that.

'True enough, my darling,' he told her tenderly,
'that Peverel was a weak fool, and I must thank him
for his folly—if I ever see him again. But it still
took courage to escape into the black night.'

Simon saw that the effort of talking had tired her,
but the look of love on her face determined him on
what to say and do next. They had lost too much
time. He would make sure that they would lose
no more.

'There is something I must ask you, Meg, before
the world arrives to part us again—but only temporarily this time, I hope—'

Exhausted though she was, Meg struggled into a
sitting position, saying earnestly, 'Before you ask
me your question, Simon, there is something I ought
to tell you. It is about my marriage. No one but
André and I knew the truth of it.

'I married him because he was handsome and
had been brave: a true Prince Charming, I foolishly
thought. The man I turned you down for. But, oh,
what a mistake I made. Young he might have been,
but he was old and jaded in all the vices of life. So
much so that our married life was a mockery. I thank
God that my aunt, who helped to make the marriage,
did not live to learn the truth of him.

'And when he decided that a young and untried
woman was no longer to his taste, he resumed his
old ways and treated me most cruelly. Oh, he did
not beat me, but he had a vicious tongue and used
it to demean me daily and to tell me all the details
of his wicked life. He died in a duel caused by his

seduction—nay, his rape—of the wife of his best friend, but not before he had tried to destroy my reputation.

The irony of it was that he had no relatives—they had all died in the French Revolutionary Terror—so that his wealth and his estates came to me. But the price I paid to inherit them was a terrible one. The very idea of marriage seemed hateful to me after André's death.

'But those who truly loved me knew the truth. And there you have it. I refused the good man who loved me—and married a roué instead. To survive I became hard and unfeeling myself. Until I met you again.'

The eyes she turned on Simon were grave and loving. Meg thought that she owed him the truth and, weak though she was, must tell him that truth before he proposed to her.

Simon took her in his arms and held her to him, his lips on her hair, telling himself that he must be gentle, that she was still weak from her illness. Though she needed love, that love must be restrained, not powerful.

'Oh, my darling, you are as honest as you are true,' he told her. He knew, from what she had revealed in her delirium, that she had not told him all the horrors of her life with André de Mortaine. But that knowledge was a secret for him to keep. It was enough that she had confessed her folly—as he had confessed his.

'Before I ask you to marry me,' he said, 'let me say this. That had you accepted me all those years ago, I do not believe that our marriage would have been a happy one. You were too young and I was too proud, too sure of my own rectitude, too certain of the rightness of my own judgement. What was worse, I knew nothing of true passion, the depth of love of a man for a woman—until I lost you for the second time.

'When I first proposed to you, I thought of marriage as a kind of bargain between us, as a convenience, a mere continuance of a long friendship, and nothing more. But life has chastened us both, and at the same time has offered us a second chance.

'Meg, my darling, before the doctor arrives to send me away, will you make me a happy man by promising to marry me? This time I make the offer with love in my heart, and respect for the brave creature that you are to survive such a marriage, and my cousin Peverel's villainy.'

'Oh, yes, Simon, yes. I offer you my love unconditionally, the past forgotten and forgiven. The present and the future must be ours.'

Meg was in his arms, where she had always wanted to be, and where she had feared that she might never be. Before them lay fulfilment and a shared life. Her face was flushed, not with fever, but with returning health. Weak she might be, but not so weak that she was not able to enjoy Simon's gentle caresses.

Cass Devereux insisted on accompanying the doctor to Meg's room as soon as she learned that Meg's fever had broken and that she was on the way to recovery.

She also insisted on entering Meg's bedroom

before the doctor did. What she saw there had her shutting the door again, and saying to the doctor, 'I should leave your examination of Madame for a little, sir. I think that the medicine she is receiving at the moment will be as helpful as anything that you might prescribe for her.'

Historical Romance™

Coming next month

FRANCESCA
Sylvia Andrew

Francesca Shelwood was mortified when Marcus Carne
reappeared in her life... He had stolen the most magical
kisses from the young and innocent Francesca. But when
her illicit actions were severely punished by her cruel
Aunt, she'd blamed Marcus and vowed never to forgive
him! But on her inheritance Marcus returned and offered
Francesca the unimaginable—marriage! She refused, sure
he only wanted her money. But when Francesca set off to
France to find her beloved childhood nurse, Maddy, she
walked headlong into danger! And only one person was
ready to sacrifice his reputation *and* life for her—Marcus...

JOUSTING WITH SHADOWS
Sarah Westleigh

Having been abandoned to the convent for the shame her
supposed illegitimacy brought to the family, Genevra had
long since lost hope of a good marriage and children.
So she was thrilled beyond belief when she was betrothed
to a highly respected knight, Robert St Aubin. Their first
meeting was the culmination of all her dreams, for he
was young and vigorous, and his smile transformed
his stern face.

But marriage brought Genevra down to earth with a bump,
for though their nights were ecstatic their days were
fraught with tension. Robert was clearly on difficult terms
with his family and when she learned he had been married
before she thought she had found the source of her
problems...but persuading Robert to love and *trust* her was
another matter entirely.

ARE YOU A FAN
OF MILLS & BOON®
HISTORICAL ROMANCES™?

If YOU are a regular United Kingdom buyer of Mills & Boon Historical Romances you might like to tell us your opinion of the books we publish to help us in publishing the books *you* like.

Mills & Boon have a Reader Panel for their Historical Romances. Each person on the panel receives a questionnaire every third month asking her for *her* opinion of the books she has read in the past three months. All people who send in their replies will have a chance of winning ONE YEAR'S FREE Historicals, sent by post—48 books in all. If you would like to be considered for inclusion on the Panel please give us details about yourself below. All postage will be free. Younger readers are particularly welcome.

Year of birth .... Month ....

Age at completion of full-time education ....

Single ☐   Married ☐   Widowed ☐   Divorced ☐

Your name (print please) ....

Address ....

....

.... Postcode ....

THANK YOU! PLEASE PUT IN ENVELOPE AND POST TO
MILLS & BOON READER PANEL, FREEPOST SF195
PO BOX 152, SHEFFIELD S11 8TE